a *Piece* of *My* *Heart*

SHARON SALA

sourcebooks
casablanca

Published by Sourcebooks Casablanca, an imprint of Sourcebooks, Inc.
P.O. Box 4410, Naperville, Illinois 60567-4410
(630) 961-3900
Fax: (630) 961-2168
www.sourcebooks.com

Printed and bound in Canada.
MBP 10 9 8 7 6 5 4 3 2 1

Broken children lead troubled lives, yearning for something they never experienced, wanting to understand their place in the world. But without love, nothing is possible. Nothing matters if you do not even love yourself. Walk gently in this world as you travel your path. Watch carefully that you do not, by some careless word or gesture, injure a young child's heart.

This story is dedicated to the broken ones, and to the hope that as they grow to adulthood, they find a special someone along the way.

Chapter 1

FROM CHILDHOOD, MERCY DANE VIEWED CHRISTMAS EVE in Savannah, Georgia, like something out of a fairy tale. The old, elegant mansions were always lit from within and decorated with great swags of greenery hanging above the doorways and porch railings like thick green icing on snowy white cakes.

The shops decked out in similar holiday style were as charming as the sweet Southern women who worked within. Each shop boasted fragrant evergreens, plush red velvet bows, and flickering lights mimicking the stars in the night sky above the city.

And even though Mercy had grown up on the hard side of town with lights far less grand, the lights in her world burned with true Southern perseverance. Now that she was no longer a child, the beauty of the holiday was something other people celebrated, and on this cold Christmas Eve, she no longer believed in fairy tales. So far, the chapters of her life consisted of a series of foster families until she aged out of the system, and one magic Christmas Eve with a man she never saw again. The only lights in her world now were the lights where she worked at the Road Warrior Bar.

The yellow neon sign over the bar was partially broken. The *R* in *Road* was missing its leg, making the word look like *Toad*. But the patrons who frequented this bar didn't care about the name. They came for the company and a drink or two to dull the disappointment of a lifetime of regrets.

Carson Beal, who went by the name of Moose, owned the bar. He'd been meaning to get the *R* fixed for years, but intention was worth nothing without the action, and Moose had yet to act upon the thought.

Outside, the blinking neon light beckoned, calling the lonely and the thirsty into the bar where the beer was cold and the gumbo and rice Moose served was hot with spice and fire.

Moose often took advantage of Mercy's talent for baking after she'd once brought cupcakes for Moose and the employees to snack on. After that, she'd bring in some of whatever she'd made at home. On occasion Moose would ask her to bake him something special. It was always good to have a little extra money, so she willingly obliged.

This Christmas Eve, Moose had ordered an assortment of Christmas cookies for the bar. When Mercy came in to work carrying the box of baked goods, he was delighted. Now a large platter of cookies graced the north end of the bar.

The incongruity of "O Little Town of Bethlehem" playing in the background was only slightly less bizarre than the old tinsel Christmas tree hanging above the pool table like a molting chandelier.

Because of the holiday, only two of his four waitresses were on duty, Barb Hanson, a thirtysomething widow with purple hair, and Mercy Dane, the baker with a curvy body.

Mercy's long, black hair was a stunning contrast to the red Christmas sweater she was wearing, and her willowy body and long, shapely legs looked even longer in her black jeans and boots. Her olive skin and dark hair gave her an exotic look, but being abandoned as a baby, and growing up in foster care, she had no knowledge of her heritage.

Barb of the purple hair wore red and green, a rather startling assortment of colors for a lady her age, and both women were wearing reindeer antler headbands with little bells. Between the bells and antlers, the music and cookies, and the Christmas tree hanging above the pool table, Moose had set a holiday mood.

Mercy had been working at the bar for over five years. Although she'd turned twenty-six just last week, her life, like this job, was going nowhere.

It was nearing midnight when a quick blast of cold air suddenly moved through the bar and made Mercy shiver. She didn't have to look to know the ugly part of this job had just arrived.

"Damn, Moose, play some real music, why don't ya?" Big Boy yelled as the door slammed shut behind him.

Moose glared at the big biker who'd entered his bar. "This *is* real music, Big Boy. Sit down somewhere and keep your opinions to yourself."

The biker flipped Moose off, spat on the floor, and stomped through the room toward an empty table near the back, making sure to feel up Mercy's backside in passing.

When Big Boy suddenly shoved his hand between her legs, she nearly dropped the tray of drinks she was carrying. She knew from experience that he was waiting for a reaction, so she chose to bear the insult without calling attention to it.

As soon as he was seated, Big Boy slapped the table

and yelled at the barmaids, "One of you bitches bring me a beer!"

Moose glanced nervously at Mercy, aware that she'd become the target for most of Big Boy's harassment.

Barb sailed past Mercy with a jingle in every step. "I've got his table," she said.

"Thanks," Mercy said, and delivered the drinks she was carrying. "Here you go, guys! Christmas Eve cheer and cookies from Moose!"

One trucker, a man named Pete, took a big bite out of the iced sugar cookie. "Mmm, this is good," he said.

"Mercy made them," Moose yelled.

Pete shook his head and took another bite. "You have a fine hand with baking. I'd ask you to marry me, darlin', but my old lady would object."

Mercy took the teasing with a grin. The men at this table were good men who always left nice tips. In fact, most of the patrons in the bar were men with no family or truckers who couldn't get home for Christmas. Every now and then, a random woman would wander in to have a drink, but rarely lingered, except for Lorena Haysworth, the older woman sitting at the south end of the bar.

She'd been coming here since before Mercy was born, and in her younger days she and Moose had been lovers before slowly drifting apart. She'd come back into his life a few months ago and nightly claimed the seat at the end of the bar.

Barb took the first of what would be multiple beers to Big Boy's table, along with a Christmas cookie and a bowl of stale pretzels, making sure to keep the table between them.

Big Boy lunged at her as if he was going to grab her,

and when she turned around and ran, he leaned back and laughed.

Mercy returned to the bar with a new order and waited for Moose to fill it.

"Sorry about that," Moose said as he glanced toward the table where Big Boy was sitting.

Her eyes narrowed angrily. "How sorry are you? Sorry enough to kick him out? Or just sorry his money is more important to you than me and Barb?"

Moose's face turned as red as his shirt. "Damn it, Mercy. You know how it goes," he said, and pushed the new order across the bar.

She did know. The customer was always right. Trying not to buy into the turmoil, she picked up the tray and delivered the order with a smile.

The night wore on with Big Boy getting drunker and more belligerent, while Barb and Mercy dodged his constant attempts to maul them, until finally, it was time to close.

It was a few minutes before 2:00 a.m. when Moose shut down the bar. There were only three customers left: Big Boy, who was so close to passed out he couldn't walk; Lorena, who was waiting to go home with Moose; and a trucker who'd fallen asleep at his table.

Mercy headed for the trucker, leaving Moose to wrestle Big Boy up and out.

The trucker was a small, wiry man named Frank Bigalow who fancied himself a ringer for country music star Willie Nelson. He was dreaming of hit songs and gold records when Mercy woke him.

"Frank. Frank. You need to wake up now. We're closing."

Bigalow straightened abruptly, momentarily confused as to where he was, then saw Mercy and smiled.

"Oh. Right. Sure thing, honey. What do I owe you?" he mumbled.

"Twelve dollars," she said.

Bigalow stood up to get his wallet out of his pants then pulled out a twenty. "Keep the change and Merry Christmas," he said.

"Thanks," she said, and began bussing his table as he walked out of the bar.

Moose had Big Boy on his way out the door, and it was none too soon for Mercy.

She handed Moose the twenty when he returned. "Take twelve out. The rest is mine," she said, and pocketed the change Moose gave her.

Within fifteen minutes, the bar was clear and swept, the money was in the safe, and Barb and Mercy were heading for the door.

"Hey! Girls! Wait up!" Moose said, then handed them each an envelope, along with little bags with some of Mercy's cookies. "Merry Christmas. We're not open tomorrow so sleep in."

"Thank you," Barb said as she slid the envelope inside her purse.

"Much appreciated," Mercy added as she put her envelope in one of the inner pockets of her black leather bomber jacket. It was old and worn, but it was warm.

Then she grabbed her helmet and the cookies and headed out the door behind Barb and just ahead of Moose and Lorena. Once outside, she paused to judge the near-empty parking lot, making sure Big Boy and his Harley were at the motel across the street.

The air was cold and the sky was clear as she stashed the cookies, then put on her helmet and mounted her own Harley. Seconds later the quiet was broken by the rolling rumble of the engine as she toed up the kick-stand, put the bike in gear, and rode off into the night.

The empty streets on the way to her apartment were a little eerie, but she was so tired she couldn't work up the emotion to be scared. The streetlights were draped with Christmas garlands and red bows, but they were all one blur as Mercy sped toward home.

A city cop on neighborhood patrol saw her, recognized the lone bike and biker, and blinked his lights as she passed him.

She waved back and kept going.

When she stopped for a red light and realized she was the only person on this stretch of street, she didn't breathe easy until the light turned green, and she moved on.

Finally, she was home. She eased up on the accelerator as she rolled through the gates of her apartment complex and parked the motorcycle beneath a light in plain view of the security cameras. She ran up the outer stairs to the second level and down the walkway to her apartment carrying her helmet and the cookies. No matter how many times she'd done this or how many times she'd moved since it happened, the fact that she'd once come home late at night to find out she'd been robbed, she never felt safe until she was in the apartment with the door locked behind her.

She tossed the helmet onto the sofa and took the cookies into the kitchen. Curious as to how much of a bonus Moose was giving this year, she was pleased to see a hundred-dollar bill.

"Nice," she said, and took it and her night's worth of tips to the refrigerator, opened up the freezer, and put the money inside an empty box that had once held a biscuit mix.

She wasn't sure how much money she had saved up, but last time she'd counted it had been over two thousand dollars. It should have been in a bank, but these days, banks cost money to use, and she didn't have any to spare, so she froze her assets.

The place smelled of stale coffee and something her neighbor across the hall had burned for dinner. She was tired and cold, but too wired to sleep, so she went to her bedroom, stripped out of her clothes, and took a long hot shower.

She returned to the kitchen later to find something to eat. One quick glance in the refrigerator was all the reminder she needed that she still hadn't grocery shopped. She emptied what was left of the milk into a bowl of cereal and ate it standing by the sink, remembering another Christmas in Savannah, her first all on her own.

———

Mercy was nineteen years old, between jobs, and as close to homeless as she'd ever been. She had come back to her apartment after a long day of job-hunting, only to walk in on a burglar in the act. She screamed. He ran with what was left of her savings, and the hours afterward were a blur of tears and a fear that she would not be able to survive the setback. The only money she had left in the world was in her pocket.

The people in the adjoining apartments were

sympathetic and curious, and a couple felt sorry for her
and gave her a couple of twenties. She was standing in
the hall waiting for the cops to clear her room when the
neighbor from across the hall opened his door and came
out. He'd moved in only two days ago, and during that
time they'd done no more than nod and smile as they
passed in the hall, but she liked his face. His eyes were
kind, and his smile felt genuine.

It was apparent he'd been sleeping and had done no
more than comb his fingers through his hair before he
opened the door. The top snap on his jeans was undone,
and he was pulling a sweatshirt over his head as he came
out. She got a quick glimpse of a hard belly and wide
shoulders before she looked away.

"What's happening?" he asked as he stopped beside
her. "I fell asleep with the TV on. When I woke up and
turned it off, I heard all this."

"I was robbed," she said.

His empathy was instant. "Oh no! Oh, honey, are you
okay? Were you hurt?"

Her voice was shaking. "My arrival scared him off."

Without hesitation, he hugged her. The unexpected
compassion undid her, and she began to cry.

And in the midst of that moment, the cops came out,
and she pushed out of his arms.

"Ma'am, we're through here. He busted the lock.
I would suggest you find somewhere else to sleep for
the night."

"I don't have somewhere else or someone else,"
she said.

They shrugged and left the building.

The neighbors all went back into their apartments.

All but him.

She sighed and started for her apartment, when he stopped her with a word. "Don't."

She turned, anger already settling in her heart. "Don't what? That's everything I own in this world. They took my money. I'm not giving up what clothes I have left too."

She walked into her apartment and closed the door.

He opened it and walked in behind her. "Get your things. You can sleep at my place tonight. Tomorrow we'll figure something out."

Mercy started to shake. "There is no *we* in my life."

"Fine. Then *you'll* figure something out. But you can stay with me tonight anyway."

She stared at his face, looking for a sign of danger and seeing none. "Yes. Okay."

"Want help gathering up your things?"

"No."

"Then do what you need to do, and knock on my door when you have everything."

She nodded.

He walked out.

She packed her bags while a cold anger washed through her. One more kick when she was down. It's how her world worked. By the time she got across the hall, she had shut herself down.

"I made a bed for you on the sofa," he said.

She left her bags by the door and then laid her coat on top of them as he locked up behind her. "Thank you," she said.

"You're very welcome. Oh, hey, I just realized I don't know your name."

She grimaced. "Oh, just call me Lucky."

"I have a feeling that's not your real name, but it will do. I'm L. J. but my friends call me—"

"We're not friends. L. J. will do," she muttered.

His eyes narrowed, but he didn't argue. He'd seen animals trapped into a corner with no way out, and the look in her eyes was about the same. "Can I get you something to eat or drink?" he asked.

"No, thanks. Just the bed. I'm tired. So fucking tired."

A tear rolled down her cheek, but he was guessing she didn't know it. "Then I'll leave you alone. If you need anything later, just knock on my door."

She nodded, dropped onto the sofa, and began taking off her shoes.

"Good night, Lucky. Sweet dreams," he said.

She made a sound halfway between a snort and a sob. He left the room.

She went to bed. And three hours later woke up screaming.

He came out on the run with a gun in his hand.

By that time she was sitting on the side of the sofa bed with her head in her hands. Her long, black hair was in tangles, and the sports bra and sweatpants she'd been sleeping in were drenched with sweat, even though the room was cold. His first thought was that she was sick.

"Sorry. Bad dreams," she said, and got up. "Where's your bathroom?"

"Down the hall, first door on your left."

She passed by him, so close he felt the heat from her body. And when she came out, she had washed up and dried off the sweat.

"You didn't have to wait," she said.

"I know. I just wanted to make sure you were okay, and that you didn't need anything..." Then he pointed at the clock. "It's Christmas."

Tears rolled down Mercy's cheeks.

"Oh hell. I didn't mean to make you cry," he said.

"Well, you did, so what are you going to do about it?" she snapped.

L. J. flinched. "We could make love."

Now she was the one who was startled. "What if I say no?"

He shrugged. "Then I go back to my room and sleep till daylight."

The rage within her was choking. She wanted to feel something besides despair. "I am numb. I don't think I will be able to feel."

He held out his hand. "I know how to make you feel again."

Mercy shivered, her mind racing. With a stranger? Just once. Just so she wouldn't have to hurt.

She walked into his arms.

The ensuing hour was nothing short of magic. Mercy turned into someone she didn't know existed. He turned her on and sent every emotion she had into overdrive. The sex was heart-stopping, and so was he. After it was over, he fell asleep with her still in his arms.

She watched his face as he slept until every facet of him was branded into her memory, but she wouldn't sleep. An hour before daylight, she slipped out of his bed, dressed in the other room, and left without telling him good-bye.

―∾―

A loud crash, and then the squall of a tomcat somewhere outside broke Mercy's reverie.

She put her bowl in the sink and walked to the window overlooking the parking lot.

The neighborhood cat was prowling around the dumpster, and she saw the vague images of two people making out in a car near the back of the lot. Angry that she cared, she turned away. Exhaustion was finally catching up. It was after three in the morning when she rinsed the bowl and then paused in the doorway, making sure everything was turned off and locked up.

The silence in the apartment was suddenly broken by the distant sound of a phone ringing in a nearby apartment. The ringtone was "Jingle Bells."

"Merry Christmas," she muttered, and went to bed.

Chapter 2

IT WAS NEARING DAYLIGHT WHEN HER CELL PHONE BEGAN to ring. She rolled over and grabbed it as she turned on the lamp. "Hello?"

"This is Mildred Starks from the National Rare Blood Registry. Am I speaking to Mercy Dane?"

"Yes," Mercy said as she threw back the covers and stood up.

"Ms. Dane, we have an emergency in your area. This is an unusual situation, and we're asking something out of the ordinary. Can you respond directly to the hospital in need?"

"Yes. Where do I need to be?" she asked as she began grabbing clothes.

"You still reside in Savannah, Georgia, and are there at this time?"

"Yes."

"Perfect. There is a small town about an hour south of you called Blessings. There's no chopper available to fly you there and no time to donate in Savannah and then have it transported. Do you have transportation to get yourself to Blessings?"

Now her hands were shaking as she realized the reality of someone's life would lie partially in her ability to get there. "Yes. Where do I go?"

"The town is small. There's only one hospital. I'm sending GPS directions to your phone. Time is crucial. Be safe and Godspeed."

"On my way," she said, and dropped the phone on the bed as she took her biker gear out of the closet. Within five minutes she was out the door, her helmet in one hand, keys in the other.

The sun was only a hint on the eastern horizon as she left the complex. According to her directions, she was to take I-16 west, then connect to I-95 south. She wasn't far from a feeder road that would take her to I-516, which then turned into I-16, so she took that route.

It was early Christmas morning and traffic was sparse. Sunrise was minutes away when she finally hit I-16, and by that time she was flying. Every mile behind her put her closer to Blessings. It wasn't the first time she'd been called upon to donate her blood, but it was the first time she'd been asked to go to the person in need. It amped the urgency to a fever pitch, making her part in it personal.

Once she hit I-95 southbound, the northbound lane was a black ribbon of flickering headlights, while she and the Harley became a two-wheeled version of earth-bound flight.

She rode with single-minded focus, keeping an eye on the traffic while making sure she didn't get caught in the draft of passing truckers. And when the new sun was just high enough in the east that she could see the landscape through which she was passing, the glimpses of houses led her to imagining what might be going on within the walls—because it was Christmas Day.

Surely joyful families were opening presents and eating breakfasts. She pictured turkeys already in the oven, pies already baked and lining sideboards and tables, and the dough for homemade hot rolls in big crockery bowls, covered and rising in a warm place on the counter. Unfortunately, that scene was nothing but her imagination because she'd never experienced anything like it. But the closer she got to Blessings, the more she realized there was no time to dwell on what she didn't have. Today, it was what she did have—an RH negative blood type—that mattered most.

She'd been on the interstate forty-five minutes when she reached the exit that would take her to her destination. According to the directions she'd received, Blessings was less than fifteen miles ahead. The roar of the engine beneath her was all she could hear as she leaned slightly forward into the ride and accelerated.

And just as she rode past the city limits sign, she came upon a roadblock and a long line of cars blocking the highway with rescue vehicles up ahead. Her heart sank. She didn't know it was the aftermath of the wreck that had caused the injuries to the person in need of her blood. But waiting around for permission to pass was not on her agenda.

She rolled out around the last car in line and kept moving forward. When she reached the accident site, she rode around two tow trucks, then took to the ditch to get around a couple of police cars and one highway patrol.

Although she couldn't hear what they were saying, she saw them shouting and trying to wave her down. She'd never outright defied a lawman in her life, but these were extenuating circumstances, and so she kept moving until she was beyond the roadblock and heading into town.

She knew she was speeding, but traffic on Main Street was almost nonexistent. Her gut knotted when she heard a siren. One glance in her side mirror, and she saw the red and blue flashing lights of a cop car coming up behind her. Stopping to explain her situation could be the difference between someone living and dying.

Led by fear, she swerved off Main Street into a residential neighborhood and accelerated. It wasn't enough. The cruiser was still behind her and closing the gap. Then she noticed an alley coming up on her right, swerved into it and sped up, trying to get back to Main. Everything in her peripheral vision was a blur, and the sound of the siren was fading as she shot back onto Main and then down to the far end of the street to the blue hospital sign with an arrow pointing east.

She followed the arrow, saw the hospital building straight ahead, and headed toward the entrance marked ER. She slid sideways as she came to a stop and then ran toward the entrance with her helmet in her hand and her hair in tangles.

It had taken an hour and five minutes to get there.

It was thirty-seven degrees, and she was sweating.

—◦◦◦—

Everyone in the waiting room looked up as the tall, leggy woman came running into ER, heading straight toward registration. They saw black leather, wild hair, and a motorcycle helmet, and frowned. Women in Blessings didn't dress like that. She was obviously a stranger.

Mercy was unaware of the stares and would have cared less had she known. She stopped at the desk.

"I'm here to donate blood to—"

A nurse came out of a nearby office.

"What's your name?" she asked.

"Mercy Dane."

The nurse threw up her hands in a gesture of thanks-giving. "Praise the Lord that you're here. They're wait-ing for you. Come with me."

They left the waiting area with haste, moving down a long hallway, then through double doors, past the sur-gery waiting room, unaware of the two men who came running out of the waiting room behind them as they passed. And when the nurse took her through another set of doors, things began to happen rapid-fire.

She'd given them her photo ID and donor card and was now flat on her back, half-listening to the frantic voices around her as they began hooking her up. It was obvious whoever needed this transfusion was someone they knew—someone they certainly cared about. And she was here, so she closed her eyes, letting the chaos go on around her without buying into the panic, just glad she'd made the ride.

———∿∿∿———

Lon Pittman clocked the biker at close to sixty miles an hour going down Main Street. He immediately hit the lights and siren as he took pursuit, and when he got close enough to ID the tag number, radioed it in. He had assumed the rider was a guy with long hair until the dispatcher radioed back. The owner was a woman named Mercy Dane. That wasn't going to change any-thing when he caught her, but it did cross his mind that this woman was surely hell on wheels. He was still in pursuit when she suddenly took a right and shot up the alley that ran along the side of Ruby Dye's home.

"Damn it," he muttered, knowing it was too narrow

to take his cruiser up that alley at this rate of speed, and had to drive to the end of the block to take a quick right, only to see her shoot out of the alley, straight across the street into another one. She was still running the alleys, one block after another.

He took off toward Main running hot, and when he finally reached it, caught a quick glimpse of the bike and rider now on Main and turning east. With lights still flashing and his siren screaming, he took the turn onto Main and followed her route.

It wasn't until he took the same turn the biker had taken that he realized it led to the hospital. He caught a glimpse of her and the bike heading north around the hospital and floored it.

The last thing he expected to see when he drove up to the ER was the big Harley parked near the entrance. He killed the lights and siren, radioed in his position, and got out on the run.

Once again, the people in the waiting room were surprised. When their police chief entered a building running, they were curious what was going on.

None of them had expected to see so much action and excitement in the hospital ER, especially on Christmas Day.

Lon quickly scanned the room, and when he didn't see anyone in black leather, he headed for the registration desk.

"Sally, did a woman wearing black leather come in here?"

"Oh…you mean Mercy Dane? Yes, she's here, thank goodness. They took her straight to the surgery area."

He frowned. "Why? Was she injured in some way?"

"Oh, no! She came for Hope Talbot. She's the rare blood donor they've been waiting for."

And just like that, all the anger he'd been feeling for the reckless way in which she'd come into Blessings was gone. He'd helped pull Hope out of the wreck. He knew she was hanging onto life by a thread, but had no idea about her blood type or the frantic call that had gone out on her behalf.

"Where did they take the Dane woman?" he asked.

"Down the hall is all I know. You might check in at the surgery waiting room. Jack and Duke are there. They might know more."

"Thanks," he said, and headed down the hall.

—⁓—

Jack Talbot and his brother, Duke, were still celebrating the blood donor's arrival when Chief Pittman entered the waiting room.

Jack immediately stood up and shook his hand. "Chief! I was told you helped pull Hope out of the wreck. Thank you so much."

"I just happened to be one of the first on the scene," he said.

"I'm still so grateful," Jack said. "My wife is the beginning and end of my world."

"So how's she doing?" Lon asked.

Jack shook his head and walked away in tears, leaving Duke to answer. "She's hanging on, but it wasn't looking good. She'd lost so much blood that they didn't think she would pull through surgery without a transfusion. The problem became getting blood for her. She's RH negative, which is a rare blood type. There wasn't any in the blood banks that could have gotten to us in time, and just when we thought it wasn't going to happen, they found a donor who lived in Savannah. She just got here a few minutes ago. There's no way to know how this is going to come out, but whoever she is, her presence was an answer to our prayers."

The image of Mercy Dane's frantic ride now made a crazy kind of sense. Now Lon was past curious. He wanted to see the woman who'd made a wild ride on Christmas Day to save a stranger's life.

"That's good to know," he said. "If you don't mind, I believe I'll wait here with you, just to see how Hope fares after the transfusion."

------~~~------

Mercy watched one nurse rush out with the donated blood while another took the needle out of her arm. The panic of getting here was over. Whatever happened now was out of her hands, save for the silent prayer she'd said for the woman in need. She was about to get up when a nurse stopped her.

"Wait, honey. Not so fast," she cautioned.

Mercy didn't argue. The room had already begun to spin when she raised her head—a combination of too little sleep, an adrenaline crash, and a unit short of blood.

The nurse helped Mercy up and walked her out, talking as they went.

"I'm taking you to the waiting room to get juice and a sweet roll from one of the vending machines before I can let you leave. I don't know if anyone told you, but the woman needing the donation is a nurse in this hospital. We are all so grateful you came when you got the call. None of this is standard donation procedure, so thank you for going above and beyond for her."

"I am happy I was close enough to help," Mercy said.

"You gave her a chance, which is more than she had before you showed up," the nurse said.

Mercy was still shaky and wanting to sit down as they walked into the waiting room. But two men who were already there stood up and came toward her so fast she took a quick step back.

However, it was the cop standing behind them who caught her eye. She thought for a moment she was hallucinating, then saw the same look of shock on his face as the one she must be wearing. Her gut knotted.

"You! You disappeared seven years ago. I never thought I'd see you again," he said.

She shrugged. "Seven years is a long time. Neither did I." She wondered if he'd stayed to give her a ticket for speeding, and then decided she didn't care.

The brothers began crowding around her, all trying to talk at once.

"Miss Dane, this is Jack Talbot and his brother, Duke. Hope is Jack's wife, and it appears they've figured out who you are. Jack, this is Mercy Dane. She needs juice and a sweet roll from the vending machine."

"I'll get it," he offered, and ran toward the machines at the far end of the room, and then yelled back at his brother to see if he had a debit card on him while the nurse seated Mercy and introduced her to the chief.

"Mercy, this is Chief Pittman. He helped pull Hope from the wreck." Then she added, "Ideally, you need to sit at least thirty minutes after you've finished eating. An hour would be even better."

Mercy nodded. "Yes, I will, and thank you."

"Oh no, we're the ones thanking you. God bless you, Mercy Dane. Have a safe trip home," she said.

Lon was in shock. Seven years ago he'd spent a week looking for this woman. She was in his arms when he fell asleep, and when he woke she was gone. He'd never forgotten her or that night, and now, fate had brought her back into his world.

"So, Lucky, long time no see," he said softly.

She nodded.

"You are one hell of a rider," he said.

Her eyes narrowed. "So, Chief, is that your way of saying I was speeding?"

She watched his eyes crinkling up at the corners as he smiled.

"Pretty much, but given the circumstances, I'm gonna let that slide. I stayed because I wanted to meet the donor who willingly interrupted her Christmas Day to save a stranger's life. I didn't know I was going to meet an old friend."

"We're not friends," Mercy said, and then blinked as she realized that was what she said before, and added, "I don't have family. Just a job. I was happy to do it."

He heard a challenge in her claim…as if daring him to remark about her solitary life. But he wasn't going to give her a moment of sympathy. "Yeah, same here. Cops and family aren't necessarily synonymous. Most days I feel like my life is the job. At any rate, you are not what you seem, and I am impressed."

All of a sudden, a quick wave of weakness washed over her. She bent over and put her head between her knees, trying not to pass out.

Lon caught her just as she was about to slide out of the chair as Jack returned with a bottle of orange juice, a packet of mini-doughnuts, and an iced honey bun. It was pure sugar overload, but Mercy knew it was what her body needed to offset the shock of blood loss.

"Here you go, Miss Dane. If you want more to drink, just let me know," Jack said, and then pulled out a chair and sat down near her.

Duke was drawn to the woman by her beauty, and unhappy that it appeared the chief and the woman were already acquainted with each other. He followed his younger brother's lead and sat nearby.

Mercy took a drink of the juice and then tore back the cellophane from the honey bun and took a bite as the chief's radio squawked. Someone was trying to locate him.

"As you heard, my presence is requested elsewhere," Lon said as he stood. "It was a pleasure to meet you again. Take care, Miss Dane, and have a safe ride home."

"Thank you," Mercy said.

She didn't want to watch, but she couldn't help it. The years had turned him into quite a man. One thing was the same though. His butt still looked good from behind.

Chapter 3

JACK SCOOTED HIS CHAIR CLOSER TO HER. HIS VOICE WAS TREMbling as he captured her attention. "Miss Dane, there aren't words enough to thank you for what you've done. Hope means everything to me, and I thought I was going to lose her. You have given her a fighting chance."

"I was happy to help," she said.

Duke picked up the conversation. "Well, we certainly appreciate it. Hope has no family, so there was no option of having a relative donate, which would have been the normal avenue. She was adopted out of foster care."

"Then she was lucky to get out. I grew up in foster care and aged out," Mercy said, and took another bite of the honey bun.

"Where do you live?" Jack asked.

"In Savannah."

Duke pointed at the helmet that she'd put between her feet. "Did you come here on a motorcycle?"

She nodded. "I don't own a car."

He frowned. "Wasn't your husband upset about you coming all this way alone?"

Mercy resisted the urge to glare. He asked too damn many questions. "I'm not married, but that wouldn't have mattered. I make my own decisions. No man tells me what to do."

Duke heard the cold tone in her voice and unconsciously sat up and leaned back.

"I'm sorry," he said. "I didn't mean to imply—"

Mercy sighed. She'd come on too strong to a family who was freaked out, and rightly so. "No. I'm sorry. I guess the defensive wall I keep between me and the world is a little steep."

She finished off the honey bun and got up to wash the sugar from her fingers. When she came back from the bathroom, she glanced at the clock. Since it was still too early to leave, she took off the leather jacket and sat back down.

The moment she removed it, Duke saw the odd-shaped birthmark on her neck and did a double take. "Unusual birthmark you have there," he said, pointing at the side of her neck.

"I guess," Mercy said. "I forget it's there."

She drank the last of her juice and then leaned back in the chair, resisting the urge to close her eyes. It wouldn't take much for her to go to sleep.

"Would you like a cup of coffee?" Jack asked. "I mean, you look a bit sleepy. I wouldn't want you to have an accident going home."

"Yes, actually I would. Coffee sounds like a good idea, but I have money to—"

"Please, let me," Jack said.

Mercy didn't argue. She understood his need to give back and closed her eyes rather than continue a conversation. This was a random meeting in their lives, and the sooner she was out of here, the better.

But Duke kept staring. After Jack handed Mercy the coffee and sat back down, Duke and Jack began talking in low tones.

Mercy wasn't paying any attention until she heard a

comment that startled her. "She sure looks like Hope, doesn't she?" Duke asked.

Jack frowned. "Maybe."

But Duke was insistent. "Same olive complexion. Same black hair and brown eyes."

Then Duke realized Mercy was staring at them. "Sorry for talking about you like that," Duke said. "It was rude."

Mercy shrugged it off as Duke continued talking. She thought he talked too much, but now that he had her attention, he launched another conversation. "Hope had a little sister when she was in foster care. Her adoptive parents left her behind, and it broke Hope's heart."

"That's too bad, but it happens," Mercy said.

"She said her little sister had a birthmark on her neck that looked like a valentine heart lying on its side."

Mercy grabbed her neck before she thought. She could feel herself flushing like she used to when a foster parent would decide she was too wild, too unwilling to conform, and her social worker would come and take her away. *Why don't you try to get along,* he would ask.

She never knew what to say. She had no words to describe that she was afraid of everything. That she'd been hurt so many times that her defense mechanism had evolved to being the first to throw a punch or disagree.

"I do remember Hope talking about that," Jack said, and looked at Mercy anew.

"She said her little sister was only three when that happened," Duke said.

Mercy stood abruptly. "What you're implying is impossible. Why are you doing this? You know my name. It was never changed, so obviously, that's not me."

"Hope said she always called her Baby Girl. I don't think I ever heard her mention anything but that."

Now the room was beginning to spin again, but this time from fear, not weakness.

All of a sudden she was remembering a gritty floor against her bare legs and old shoes on her feet so scuffed they no longer held color. Someone was hugging her and patting her on the back. *Don't cry, Baby Girl. I'll tie your shoes.*

She blinked, and the memory was gone, but she felt off-center and anxious. When she began gathering her things, Duke stood.

"Aren't you curious?" he asked. "What are the odds that a donor with the same rare blood type as Hope's, who also looks like her, has the same general coloring, and the same identifying birthmark as the missing sister, isn't connected?"

Mercy was beginning to shake. She'd been alone all her life, and this felt scary. She was afraid to buy into something only to be disappointed again when it wasn't true. "It's not possible," she said.

"Then let's determine it right here and now," Duke said, and pulled out his phone and sent a quick text to a friend who worked in the hospital.

Within moments he got a text back. "My friend, Mark, works in the lab. He's coming up to get a swab for a DNA test. Is that okay?"

Mercy wanted to run, but the thought of actually having family was beyond anything she'd ever dreamed. "I guess," she said, and sat back down.

A few moments later, Doctor Barrett, the surgeon who had operated on Hope, came into the waiting room.

Jack immediately stood. "How is she, Doctor Barrett?"

"I'm cautiously optimistic," he said. "I just wanted to let you know her vital signs are improving. She's not out of the woods by any means, but getting that transfusion was vital."

"Oh, thank God," Jack said, and grabbed both of Mercy's hands. "And thank you again."

"You're the donor?" the doctor asked.

"Yes."

"Then I'm thanking you too. Hope is a good woman and a fine nurse. What you gave her was a chance to live."

Mercy was blinking back tears as the doctor left and fighting an urge to run. But if she left now without following through on this sister thing, she would live the rest of her life wondering what would have happened had she stayed.

A few minutes later, a short redheaded man in a lab coat came hurrying into the waiting room. "Is this the lady in question?" he asked.

Duke nodded. "Mark, this is Mercy Dane. Mercy, this is my friend, Mark Lyons."

Mark smiled. "Hello, Miss Dane. This will only take a few seconds. I just need to get a swab from inside your mouth, okay?"

She nodded.

When he pulled the long swab out of the wrapper, she opened her mouth.

Mark got the sample and secured it. "All finished. When we get the test results, I'll let Duke know."

"How long will it take?" Duke asked.

"Hard to say. They'll take all of the regular requests for people who are waiting for treatment first."

"Okay then," Mercy said, and headed for the door.

"Wait!" Duke said. "How can I contact you?"

She wasn't about to give him her phone number or address. "You can reach me at the Road Warrior Bar in Savannah," she said, and walked out of the waiting room, then out of the hospital.

The sun was bright as she headed toward her bike. The urgency of her arrival was no longer an issue as she slipped the helmet over her head, mounted the Harley, and started it up. The pipes rumbled as she rode out of the parking lot and back toward Main Street.

———

Lon was standing outside the police station talking on his cell phone when he heard the motorcycle. He ended the call as she approached, and on impulse, waved her over.

Mercy sighed. This meeting had to happen to get past it, so she turned toward the curb and pulled into a parking space. She killed the engine, took off her helmet, and cradled it in her lap as he walked toward her. "Am I in trouble again?" she asked.

"No ma'am, you are not," he said, and handed her a card. "This is my business card, but the number on the lower left is the number to my personal cell phone. I would sincerely appreciate it if you gave me a call when you get home, just to let me know you arrived safely. I am a bit concerned about the long ride you're going to have to make so soon after donating blood. I want to know you made it home in one piece. Unlike the last time we parted, when I worried myself sick for some time, wondering what happened to you. Wondering if that thief had come back and taken you away."

Mercy's heart skipped a beat as he laid the card in her palm. She'd been so beaten down and wounded by life that she never thought of his feelings when she'd left. "Are you serious?" she asked.

Lon frowned. "Yes, I'm serious. Why would you doubt that?"

She shrugged. "Nobody ever cared."

He heard a slight tremble in her voice. "Well, I'm not nobody, and I cared before, and I care now."

She slipped the card into one of the pockets in her jacket and then zipped it up for safekeeping. She didn't what to think about him. "I never had to check in with anyone before."

Lon felt like he'd been sideswiped, but didn't let on. He'd thought it that night together so long ago, and he was thinking it again this Christmas Day. He'd never met anyone like her—a matter-of-fact woman who said what she thought and didn't use the situation in her life to gain attention or pity.

"You're not checking in with me, Mercy Dane. If this insults you, then don't call. But like before, be aware that I will worry, and I will wonder if you ever made it home. I will be grateful if you call. Ride safe. Both times we have crossed paths in sad circumstances. I never got a chance to say it before, but I am truly glad to have met you."

All of a sudden Mercy was looking at him through a veil of tears. She took a quick breath and jammed the helmet back on her head.

"Thanks for not giving me a ticket," she said, and started the engine and rode off.

Lon stayed where he was and watched until she

disappeared from view—still remembering what it felt like to come apart in her arms.

———〜〜〜———

Mercy was shaken by the encounter and didn't feel easy until she'd put several miles between herself and Blessings. The town was small by Savannah standards, but there was something about it. Some people might have called it quaint. But that wasn't the adjective Mercy would have used. It took her a few moments to put a name to the vibe she'd gotten just from being there, but when the word came to her, it felt right.

There was an innocence to it. Maybe it had to do with small-town living. She'd never thought about living in a place where you knew most everyone who lived there and had known them since birth. She kept thinking about the depth of concern everyone had for the injured woman…for Hope Talbot. Everyone seemed so friendly, so kind and caring, both for her health and safety, and for Hope.

As for that cop, she didn't quite know how to feel about him. He didn't hit on her. He didn't ask for her number like most of her customers did in the bar. He just wanted to know that she made it home. How had he worded it? Oh yes. In one piece. If she made it home in one piece.

Almost as suddenly as that thought slid through her mind, a car on her left in the passing lane suddenly swerved toward her. She turned toward the ditch, certain he was going to hit her. At the last moment, he overcorrected too much and drove into the center median.

She caught a glimpse of the car as it began to roll and

breathed a shaky sigh of relief that she wasn't the one rolling. She glanced in her side mirror and saw a number of cars were already stopping, so she kept on going, grateful it had not slowed her mercy mission.

About forty-five minutes later, she hit the city limits of Savannah and took an exit ramp that would take her home.

Fifteen minutes more, and she had arrived at her apartment complex and locked up her bike. She paused to stretch before going upstairs and gazed around the complex, noting the number of Christmas wreaths and big red bows decorating doors and balconies.

It was almost noon on a clear, cold Christmas Day.

She thought about the cop's card in her pocket, and on impulse pulled it out and gave him a call. When he answered, she realized she'd been holding her breath for the sound of his voice. "Hello?"

"It's me, Mercy. I'm home."

"Good news! Are you feeling okay?"

She shivered as the deep rasp in his voice rolled through her. "Yes, Chief, I'm fine, and thank you for asking."

"Thank you for calling to ease my mind. Next time we meet, call me Lon. Merry Christmas to you, Mercy Dane."

"Merry Christmas to you too," she said, and disconnected.

She started up the steps to her apartment with a bounce in her walk. It was a good day.

—⁓—

Lon was still smiling as he dropped the phone back in his pocket. For a day that had started out in a near tragedy, it was turning into a really good day.

Chapter 4

Ruby Dye, who owned the Curl Up and Dye hair salon on Main Street, was at home in her kitchen and taking a pecan pie from the oven. The pie was for tonight. She had friends coming over to watch a football game, and she always had desserts ready for them to snack on. And then, in the middle of her party preparations, she thought again of the crazy way her day had begun.

The first incident had been a knock at the door, but by the time she answered, no one was there, just a beautifully wrapped present and a card from a secret admirer.

Before she could go back inside, she had heard sirens and then the sound of a motorcycle racing through the streets. Suddenly, the motorcycle shot out of the alley to the left of her house and went straight up the alley across the street and disappeared.

She only had a glimpse of the rider—black leather, long legs, and a swath of long, dark hair flying out from under that silver helmet like a cape, before he disappeared from view.

The sirens were louder now. He was obviously being chased.

In a fit of good cheer, and because it *was* Christmas Day, Ruby had shouted aloud, "Ride safe and ride fast, whoever you are. God is in His heaven, and the Devil's on your tail."

Then she went inside out of the cold and sat down to

open her gift. An hour later she was still puzzling over the identity of her secret admirer. Whoever he was, he had good taste. The ruby glass candy dish that had been in the box was now sitting in a place of honor on the dining room table, catching bits of sunlight in the facets of the glass.

She hadn't had a man friend since she'd come to Blessings. She'd arrived here straight out of an ugly divorce, and the last thing she'd wanted was another man in her life. And all this time, she hadn't even given a single thought to looking for one.

Now this.

But the idea was intriguing, and certainly something to think about for the upcoming year.

———

Mercy had been home two days and was finally on her way to the grocery store. She had just pulled up and parked when her phone signaled a text. She frowned, wondering if Moose was calling her in to work. It was her day off, and she sure hoped it stayed that way.

Then she pulled up the text.

It's me, the cop, wanting you to know someone is thinking of you. Hope you are well. I have the flu. Feeling sorry for myself. Going back to bed now.

Mercy smiled. It was an unexpected hello she never thought she would receive.

Stay in bed, Lon. Drink lots of liquids. I am fine.

Then she put the phone in her jacket pocket and headed into the supermarket, still smiling.

Back in Blessings, Lon heard the ding and knew she'd sent something back. He reached for a tissue as he pulled up the text, read it, and sighed. He felt like hell, but she'd called him Lon. He blew his nose, rolled over in bed, pulled the covers beneath his chin, and saw Mercy's face as he drifted off to sleep.

Chapter 5

TWO NIGHTS LATER MERCY WAS JUST GETTING OFF WORK. She stopped in the hall of the bar and checked her phone before she headed home. When she saw a text from the cop, she grinned.

> It's me, the cop. I'm still alive. Are you? I'm somewhat better, almost well, and went back to work today.

She never even thought about ignoring it as she sent back a quick answer.

> I'm alive. Just getting off work and ready to head home. Glad you are feeling better.

Lon was working the night shift for one of his deputies, who was out sick with what he had just gotten over. When he heard his phone signal a text, his heart skipped. And when he saw it was from Mercy, he grinned. He read the message, delighted that she had answered him, and then realized what time it was and frowned.

At 2:00 a.m.? She gets off work at 2:00 a.m.? He wouldn't let himself think about her riding through the streets of Savannah at that time of the morning. She'd been taking care of herself long before their paths ever crossed. Still, he said a silent prayer for a safe journey

home as he turned around at the end of Main Street and
started down the other side of the street, flashing his
searchlight and checking storefronts to make sure everything was secure.

———

Mercy had been home about ten minutes when her cell
signaled a text. She didn't hesitate anymore, and looked
forward to their sparse and irregular communication.
Then she read the message and frowned.

> It's me, the cop. Hope I didn't wake you. It's been
> a rough night. Had a house fire on the outskirts of
> Blessings. A man died. Had to call his daughter in
> Illinois. Downside of my job.

Mercy's shoulders slumped as she sat on the side of
the bed. She started to send a response and then stopped.
What the heck would she say? How do you comfort
someone you barely know?

She sat there a minute and then instead of a text, she
called, and when she heard the surprise in his voice, she
knew she'd made the right move.

"Mercy? Is that you?"

"It's me. I'm sorry you're sad."

Lon was floored. "Well, honey…this call has gone a
long way toward cheering me up."

"I didn't know what to say, so I thought if I called,
you could do the talking, and I would listen. Sometimes
you just want to be heard."

Lon pinched the bridge of his nose to keep from
crying. "For a girl, you're actually pretty smart."

She frowned and was about to light into him for such an antifeminist remark, and then thought she heard him chuckle. "Are you laughing?" she asked.

"Not quite."

She sighed, and curled her feet beneath her. "Are you okay?"

"I am now," Lon said. "Thank you for caring enough to do this."

"When do you get off work?"

"At 7:00 a.m. I'm covering for one of my deputies. Everyone has the flu."

"Get a new toothbrush, and wipe down your home with a disinfectant cleaner."

"What?"

"It's what one of my foster mothers did when we all got sick at once. She threw away our toothbrushes when we got well and washed away the germs."

"Thank you for the tip," Lon said. "It makes sense."

Mercy smiled, more than pleased that he thought what she'd said was a good idea.

"It's time you were in bed, so I'm going to say goodbye. This has been an unexpected joy on a really awful day. Thank you. I won't forget this."

"You're welcome," Mercy said and disconnected.

She sat in the silence of her apartment, thinking about what it would be like to be the constant bearer of bad news and was glad she was not a cop. Then she got beneath the covers and turned out the lights. But even after she closed her eyes, she still saw his face.

She remembered what it felt like to come when he was inside her. She had yet to realize he had long ago laid claim to a tiny little piece of her heart.

—⁓—

Hope Talbot remembered seeing the pickup truck cross-ing the center line only seconds before impact, and then nothing until she woke up in intensive care nearly thirty-six hours later.

You nearly died, they told her. *A young woman came from Savannah and donated blood that saved your life.*

She heard the words, but there was too much pain to focus, and she fell asleep again.

The next time she woke, Jack was standing by the bed, crying.

"Am I dying?" she'd asked.

"No, baby, no. You're getting well," he'd said.

She slept again and dreamed of standing on the street in front of a house, watching a car drive away, and the smaller it appeared, the more panicked she became. "Mommy!" she screamed.

"Hope, Hope, you're okay," someone said, laying a hand on her forehead.

She tried to wake up, but the pain was still between her and daylight.

It wasn't until the fourth day after the accident that her doctor had her moved out of ICU. After that, she was able to stay awake for short periods of time, and by the seventh day had improved so much they talked about sending her home.

On the eighth day, Jack was cleaning up the kitchen after breakfast when his cell phone rang. He grabbed a towel to dry his hands, noticed the call was from the hospital, and quickly answered. "Hello?"

"Jack, it's me."

He leaned against the cabinet, smiling at the sound of her voice. "Hope! Baby! How are you doing this morning?"

"The doctor already made his rounds this morning. He said I could go home."

"Oh wow! That's the news I've been waiting for. I'm on my way!"

Hope smiled. "Don't forget to bring me something to wear. They burned the clothes and coat I was wearing in the wreck. They were full of glass."

"I remember. I've already got the bag packed."

"See you soon," she said, and hung up the phone.

She swung her legs off the side of the bed, steadying herself as she stood. It was a miracle she was alive, and she knew it.

Her spleen had ruptured in the wreck. She'd nearly bled to death before they got her into surgery. One lung had collapsed, and that had to be dealt with as well. After surgery, while she received a transfusion, the doctor and nurses had picked splinters of glass out of her neck and face. She didn't remember any of that.

Until this morning, she'd had a good dozen staples in her belly from the surgery, and a total of six in two different places on her scalp. She'd seen the bruises on the front of her body, but knew there were bound to be more. Her ribs were sore—two had cracked, but she was healing, and thanks to a skillful surgeon and a stranger's blood, she was going home.

She made her way to the bathroom, and when she was finished, stopped at the sink to wash her hands. As she was drying, she glanced at the mirror and frowned at her reflection.

It was difficult to see herself beneath the swelling

and bruising. Her hair was still black. Her skin still held the color of her Italian heritage, and her eyes were still that dark, fathomless brown. But her face and neck were peppered with tiny scabs from the shattered glass. There were places on her scalp missing hair, but at least they hadn't shaved her head. The large contusion over her right eyebrow was getting better. The swelling had gone down enough so she could finally see out of that eye, and her arms and most of her upper body had been somewhat protected from flying glass because she'd been wearing a heavy winter coat. Something else to be thankful for.

She'd been told that a preacher prayed over her, but she didn't remember. He said the whole town of Blessings had prayed day and night for her recovery. Suddenly struggling not to cry, she took a deep breath. Thank God their prayers were answered. She wasn't nearly through living.

Hope laid her palm against the glass, partially covering her reflection. She was still Hope, yet not the woman she'd been. She was more. More because of the woman whose blood now ran through her veins—because of the woman who'd saved her life.

Then the door opened. Hope's friend and fellow nurse, Georgia Frost, came in smiling. "I hear you're going home today," Georgia said.

Hope nodded. "Yes, I've already called Jack."

Georgia took her by the elbow. "Come lie back down while you wait. You don't need to overdo this 'feeling better' phase, or it won't last long."

"I know, but it's hard to be still when you're used to staying busy."

"You nearly died," Georgia reminded her.

"Right," Hope muttered. "So I'm lying down now," she said as she eased herself onto the bed and stretched out.

Georgia pulled the covers up to keep her from getting cold and then leaned against the side of the bed. "Did you hear about the guy who hit you?"

"I haven't heard anything. I don't even know his name. Was he from around here?"

"No. Out of state plates, but this is what burns me. He was driving with a revoked license. He'd just been released from jail for drunk driving. I heard that when he gets out of the hospital in Savannah, he's going straight to prison. This was the fifth drunk driving charge. I personally hope they keep him. He came close to killing you." Georgia patted Hope's leg as she changed the subject. "We just wanted to let you know how happy we are that you will be home, getting well, and that we'll see you again."

"Thank you," Hope said, and then Jack came in, and the visit with Georgia ended.

He gave Hope a quick kiss and smoothed the hair from her forehead. "They're getting your release papers ready. I told them I'd help you dress. Do you feel okay to do that now?"

"Yes. I just want to get home and sleep in my own bed."

"I will be glad to have you there." Hope heard the tremble in his voice as he lifted her fingers to his lips. "I've missed you."

"Someday, this will just be a story we talk about at the dinner table," she said.

"That's for sure," Jack said as he set the bag he'd brought on the foot of the bed and took out all the clothing. "If I help, can you manage panties, or do you want to go home commando?"

She pointed at the clothes he'd laid out. "I'll take the panties. It's too cold to be all that airy."

He grinned, and together they got her dressed. By the time Georgia came back with a wheelchair and release papers, Hope was in sweatpants, a zip-up sweatshirt, and fuzzy house shoes over thick wool socks.

"Ready to go for a ride?" Georgia asked.

"If it gets me home, I sure am," Hope said.

Since her coat was not salvageable, Jack had brought one of his. The tan goose down jacket was too big, but it served its purpose as he helped her to the wheelchair.

"Georgia, I'll meet you at the front entrance. I'm going ahead to get the car," Jack said, blew Hope a kiss, grabbed the empty bag, and left on the run.

Georgia pushed Hope toward the door. "Your husband is a cutie-pie," she said.

Hope beamed. "I like to think so."

"He reminds me a little of that actor, Ryan Reynolds, but with darker hair and green eyes."

"He'll get a big head if I tell him that," Hope said as they headed up the hall toward the elevator.

Georgia giggled. "He's better looking than his brother. Not that Duke isn't good-looking, you know. But Duke is always frowning, like he's a little displeased with the world in general."

Hope had to laugh. "Oh, Georgia, do you ever have Duke pegged. Oh, don't get me wrong. He's a great brother-in-law, but he's really hard to please. Probably why, at the age of forty, he's still a bachelor."

Georgia reached the elevator and punched the button

to go down. When the doors opened, she rolled Hope inside. Down they went to the ground floor as Georgia wheeled her toward the exit. "There's Jack-on-the-spot, already waiting," Georgia said.

Hope sighed. It was such a relief to be going home.

She got in the truck and was safely buckled up as Jack drove away. Hope was seeing Blessings with new appreciation as they drove down Main. They were leaving the city limits when Jack patted her knee, and then tucked in a corner of the blanket he had over her legs. "As you can see, it's starting to sprinkle. Are you warm enough? I can turn the heater up if you need," he said.

"No, I'm fine," Hope said, and then felt her eyes well.

Jack panicked. "Honey? What? Are you in pain? Do I need to turn around?"

"No, I'm just emotional," Hope said. "We just passed the place where the wreck occurred."

"Ah...yes, we did," Jack said. "I'm sorry."

"It's nothing. It's silly. I need to get over that because it's the road we always use to get to and from Blessings."

Jack turned on the windshield wipers and drove a little further in silence, debating with himself whether to tell her about the woman and the DNA test, then decided she, of all people, had the most right to know. "I have something to tell you. It's about the woman who donated blood for you."

"Please do. I can't get her out of my mind. She's the reason I'm still alive."

"She was something to see. She sure took the starch out of old Duke. You know how he is...always trying to boss people around."

Hope grinned. "Tell me."

"She rode a Harley all the way from Savannah, and I can only imagine what a ride that was because of the timing. Started out in darkness and then rode into daylight all the way to Blessings, only to get stopped by the roadblock from the wreck. Then Chief Pittman tried to chase her down to give her a ticket for speeding, and she took off through the alleys and outran him to the hospital. By the time he got there, they'd already taken her back to draw blood."

Hope laughed. "A bit of a hell-raiser. I like that. Maybe some of her daring will rub off on me. I'm a little too passive sometimes."

"You're perfect," Jack said. "But there's more."

"Then tell me."

"They brought her into the waiting room after she'd donated blood. The chief was there. I think he wanted to see her after she eluded him to get to you, and then it was the strangest thing. They realized they knew each other. She sat down to drink some orange juice and eat some sweets before she could leave, so I got her the stuff from the vending machines. The chief left, and Duke and I talked to her while she ate."

"Was she nice?" Hope asked.

"She seemed very nice. She works at a place in Savannah called the Road Warrior Bar. She's lived in the city all her life, and she's not married."

"Sounds like someone who's had to take care of herself and is doing a good job of it."

Jack reached for her hand and gave it a light squeeze. "Duke was telling her that because you'd been adopted out of foster care, there were no blood relatives who might have been a match for your rare blood type. She said you were lucky, because she grew up in foster care and aged out."

Hope frowned. "That's tough. I know it happens to a lot of foster kids."

Jack hesitated again, trying to feel his way through the rest of this story. "So after she ate some of the food, she took off her leather coat. Oh…did I tell you she was wearing all leather…tight black pants and a big black bomber jacket? She was so tall and so damn beautiful, she could have been a runway model. But that silver biker helmet she had was bothering Duke. He couldn't get over the fact that there was no man running herd on her, and of course, Duke being Duke, made a male chauvinist comment. I thought she was going to take the hide off him. If I hadn't been so worried about you, I would have laughed."

Hope was laughing just imagining how it all played out. It felt good to be happy again. "I can see that. Lord, I wish I could have met her."

Jack gave her hand another little squeeze. "That's part of what I needed to tell you. Hope, when she took off her jacket, there was a birthmark on her neck that looked like a valentine heart lying on its side."

Hope gasped. "No, oh my God, no. Jack. Tell me you got her name. Where she lives. Something!"

"Thanks to Duke's insistence, we got more than that. She agreed to a DNA sample. Mark Lyons came up from the lab and took a swab. We're waiting for results any day now."

Hope was shaking. "What did she look like?"

"Duke thinks she looks like you, but taller. She has black hair, the same olive complexion, and dark brown eyes. And there was the birthmark, and the fact that she grew up in foster care."

"What did she say?" Hope asked.

"At first she got angry when the connection was suggested, but I think it scared her. She doesn't remember having any family. She is about as alone in the world as a person can be. She said she couldn't be your sister because she'd never changed her name, and since we already knew what it was, and no one mentioned a connection, it surely wasn't her."

Jack continued. "But then we told her you never mentioned her given name…at least not to our memory. All we ever remembered was that you called her Baby Girl. She got this funny look on her face and clammed up. She let Mark take the DNA swab and then left. She wouldn't give Duke her phone number or address. She just told him where she worked."

"Jack, what was her name?"

"Mercy Dane."

Hope let out a wail and then covered her face and started to weep. "Oh my God. That's my sister, Jack. I don't need a DNA test to prove it. I had to nearly die to find her, but God gave her back to me. I will never ask for another thing in this life as long as I live. We have to go get her. I need to see her. I need to explain I didn't want to leave her behind. It wasn't my fault, but the guilt has colored my entire life."

"Well, not today, you're not. She's not going anywhere, and I need to get you home," Jack said.

"I can't believe it. I just can't believe it," Hope kept saying. "All these years, she was still in Savannah."

Chapter 6

DUKE WAS WAITING AT THE HOUSE WHEN THEY DROVE INTO THE yard. He came out onto the porch smiling, ready to help Hope inside, only to see her get out of the car in tears.

"What's wrong?" Duke asked.

"Nothing's wrong," Jack said as he steadied Hope's pace.

"It was my sister who saved my life," Hope said.

Duke frowned at Jack. "Why did you tell her? We still don't know if—"

"I know!" Hope cried. "Mercy Dane. That's my sister's name. I was Hope Dane until I was adopted. She's my sister, and I want to see her!"

Duke's frown deepened. "Well, Mark Lyon took a DNA swab, and we may as well wait until there's hard proof before—"

"That's not your decision to make, Duke Talbot. If you don't go get her, I will find a way to get her here without anyone's help."

"Now see here, Hope. She—"

Hope stopped at the bottom of the porch steps. "Shut up, Duke. Just shut up right now before you say something I won't forgive," she muttered.

Jack frowned. "Back off, Duke. What's the matter with you?"

Duke held up his hands and stepped aside. "I'm sorry. I was just trying to take care of you. Not wanting you to get your feelings hurt if all she wanted was a handout."

"She didn't know us from Adam. She came to help Hope from the goodness of her heart. She was leaving, and you're the one who insisted she give a DNA sample," Jack said. "Now you're acting like she's going to steal something. Hope's right. Stop talking now and help me."

Duke hurried down the steps and then gave Hope a quick hug. "I'm sorry, honey. I didn't mean to upset you."

Hope didn't say anything as they helped her up the steps and into the house. The ride home had been uncomfortable, and now she was upset as well. She just wanted to be in her bed and out of earshot of Duke's dictatorial voice.

And then Duke's phone rang. He glanced at caller ID and frowned. "I need to take this. Jack, can you get her to the bedroom on your own?"

"Yes. We're good," Jack said, then helped her down the hall into their bedroom and pulled back the covers on their bed as she sat down.

"Oh my lord, I am so sore," Hope said.

"I have your pain pills in my pocket, baby. Do you want to change into some pj's?" Jack asked.

"No. I just want to lie down for now."

Jack ran into the bathroom to get a glass of water, then came back, handed it to her, and then dropped to one knee beside her chair as he dug the pills out of his pocket.

"Here you go. It says to take two," he said as he put them in her hand and then watched her swallow them. "I'm so sorry Duke hurt your feelings. I'd go talk to your sister myself tomorrow, but I'm not leaving you here alone. If I can get someone to stay with you, I'll make it happen. This is a miracle for you, and I know it. I can't wait for you to meet her all grown up. She's just a younger, tougher version of you."

Tears were rolling down Hope's face again. "Bless her heart."

"Honey, you two will have the rest of your lives to catch up. She's not lost anymore, right?"

"Right," Hope said. "I'm ready to lie down now."

Jack helped her into bed, then leaned down and kissed her square on the lips. It was a gentle kiss, but one of longing as he pulled away.

"I love you so much, Hope, so much. I'm grateful you are home."

"I love you too," Hope said.

Jack patted her shoulder and then closed the door as he left the room, only to meet Duke coming out of the kitchen with a smile on his face.

"That was Mark Lyons at the lab. The DNA test came back positive. Hope and Mercy Dane are full-blood sisters."

Jack's eyes narrowed. "Yeah, well, she already told you that, so—"

Duke sighed. "Look, I already apologized, and I'll go to Savannah myself and give the woman the news."

"And you will invite her to stay here, and you will not be an ass about anything. Do you understand?" Jack asked.

Duke didn't like to be called down by anyone, especially his younger brother, but he was already walking on shaky ground here, and let it slide. "Yes, of course. I'm not heartless."

"Fine. As long as we understand each other," Jack said. "I'm going to make some lunch. Hope is resting now."

"And I'm going out to see about that broken fence wire on the road. Last thing we need is cattle getting out."

"Okay," Jack said, and went to the kitchen as Duke went out the back door.

It had been nine days since Mercy's return from Blessings, and she hadn't had one solid night's sleep since. If it hadn't been for the intermittent texts from the cop, she wouldn't have had one good thing to say about that crazy ride to Blessings other than someone's life was saved.

She was having dreams that felt more like memories, dreams of crying in the dark and soft hands and a gentle voice pulling her close, but she couldn't tell if they were real or wishful thinking. She also dreamed about the cop and that night they'd spent making love.

Yesterday was her day off. She'd spent the day cleaning her apartment and doing laundry, and today she'd been baking before going to work. It's what she did when troubled.

Now, the aroma of pumpkin muffins in the oven filled the apartment. She'd made too many. She always did when she baked because the foster mother who'd taught her to cook always had a lot of mouths to feed. And since she had to go to work in a few hours, she would take most of the muffins to the bar. A few minutes later, the timer went off. She took them out of the oven, turned it off, and set them aside to cool as she cleaned up the kitchen.

It was 3:00 p.m. by the time she was through. She hadn't eaten lunch, and there wasn't much left in the refrigerator, so she sat at the kitchen table with a glass of milk and a hot muffin, slathered it with butter, and ate with the melting butter dripping through her fingers onto the plate. Unwilling to waste anything this delicious, she sopped up the drips with her last bite and popped it in her mouth. She thought about eating another, then happened to glance out the window.

She sighed. It was raining, one of those days she wished she had a car.

—⁓—

Moose was counting out change for the till when Mercy got to work. When he saw the container she carried, he grinned. "Please tell me you baked something."

"I baked something," she said, and slid it across the bar.

He opened the lid on the plastic container then groaned. "Oh man, oh man, oh man. Muffins! Smells like pumpkin bread. Is it pumpkin?"

"All day long," she said, and disappeared into the back room to lock up her stuff before she came back, tying on her bar apron and slipping a new order pad into the pocket.

Within a couple of minutes, Barb arrived along with Farrah Welty, another of the five rotating waitresses Moose employed. Farrah had a sharp tongue and a wicked wit. Once she'd been a looker. Now she was just a Botox version of her former self and was working at the bar to save up for a boob job. After four kids and forty-five years of hard living, she claimed her boob size had become a 36 long and wanted that fixed.

When the girls saw the container at the end of the bar and the muffin in Moose's hands, they both squealed.

"Did Mercy bake again? Oh lord, I want one of those," Farrah said.

"Like eating the best pumpkin bread you ever tasted," Moose said.

Barb groaned. "Well, hell, there goes my diet. I didn't last twenty-four hours this time," she said as she helped herself.

Mercy smiled. It wasn't often she felt proud of anything she'd done, but she knew she was a good cook and an even better baker.

By the time eight o'clock rolled around, the Road Warrior Bar was loud and rocking. Moose had the sound system keyed in to country music, and chili heating on the stove in the back. A half dozen truckers had pulled into the parking lot for the night. After beer and chili and a few games of pool, they would spend the rest of the night in the sleeper cabs.

Most of the others were regulars, including Big Boy and a couple of his biker buddies. So far they'd been too involved in getting drunk to worry about harassing the waitresses.

Mercy was on her way back to the bar with another order when the door opened, and Duke Talbot walked in. Her heart skipped a beat as she saw him scanning the room, and when he spied her and grinned, she started to shake. By the time he stood in front of her laughing and talking, she couldn't hear a word he was saying for the roar in her head. And then he took her by the shoulders. She heard the words "full-blood sister" and "can't wait to meet you" right before the earth shifted beneath her feet, and everything went black.

Duke caught her before she hit the floor and scooped

her into his arms. Her head dangled limply against his arm as both waitresses came running, yelling for Moose. "What did you do to her?" Moose growled as he yanked her out of Duke's arms.

She flopped like a rag doll as he carried her past the tables of shocked customers toward his office.

Duke was at his heels, explaining as he went. "I didn't do anything. I was just giving her the news about her sister, and she fainted."

Moose laid Mercy on the old sofa in his office and yelled at Farrah, who was standing in the doorway. "Bring me a wet bar rag, and make sure it's clean," he said, and then turned and poked a finger at Duke's chest. "Mercy doesn't have a sister, so you better come up with another excuse, buddy."

Even though the guy was twice his size, Duke didn't back down. "She does have a sister. She just didn't know it. They figured it out when she came to Blessings to donate her blood."

"I don't know anything about any blood donation!" Moose said.

"I do," Barb said. "Over a week ago. Some woman was dying and needed a blood transfusion, but had a rare blood type. The same type as Mercy."

Farrah came running with the wet cloth, folded it, and placed it over Mercy's forehead. "Mercy, honey, wake up," Farrah said.

Mercy groaned.

Duke frowned. This was not the reaction he had expected, and he was trying not to be judgmental about this bar or the low-class people who were obviously Mercy's friends.

Mercy shoved the wet cloth off her forehead, swung her legs over the side of the sofa, and sat up. "You fainted," Moose said.

"I never faint," Mercy muttered, and then saw Duke again and remembered. "Say it again."

"Hope is your sister. She's out of the hospital and so excited to see you. I came to take you to Blessings."

Mercy frowned. He was doing it again—making plans without giving her a chance for input. "You're not taking me anywhere," Mercy said, and stood up.

Duke frowned. "Don't you want to meet your sister?"

Mercy's eyes narrowed. "Yes, but I'll get myself there."

"But—"

She held up a hand. "Just stop. Please."

Duke's frown deepened. He wasn't used to people disagreeing with him about anything.

Moose glared at the stranger. "So Mercy has a sister. What business is it of yours?"

"Mercy's sister, Hope, is my sister-in-law. She and my brother have been married for almost ten years. I'm the one who suspected the connection between them. I'm the one who urged her to have a DNA test. I found out yesterday and came here tonight to give her the news."

"And now she knows," Moose said. "It's up to her what she does, right?"

"I guess," Duke said.

Mercy sighed. "Moose…I'm sorry, but I need some time off. I need to explore this revelation, and see how it plays out in my life."

Moose patted her on the shoulder, but there were tears in his eyes. "I understand, and we're all happy for you, girl. You know that. You do what you have to do, just know you'll always have a job here, if you want it."

"Thank you," she said, and when she saw Barb and Farrah crying, she fought back tears of her own. "You guys! Don't make me cry too."

They hugged her. "We're happy for you. It's just that we'll miss you," Barb said.

"And your baking," Farrah added.

Duke could see that her ties here were strong. The sooner she got into a decent environment, the better off she would be.

"Go on home," Moose said. "Get a good night's sleep, and safe travels."

"Thank you all. I'll stay in touch. I promise."

They went back into the bar, leaving Mercy alone with Duke. "So?" he asked.

"I'm going home to pack. You can follow me. We'll talk more there."

The invitation pleased Duke. Now they were getting somewhere.

She got her things and led the way through the bar, then out the door.

Chapter 7

BIG BOY WAS DRUNK AND ALMOST MISSED SEEING MERCY leaving with a stranger. It ticked him off that she wouldn't give him the time of day. He wondered what that man had on her, then decided he might be some kind of cop.

He grabbed at the tail of Barb's shirt as she walked past his table. "Hey, where's your buddy going? Is she getting arrested?"

Barb slapped at his hand and moved out of his reach. "No, he's not a cop, and it's none of your business where she goes. But I hope wherever it is, she doesn't ever have to come back to put up with your crap."

Big Boy was startled that her exit might be permanent. This didn't fit in with his plans. The fact that she rode a Harley had been what first attracted him to her. He'd spent months aggravating her, believing that he'd finally break her down and turn her into his bitch. He didn't like to think that was the last he'd ever see of her, but he'd worry about that tomorrow.

"Then bring another round of drinks to the table, and bring us some chili and crackers. We're hungry!"

Mercy took the usual way home, super-conscious of the headlights on her tail. She was so overwhelmed by the news Duke Talbot had given her that she was struggling with an urge to cry. She didn't know how she was supposed to feel at this point, but she was scared. She didn't know how to be a sister. She didn't know what being part of a family was about.

By the time she rode up to her apartment building, she'd erected one heck of a mental wall. She didn't like Duke Talbot. He was too pushy, and the sooner she set boundaries, the better off she would be.

"Follow me," she said as she locked up her bike and headed up the stairs and into her building.

Duke followed, already forming an opinion of her living conditions, and didn't think any more of them than he had her place of work. He was happy for Hope's sake that they'd found her missing sister, but if all of this was okay with Mercy, they had their work cut out getting her to a presentable mind-set.

Mercy entered the building with Duke on her heels. She unlocked the door to her apartment and turned on a light as she entered. "Have a seat. We need to get on the same page before I go to Blessings. First, I need directions to where she lives."

He frowned. "She? Her name is Hope."

"Right now you know her and I don't," Mercy said. "Directions please."

Duke sighed. None of this was going as he'd imagined. Here he'd been imagining her taking advantage of their lifestyle, and now he wasn't sure she even wanted to come.

"Actually, the directions are a little complicated. We live in the country, and there aren't street signs to get you there."

She frowned. "We? She and her husband live with you?"

"Jack and I inherited our family farm. We both work it. We live in the home we grew up in, but it's a big two-story house. Besides the two rooms we occupy, there are still three empty bedrooms upstairs. Staying there will give you and Hope lots of time to get to know each other again, and plenty of time for her to fill you in on whatever you can't remember. It will be weeks before she's strong enough to return to her job."

Mercy relented. It made sense to be as close to Hope as she could, especially while she was recuperating. "Yes. Okay."

"Good, then it's settled," Duke said. "Are you coming tomorrow?"

"Yes."

He handed her a business card. "When you get to Blessings, call me. I'll come to town, and you can follow me back to the farm."

She slipped the card into her pants pocket. "I'll see you tomorrow."

"Look, if you have a lot to bring, why don't you pack up what you can tonight, and let me take it back for you?"

She started to tell him no, but then changed her mind. "Yes, alright. There's the TV, and the remote is on the sofa. You can start with loading that first while I pack clothes and dishes."

"Oh, you won't need dishes," Duke said. "We have everything you'll need."

Mercy looked at him as if he'd just lost his mind. "I am not leaving *my* things behind. I am not living with you for the rest of my life. I will need them again."

"Oh, I didn't mean—Uh, yes, of course. I'll start with your TV," he said, and began unhooking the connections.

Mercy tried not to panic as she headed for her bedroom, but oh my God, she had a sister! She was no longer alone in this world, and she was going back to Blessings. Surely, she'd see the chief of police now and then.

———∿∿∿———

Hope was asleep by the time Duke got home with all of Mercy's belongings. He stacked the boxes in the garage for the night and carried the television into the house and left it in the kitchen.

She woke up the next day with Mercy on her mind. She remembered Jack saying Mercy had no memory of a sister, and it broke her heart. She tried to think of things she might tell her that she would remember and then gave up. They were going to have to start from this moment and not try to make the past fit into their lives.

Jack knew she was worried and sad and wanted so desperately to make everything right. He wandered into the bedroom to check on Hope and caught her with the TV on mute, staring out the window.

"Honey, what can I do for you?"

Hope turned off the TV. "Hug me."

He sat down on the side of the bed and gently took her in his arms. She had been hurt in so many places he was afraid to squeeze, so he kissed the top of her head instead. "It's going to be okay, baby. You'll see. She's coming here today. Duke brought home most of her things last night. Since she only has the Harley for transportation, he offered to bring everything she couldn't carry."

Hope's eyes widened. "Oh my gosh! She'll be here today! We have to get a bedroom ready for her. Let's give her the big room upstairs. The sheets need to be changed. It needs to be dusted, and the floors cleaned."

"I can do that," he said. "What else?"

She smiled. "How did you know there was something else?"

"Because with you, there's always something else."

She brushed her fingers across his hand, absently rubbing his wedding ring with her thumb.

"There's an old blue box in the attic. I think it's beside your mama's trunk. Will you bring it down here to me?"

"Sure, honey. What's in it?"

"It's what I took with me from the last foster home when my parents adopted me. I haven't looked at it in years and not sure what's in it anymore, but I'm hoping there might be something that would ring a bell for Mercy."

"Oh, good idea. I'll get that for you first and then get busy on the bedroom, okay?"

She nodded, and when he started out of the room, she stopped him. "Jack?"

"What, baby?"

"I'm scared she's going to hate me."

Jack shook his head. "No. I think you're wrong about her. I only met her that one time, but she didn't strike me as someone who held grudges. She's pretty straightforward and giving. Otherwise, she wouldn't have signed up on that blood registry or made that frantic ride to Blessings before it was even daylight. Don't count her out, okay?"

"Yes, okay," Hope said, and sent him off with a smile.

But the moment he was gone, she closed her eyes. Even then, the tears slipped down her temples before disappearing into her thick, dark hair.

Ruby Dye opened the Curl Up and Dye with a bounce in her step, then paused in front of the mirror at her workstation to recheck her new hair color. She often changed the color as an advertisement for the shop, but this time she'd done it for new beginnings—something she had never expected to come her way again.

The sunlight coming through the windows caught in the rich highlights. She'd never done strawberry blonde, but the longer she looked at herself, the wider her smile became.

She was forty-five years old and feeling pretty wasn't anything she gave much thought to these days, but right now, she *was* feeling pretty—at least as pretty as Ruby Dye had ever felt. There was a fresh bouquet of flowers on her dining room table—another gift from her secret admirer.

The back door opened then banged shut as Mabel Jean came in carrying a big stack of clean towels. "Oooh, Ruby! Sister! I love that color on you."

Ruby beamed. She loved the Southern way of being called Sister. It made her feel like she belonged. "Thank you. I thought it was past time to change my look."

"Well, you hit this one out of the park," she said, and then carried her towels to the shelf behind her manicure station. "I have an early appointment this morning. Rachel Goodhope is coming in to get a manicure. She said her last guest at the bed-and-breakfast left last night, and her nails are a mess."

"Okay. Since you're here, I'm going to leave you with the shop and run to the bank for change. Do you need any?"

"No, I'm good, but thanks," Mabel Jean said. "However, if you're bringing back sweet rolls, I'll take one."

Ruby grinned. "Why am I not surprised? You have such a sweet tooth."

Mabel Jean giggled as she patted her extra-curvy hips. "And the figure to go with it," she said.

"It's all good," Ruby said. "I won't be long."

She grabbed her purse and headed out the back door.

———

Jack came down from the attic carrying the blue box Hope wanted and hurried to their bedroom, curious to see what all was in it, but she'd fallen asleep, and the box was tied with heavy cording. He would see it later, so he set it at the foot of the bed and put a pair of scissors on the bedside table before tiptoeing out of the room.

———

Peanut Butterman was coming out of Granny's Country Kitchen with a belly full of buckwheat pancakes and sausage links when he saw Ruby Dye drive by in her car.

He paused, always interested in what she was up to, and smiled when he saw her park in front of the bakery, thinking about saying hello when she got out of the car. At that point, his breath caught in the back of his throat and he was getting dizzy until he remembered to breathe.

He'd known her since the day she set up shop in Blessings and had been her steady customer for the past three years, since the local barber retired. He'd seen her hair in just about every color under the sun, but he'd never seen her as a strawberry blonde before, and she was stunning.

He was still watching when she came out of the bakery carrying a box. He finally lifted a hand in hello, and when she waved and smiled, he groaned. He'd always been a sucker for blondes, and now, he wondered what he'd been missing.

"Morning!" she called out, and then put her box in the backseat, got in the car, and drove away.

Peanut's hand was still in the air as she drove down the street to her shop, took the turn at the corner to park in the back, and disappeared from view.

"Hey Peanut, what'cha pointing at?"

Peanut blinked, dropped his hand, and then muttered something about stretching a muscle in his back and drove off without even looking to see who'd asked the question.

———

It was nearing noon when Lon Pittman rolled into the Stop and Go to fill up the cruiser. Duke Talbot pulled up on the other side of the pumps and began to do the same.

"Morning, Chief," Duke said.

Lon nodded as he swiped his card at the pump. "Good morning, Duke. How's Hope doing? I heard she was released yesterday."

"Yes, she's home, but still has to take it easy. We're really glad to have her back."

"That's great news," Lon said.

"And there's more news," Duke said. "Remember that woman you recognized in the hospital who came here to donate blood for Hope?"

I'll never forget her. "Yes, I remember."

"It turns out she's Hope's long-lost sister. Hope was adopted out of foster care, and her adoptive parents left her little sister behind. I think Mercy was around three years old when they were separated."

Lon's heart skipped a beat. "Her sister? So she's coming back to Blessings?"

"Yes. Sometime today."

"And she knew none of this when she came to Blessings?" Lon asked.

"Oh no! In fact, she didn't know she had family anywhere. She aged out of the foster care system and has been on her own ever since. I suspected a connection when I saw the birthmark on her neck at the hospital... something Hope had mentioned numerous times over the years. We talked her into giving a DNA sample, and we got the call a couple of days ago that it's true. Jack didn't tell Hope about any of this until he brought her home, so she's over the moon, as you can imagine."

Lon felt like he'd been given the keys to the city but tried not to show it. "That's amazing," Lon said, and then his pump kicked off. "So I guess we'll be seeing more of her here in Blessings."

"Yes. She'll be staying with us, of course, but we hope she makes Blessings her home."

A slow smile spread across Lon's face. Some days started out better than others, and this day had just taken a turn to the good. "That's great. You give Hope my best," he said, pocketed his receipt, and drove away.

Duke finished gassing up, then headed downtown to the bank before going to the feed store. He needed a load of cattle cubes and a couple of blocks of salt and hoped she'd arrive in Blessings before he left town, so he wouldn't have to make two trips.

The idea of seeing Mercy Dane made his heart skip a

beat. She was too outspoken for his tastes, but she was damn beautiful, and since she'd be living with them, he was giving thought to shaping her into wife material. Brothers marrying sisters would be the perfect way to keep two women happy under the same roof. He had yet to give falling in love much thought.

—⁓—

Mercy left the past behind her on a cold, clear Savannah morning with a duffel bag tied onto the back of her Harley and the cash she'd been saving in the freezer inside a money belt beneath her jacket. She was anxious to meet this sister and hopeful that life was taking her in a positive direction. The fact that the cop was the one man from her past she didn't regret gave her hope they might turn a one-night stand into more.

The miles on the interstate unrolled behind her like ribbon from a spool, leaving what was ahead in the unknown. The rumble of the engine and the wind whistling past her helmet sang a new song. She didn't know all the words and had yet to hear the end, but the music was all for her.

Sister.

She had a sister.

A sister they said she looked like.

A sister whose life she'd saved.

Mercy so got the irony. A woman she helped save was about to save her as well. She'd never had family. She had never belonged to anyone or anyplace before. Would Blessings be a blessing for her? Would she be accepted enough to belong?

By the time she rolled into Blessings it was half past

ten. She stopped at a small gas station just inside the city limits to fill up and go to the bathroom. She dismounted the Harley, took off her helmet, and hung it over the handlebars before stretching to ease her legs and back.

George Franklin was on the other side of the pumps filling up the delivery van from their florist shop while his wife Myra was in the van, talking to a floral supplier. Unbeknownst to each other, they both saw the biker ride up and park.

Myra frowned when she realized the rider was a woman, and frowned again as she watched her shake out all that long hair and stretch herself in a most unladylike manner. Her black leather pants were enough to start a rumor on their own, and when she saw George gawking, she tapped her phone on the window to get his attention.

George heard her tapping, and when he turned around and saw her shake her head in a disapproving manner, he sighed. A man couldn't even look at a pretty girl anymore without getting in trouble somewhere. So he ducked his head and focused on an oil spot on the concrete beneath the right rear wheel.

———

Unaware she had become a topic of conversation between two people she didn't know, Mercy pumped gas into the Harley, then grabbed the keys and her helmet and went inside to use the bathroom.

When she came out, the van was gone, and an old man was pumping gas into his truck. She got on the Harley and rode into town, looking for a central place to park and wait for Duke Talbot to arrive. When she saw the large lot in front of the Piggly Wiggly, she rode all the way to the front of the store. The wind was sharp, and when she got off the bike, she quickly moved into an alcove out of the wind to call Duke. Her call went to voice mail, so she told him where she was and sat down on a nearby metal bench to wait.

It wasn't long before she felt the chill of the weather again and got up to pull the bench out of the wind, then gave the town of Blessings a closer look.

Chapter 8

MERCY HADN'T BEEN WAITING LONG WHEN A CUTE LITTLE blonde wearing black pants and a pink uniform top drove up. Once she got out, she made a beeline for the entrance.

Mercy was surprised when the woman glanced her way and made a quick turn toward where she was sitting. "Hi honey! You're Mercy Dane, aren't you? You look just like Hope."

Mercy couldn't help but smile. The woman was adorable. "Yes, I'm Mercy."

"I'm Ruby Dye. I have a hair salon on Main called the Curl Up and Dye. We're all so happy for you girls. Everyone in Blessings is calling it the double miracle… you know…you saved her life and found a lost sister to boot."

Mercy smiled. "Nice to meet you, Ruby."

"You tell Hope when she feels better to come into the shop for a free hairstyle. And that applies to you too. Call it your 'welcome to Blessings' gift from me."

"Thanks," Mercy said. "I'll tell her, and thank you for the comp."

"You're welcome," Ruby said. "Sorry to run, but I need to pick up a few things before my next appointment. Have a good day, honey, and welcome to Blessings."

Mercy was still smiling when Ruby disappeared inside the store. She shifted her position on the bench and looked up just as a police cruiser drove into the lot. Her heart skipped a beat. It was the cop—her cop.

When he stopped beside her bike, the hair rose on the back of her neck. Now they had more than one night of sex between them. The nights of phone texts had been added to their strange relationship, and she wondered if he would stop sending them. The thought made her sad.

―∾―

Lon Pittman had been cruising the north end of Main Street when he saw a motorcycle ahead of him, and when it turned off Main into the Piggly Wiggly parking lot, he followed it because he recognized the bike and the rider. He tried not to buy into the excitement he felt, but she was here! He was going to see her again. He didn't know what might come of their unusual acquaintance, but texting her had started out innocently, and now had become a big deal. The brief sexual connection they'd shared so long ago was one thing, but the emotional connection he felt now was strong, and he wondered if she felt the same.

He cruised all the way down to the south end of Main before turning and retracing his route to the store. He saw the Harley, but didn't see her until he got closer. She was alone and waiting in the cold, probably for the Talbots. He could only imagine what she must be thinking as she waited to meet family she never knew she had.

It wasn't until he got closer to the front entrance that he finally saw her face again, and just like when she'd walked into the hospital waiting room, he felt sucker-punched. She was as beautiful as he remembered, and she was a daredevil on wheels. The way she sat on that Harley, like a cowboy busting a mustang as she made that crazy ride through Blessings, was pretty damn sexy. She was wild *and* beautiful, and she made him sweat. Whatever the hell he felt was scary good.

He pulled up behind her Harley and caught her watching him as he got out. All he could think was *don't stumble*. He stopped a few feet away from the bench, took a deep breath, and looked her straight in the eyes. "So, Mercy Dane, all these years I've been thinking of you as Lucky. I'd say it was more than luck that made our paths cross again, but I am damn glad they did. And I hear you're moving to town. Seeing you in person is so much better than a long-distance text. I'd like to give you a warm welcome to Blessings, but you're obviously freezing in this weather."

She refused to discuss their past and focused on what was happening now. "Thanks. I suppose you know why I'm here."

Lon grinned. "Well, yes, I do. In fact I imagine nearly everyone in Blessings knows your story. That's kind of what small towns are all about. We love Hope Talbot and are really happy there was such a good outcome from such deadly circumstances." He reached for her hands. "And, selfishly, I'm really glad you're here too." And then he added, "Your hands are cold."

She snatched them away, a little embarrassed for no reason at all. It was winter. Everyone's hands were likely cold.

"I took off my gloves after I stopped," she said.

He nodded. "Well, now. Since I see that you're wait-ing, is there anything I can do to help?"

"No. I'm just waiting for Duke Talbot to text me back and let me know he's on his way. I'm going to follow him to their farm to meet my sister."

"You're welcome to wait inside the cruiser with me. The heater is on."

The offer sounded good, but she hesitated too long.

"That's okay. No harm. No foul. I've got a quick errand to run. Back in a jiffy," he said, and hurried inside the store.

Mercy was rubbing her hands together as she sat back down and caught a faint scent of his cologne. She lifted them to her face and took a deep breath. Now his scent was in her memory and on her skin. He smelled good enough to eat.

While considering what the possibilities were of them ever having a relationship, her phone signaled a text from Duke Talbot.

Let me be the first to welcome you to Blessings! I'm on my way.

There was a slight smile on her face as she dropped the phone back in her pocket. "But you're not the first," she muttered, and looked up to see Lon hurrying out of the store carrying a Styrofoam cup.

"Here," he said, thrusting it into her hands. "It's hot chocolate from the deli. It'll warm you from the inside out, and be careful. It's always a little too hot at the start."

"Thank you," she said, curling her fingers around the warm cup. "Oooh, that feels so good."

Lon hoped the grin on his face wasn't as goofy as he felt. "It tastes pretty good too. So, I'd be happy to show you the way to the Talbot farm, if you don't hear back soon."

"Oh, Duke sent a text while you were in the store. He's on his way."

Lon nodded. "Then he won't be long. It's not far from here and pretty easy to find."

Her eyes narrowed. "That's interesting, since Duke insisted it was too difficult to tell me how to get there and said he needed to guide me instead."

Lon didn't know how to respond, but he didn't want her arrival to get off on a bad start. "Well, he may be right in one respect because there aren't street signs or the like. Just some numbered roads put in place when the 911 system was installed a few years back to give ambulances and fire trucks a way to locate their destinations. I imagine it would be confusing for newcomers."

Mercy took a quick sip of her hot chocolate, and when she licked the foam off of her upper lip, Lon took a deep breath.

Lord have mercy. Quit staring at her, you fool. And then he exhaled slowly as the little cloud of condensation around his face dispersed.

As he glanced toward Main Street, he saw Duke's black Dodge 4x4 driving into the parking lot. "Here he comes now," he said, pointing.

Mercy shivered with excitement. She was that much closer to meeting her sister.

———

Duke frowned when he saw the police chief talking to Mercy and then chided himself. She had every right to speak to whomever she chose, and it was expected that Pittman might speak to her, considering they already knew each other.

He got out with a smile on his face and came toward her in long swift strides. He was about to open his arms and give her a welcoming hug when he caught the shift in her gaze and her body language. So this was as far as he dared to go. "Hello, Mercy! I hope your ride here was uneventful."

"It was fine," Mercy said.

Duke turned to acknowledge Lon's presence. "Chief. Good to see you."

"And you," Lon said. "Give my best to Hope and Jack." Then he winked at Mercy. "I'll be seeing you around."

Mercy watched him get back in the cruiser and drive away, then took one last drink of the hot chocolate and dumped it in the trash. "Okay. I'm ready," she said. "Lead the way."

"I won't go too fast," he said.

"If you go too slow, I'll likely run over you," Mercy said.

Duke looked a little startled, then quickly got into the truck and left the parking lot with Mercy behind him.

———

Hope woke slowly, giving herself time to think about moving, and then she saw the blue box sitting at the foot of her bed. Anxious to revisit her childhood keepsakes, she shoved aside the covers and pulled it close to where she was sitting.

Originally, the box was with her and Mercy when the police took them to the station from the scene of their mother's murder, and it went with them when a man from social services took them to their first foster home. It went with them from home to home until Hope was adopted. At that point, it went to her new home. Early on, it had been the source of much conflict until June, her adoptive mother, angrily put it away in the attic.

Hope never saw it again and had almost forgotten it ever existed, and then June had it sent with their wedding presents when she and Jack got married. Even though she'd seen it among the boxes when she moved, she had never looked at it again. But today she hoped for inspiration—something that might be familiar to Mercy.

She reached for the scissors. One snip, and the cords were lying loose upon the bedspread. She lifted the lid, laid it aside, and pulled out the tissue paper.

There was a note lying on top of the contents. She felt a little twinge of regret when she recognized her adoptive mother's handwriting, then scanned the note and sighed. June knew Hope had never forgiven them for leaving Baby Girl behind and had tried to make amends.

> *I knew you would want these. I'm sorry for your heartaches. Make beautiful memories with your Jack. We love you.*

She wondered if her mother had expected her to respond to this note? If so, Hope had missed her chance because both of her parents were gone. She lost her father in an accident, and then her mother three years later from a heart attack. She had loved them and grieved their passing, but the ache for the sister she'd lost had been ever-present until today.

Today that was coming to an end.

Her hands trembled as she picked up the large pic-ture book lying on top. *The Velveteen Rabbit*. It was the last gift her birth mother, Maria, had given her before she was murdered. She opened the book and traced her mother's handwriting with the tip of her finger.

For Hope. Happy 8th birthday, sweet girl.

Hope took a slow, shaky breath. Not for the first time, she wondered what their lives would have been like if her mother had lived.

She laid the book aside and sifted through a couple of Valentine cards, a geode someone had given her, and then she picked up something wrapped in tissue paper. She unwrapped it, and when she realized what it was, she started to cry.

It was her little sister's rag doll. The yarn hair used to be yellow but was the color of dirty dishwater now, and the little pink dress was in tatters. She'd been horrified the day she went home with her new parents and found out their foster mother had accidentally put Baby Girl's doll with her things. She'd begged them to take her back so she could give it to her, but they wouldn't. Then she'd begged them to adopt her too, but again, they would not. Hope couldn't remember much about that time except sorrow.

She tried to smooth the doll's hair, but it was hopeless, and the dress had nearly rotted away. "Poor Dolly," Hope said, and laid it aside.

The last item in the box was the photo, and seeing it still hurt. Mother had been so pretty, and it was what got her killed.

"We looked like her," Hope said.

Even as children it was easy to see. One child was leaning against her leg, the younger one was in her arms—both smaller versions of Maria Dane.

Hope glanced at the clock and repacked everything except the picture and Mercy's doll. It had been a long time coming, but today she was giving it back. She left the box for Jack to take back to the attic, then went into the bathroom to wash.

Jack was waiting for her when she came out. "Hey, honey, how do you feel after your nap?"

"I'm okay, just sore. Thank you for bringing the box down."

"You're welcome," he said, and gave her a quick kiss. "Are you ready to meet your sister?"

Hope gasped. "Is she here?"

"Duke went into Blessings to meet her, and they're on their way home."

"Oh no! I look terrible, and it's nearly noon and…"

"You look wonderful. You're alive, and you're home, and I've already made some food."

Hope leaned her head against Jack's chest. Ever since she'd known him, just when she thought the world would overwhelm her, he came through for her every time. "Thank you, my Jack. The best thing that ever happened to me was you."

"In sickness and in health, honey, all the way," Jack said. "Let's go to the living room to wait, okay?"

She grabbed the picture and the doll and let him walk her down the hall into the living room. She set the doll and the picture on an end table, but she was too jumpy to sit down and moved to the window instead. "I'm scared," she said.

"It's going to be okay. You'll see," Jack said, and then heard Duke's truck coming down the drive and looked out the window. "They're here."

"I don't want to wait. Let's go out to meet them!"

"I don't think you should—"

"Please!" she said, holding out her hand.

He nodded, then steadied her steps as they went onto the porch together.

——~~——

Mercy couldn't help but check out the countryside on the way to the Talbot farm. The roads were black-top, and the houses they passed were mostly ordinary homes. Some were brick, some double-wide trailers, but the ones she liked best were the older two-story frame houses with wide front porches and gingerbread cutouts.

As she rode, she made a mental note of each turn Duke took so that she wouldn't depend on anyone to find her way around. When she realized he was about to turn from the blacktop onto a one-lane driveway, she slowed down to follow.

The drive was bordered on both sides by Georgia pines and curved to the left before it straightened out. She saw the house, and then the barns and fences and sheds spread out around it. It was postcard perfect—a two-story house straight out of the early 1900s, gleaming snow-white against the winter landscape. Wooden and wicker furniture graced the wraparound porch, and a green, winter-themed wreath hung on the front door. The family farm Duke had mentioned was Christmas card quaint, right down to the small herd of cattle in the pasture behind the house.

As Duke parked, Mercy pulled up beside him and killed the engine. The front door opened as she untied her duffel bag, and when she turned to look, Jack and her sister walked out onto the porch.

Breath caught in the back of her throat—her heart started to pound. She left the bag on the bike and walked toward the porch, and the closer she got, the shakier she became.

My sister? Obviously, still healing. Hope?

She looked as nervous as Mercy felt.

When Mercy started up the steps, Hope pushed away from Jack and went to meet her.

Mercy took a deep breath. The only memory she had from her childhood was a girl with dark hair who had cuddled her when she cried. Was this her?

Hope.

"My Baby Girl," Hope whispered, and opened her arms.

The name echoed in Mercy's memory as she walked into Hope's arms, remembering just in time not to hold her too tight. Hope went from hugging her to cupping her face with both hands. "Look at you! Just look at you, Mercy! You look just like Mama. So beautiful. So very beautiful!"

"You remember our mother?" Mercy asked.

The shock of that question rolled through Hope as she took Mercy by the hand. "Oh, honey. Come inside with me. There is so much we have to talk about."

Jack was in tears as he walked in behind them, while Duke picked up Mercy's bag from the Harley and followed them into the house.

Chapter 9

"DUKE, PLEASE TAKE MERCY'S BAG TO HER ROOM," HOPE said.

"We're going to leave you two alone," Jack said. "I'll be in the kitchen finishing up dinner. If you need anything, just call out."

Hope eased herself onto the sofa and then patted the seat beside her. Mercy took off the leather bomber jacket and straightened the sweatshirt she had on under it as she sat.

Hope couldn't quit staring. There was the birthmark. And she was wearing Mama's face, but without a smile. Yes, Mercy was stunning, but she felt the wall between them and was uncertain if it had to do with what life had done to her or resentment from Hope's abandonment.

"There's something I have to say first," Hope said, and reached for Mercy's hand. "I begged my adoptive parents to take me back to you, but they wouldn't. I begged them to adopt you, but they wouldn't. I'm sorry you were left behind. I'm so, so sorry."

Mercy shrugged. "We were children. Children without a voice. It wasn't your fault."

Hope was sick. The damage was worse than she'd feared. She couldn't bear the matter-of-fact tone in Mercy's voice.

Desperate to tap into emotion, she reached behind

her and picked up the photo and handed it to Mercy. Mercy's eyes widened. "Is this our mother?"

"Yes. You look just like her."

"I don't remember her," Mercy said.

"You were so little when she was killed."

Mercy frowned. "How did she die?"

"Our father killed her in a fit of jealousy."

Mercy frowned again. "Are you serious?"

"Yes. Men were always noticing her. Even though it wasn't her fault, it made him crazy."

"Where is he now?"

"He died in prison."

Mercy handed the photo back to Hope.

Hope sighed. Nothing but a frown. She had one more card to play and reached for the rag doll. "I've been waiting to give this back to you ever since they took me away. Our foster mother accidentally put it with my things, but it was yours."

When Mercy saw the doll in Hope's hands, the first word that popped in her mind was "Dolly?"

Hope's heart skipped a beat. She remembered the doll's name. "Yes, that's what you called her."

Mercy suddenly saw a doll floating facedown and felt a momentary sadness. "Dolly drowned."

"Yes. She fell in the bathtub, and Mrs. Hooper wouldn't let you sleep with her because the sheets would get wet. You cried yourself to sleep in my arms."

Mercy nodded.

Hope could tell Mercy was uncomfortable, and while this was a disappointing reunion, she was elated that she'd been found. "Thank you for saving my life."

Mercy reached across the space between them and

took Hope's hand. "I'm so glad I was close enough to make that happen. I know all of this is fate's way of giving me a second chance at life too, and don't think I'm not grateful. I wanted to belong to someone my whole life, but I don't know how to belong to a family yet. I don't know how to belong to anyone. Give me time, okay?"

Hope gave Mercy's hand a quick squeeze. "We have all the time you need. I'm just so grateful you've been found."

Mercy finally smiled, and Hope relaxed. It was past noon, and she could smell corn bread. She guessed Jack had just taken it out of the oven. "I hope you're hungry. Jack has food ready. Why don't you go up and check out your room, wash up, and follow your nose back downstairs to the kitchen?"

"It smells good," Mercy said.

"Your bedroom is the first door on the left after you get upstairs. It has an adjoining bathroom, and Jack has been getting everything ready for you, but if he's forgotten anything, please let me know."

"I'm sure it will be fine," Mercy said as she stood. "I won't be long."

Hope watched Mercy start toward the stairs, and then she paused and turned around. "Did you sing to me?" she asked.

Hope nodded. "Every night when we went to sleep."

"'You Are My Sunshine'?"

"Oh my God, yes!" Hope said, and started to cry. "I sang you to sleep every night because it was the song Mother sang to us."

Mercy went back to Hope and knelt in front of her. "All these years, I didn't know I belonged to a family. I thought there was just me. How did I forget this? How did I forget you?"

Hope cupped Mercy's face with both hands. "You weren't quite three years old and barely potty-trained. You sucked your thumb and were afraid of everything. The police thought you witnessed the murder, but there was no way to know. All I knew was that you cried if I was out of your sight. It was part of why my adoptive parents wouldn't take you. They didn't want a child with emotional issues. I still haven't forgiven them for that."

"Are they still alive?" Mercy asked.

"No."

Mercy saw the shadows in Hope's eyes. "I'm so sorry you were hurt. I'm so sorry you've carried such a burden," she said.

Hope kept patting Mercy's arm and then her face. "We're together now, and that's all that matters. We belong to each other, Baby Girl, and don't you ever forget it," Hope said.

Mercy was in tears, but the words wouldn't come, and it was Jack who ended the moment with a shout from the kitchen. "Dinner in five minutes!"

Hope kissed Mercy on the cheek and then reluctantly let her go. "You heard the man. Go check out your room. We'll be in the kitchen."

Mercy gave her a quick hug and left on the run.

Hope watched Mercy leaving the room, then those long legs of hers taking steps two at a time as she ran up the stairs. In her mind, she saw their mother and not her sister. Mercy wasn't the only one who had adjustments to make.

Mercy walked into what would be her bedroom for

the time she was here. The walls were a soft lilac with white sheer curtains at the windows. The bedspread was white with splashes of yellow and lilac, and the area rug over the gleaming hardwood floors was a deeper shade of yellow. Her bags, even the ones Duke brought the night before, were all inside the walk-in closet, leaving her to empty the contents where she chose.

She backed out of the closet to check out the adjoining bathroom. Walls were painted in the same pale lilac as the bedroom, with white subway tiles in the shower, and a white jetted tub beside it. The bright yellow rugs and stool cover matched the area rug in the bedroom, and when she noticed the handmade soaps in the dish were yellow and lilac, she grinned. It was the girly room she'd always wanted and never had.

Hope did good. This was a welcome to remember.

Then she remembered they were waiting and quickly washed up, brushed her hair, and added lip gloss. She saw cookies on a table by the bedroom window as she went to get a band to tie back her hair.

Chocolate chip. One of her favorites. She fixed her hair, then picked up a cookie, eating it on her way back downstairs.

Duke couldn't help but notice the sway of Mercy's hips as she entered the kitchen. Those long legs were really something, but when he saw she was eating a cookie, he frowned. "You're going to ruin your dinner."

Mercy waved it in the air. "The cookies were in my room. That is an invitation to eat one, so I am."

He blinked.

Jack hid a grin as he began dishing up stew. This might be the best thing ever to happen to his brother. Mercy Dane was definitely not a woman to knuckle under to Duke's bossy ways.

She put the half-eaten cookie on a plate. "This marks my spot," she said, grinning at Hope. "What do you need me to do?"

"Just sit here with me," Hope said. "The boys will bring the food to us."

Mercy nodded, reclaiming her cookie as she sat. "My room is beautiful. Probably the prettiest room I've ever had. Thank you."

Hope beamed. "I'm so glad. I want you to feel comfortable and welcome."

Mercy lifted the cookie. "Cookies are my kind of welcome. And they're really good. Did you make them?"

Hope shook her head. "No, we get them at the bakery in town. I'm not much of a baker."

"I bake," Mercy said. "I'll make some for you whenever you want."

"That's great!" Hope said.

Jack carried bowls of the hot stew to the table and set them on their plates. "Beef stew," he said. "Corn bread coming up."

"Sounds wonderful," Mercy said. "Something hot to warm us up."

"I suppose riding a motorcycle is cold traveling in the winter," Duke said.

"And wet when it rains, miserable when it's hot, and scary when you're riding at night with nothing between you and the semi beside you but the draft of passing air," Mercy added.

Duke frowned. "Then why choose such a dangerous mode of transportation?"

Mercy shrugged. "I didn't choose it. An old biker who used to come to the Road Warrior died and willed the bike to me. Before that, I didn't have any transportation."

"Did you know how to ride it?" Jack asked.

"Not when it was given to me, but I learned, and I learned the hard way. Now when I ride, I wear leather because the first wreck I had on that bike took most of the hide off my legs and arms."

"Oh my word!" Hope said.

Mercy shrugged again. "Life teaches you to cope. I'm good at coping."

Hope's eyes welled with tears all over again. "You were cheated out of so much," she said, wiping away tears.

"Not really," Mercy said. "The deal is, when you've had nothing, every little gain in life is a big deal. I felt pretty darn lucky when I got the Harley. I learned how to fix it and how to ride it. When you expect nothing, windfalls are golden." Then she glanced at Duke. "It's a good thing I had it, or I would have had no way to get to Blessings to donate that blood."

Duke was embarrassed that she'd had to point that out. "I'm sorry. It was a pointless question and some-what rude."

"Then why ask it?" Mercy said.

"Because sometimes I am pointless and rude?" Duke muttered.

Mercy laughed. "And sometimes honest, so you can't be all bad."

He grinned, relieved that she wasn't really angry.

Jack set a platter of thick crusty squares of hot corn

bread on the table as Duke got butter from the fridge and a pitcher of sorghum molasses from the pantry.

"For the corn bread," he said as he set it on the table.

Finally, they were all seated at the table, two brothers—two sisters. It felt strange, and yet somehow, so very right. "Thank you for this," Mercy said.

"You mean the meal?" Jack asked.

Mercy's chin trembled. "No, the welcome, and insisting I submit to the DNA test. This is the best thing that's ever happened to me."

"Today is a dream come true for me, and there are many more good things to come," Hope said.

And so the meal ensued. Oddly familiar when it shouldn't have been. Even comfortable enough for Mercy to object every time Duke's conversation turned into judgmental comments or orders.

By the time the meal was over, Duke's face was flushed and Mercy's chin was set. Jack was grinning and Hope just rolled her eyes.

Finally, Duke had to speak up or bust. "Mercy Dane, you are a beautiful woman, and I am so glad our Hope has found the sister she has grieved for so long, but you are a damned hardheaded woman."

"Why? Because I don't agree with you?" Mercy said.

Duke shrugged. "No one else is so perverse with me."

Hope frowned. "Duke! Really! This is her first day here and her first meal with us. You could try to be more agreeable."

Mercy looked at her sister. "I'm not insulted. It's obvious why Duke's still a bachelor. He's bossy. No woman likes being told what to do."

If Duke hadn't been so floored, he would have

gotten up and walked out of the room, but then Jack laughed and Hope snickered, so he sat there, too stunned to respond.

"I've told him that a dozen times myself," Jack said. "It appears he took it better from me than he has from you."

Mercy glanced at the angry jut of Duke's chin. "I'm sorry, Duke. I don't mean to be antagonistic in any way, but you've been more than blunt with me. I assumed if you needed to dish all that out, that you were man enough to take it. However, you need to understand something about me. Foster families are hard. One or both parents will usually be rough taskmasters. Nothing you do suits them. Everything you do is never enough. If they have kids of their own and also take in fosters…those kids often delight in reminding you you're not living under the same rules. I bit my lip for eighteen years. I didn't talk back. I did everything I was told, even when it was to my detriment. The day I aged out of the system was the first day of *my* life. I was in charge. I made the decisions. I made the rules. It was an empowering feeling to just say, 'No, I don't want to.' Do you understand?"

Duke was shocked, and for the first time in his life, truly moved by the story of someone else's life. "I'm sorry. I never thought…I didn't mean…"

Mercy leaned across the table and tapped his hand, then offered hers. "Truce?"

He nodded.

"Shake on it," she said.

And he did, wincing slightly from her grip.

Hope leaned back with a sigh. "Finally, peace at the table. There are cookies for dessert."

"Or corn bread and molasses," Duke said.

Mercy felt the need to make peace. "I'd like to try some of that corn bread and molasses. I've never had that before. I've eaten it on pancakes but not corn bread. Sounds tasty."

Duke was so pleased by her request that he fixed a serving for her. "Hope you like it," he said. "But if you don't, you won't hurt my feelings."

Mercy knew everyone at the table was waiting for a response, and then to her surprise, she didn't have to fake it. "This is good!" she said, and forked another bite into her mouth and chewed. "This might be my new favorite thing."

Duke slapped his knee in delight. "I knew it! I knew you'd like it alright!"

Mercy grinned at Hope and winked. Hope leaned back, her eyes twinkling. She was watching the dethroning of Duke, the tyrant. He just didn't know it yet.

Once dessert was eaten, Mercy got up to clear the table, but Jack stopped her. "Not today. Today is your welcome home. Duke and I have this covered, and Hope needs to lie down. Do me a favor and take her back to her room, okay?"

"With pleasure," Mercy said, and held out her hand.

Hope clasped it firmly and let Mercy help her up. They left the room with their heads together, already talking.

There was a lump in Jack's throat as he watched them leave the kitchen. "Who knew that wreck would yield such a blessing?"

Duke shrugged. "I'm still out on that verdict."

Jack laughed and punched him on the arm. "Get over yourself, brother. She just calls you on your bossy bullshit. You're a nice guy and a decent brother, but you're getting as set in your ways as an old maid."

Duke's eyes widened. "Please! Say what you really think."

Jack laughed again. "I just did. Relax, Duke. Life is short. Eat cookies."

Duke grinned and shook his head.

Chapter 10

LON WAS COMING OUT OF GRANNY'S COUNTRY KITCHEN WHEN his radio squawked: "Dispatch to Chief Pittman."

He jogged to his cruiser and slid into the seat. "Pittman to dispatch, go ahead."

"Requesting your presence at the precinct."

"On the way," Lon said, and left the parking lot.

By the time he got to the station and parked, he could tell something was up. There were two pickup trucks parked in front, and as he neared the back door of the station, he could hear pigs squealing. "What the hell?" he muttered, and entered the building.

Even as he walked up the hall he could hear someone bawling, two people yelling, and Avery's voice was lost somewhere in the pig squeals.

"What the hell is going on in here?" he shouted.

Avery groaned aloud. "Thank God, you're here."

Lon identified Bo Weaver as the one bawling. Bo's brother, Joe, was the one arguing with Buzz Higdon, a pig farmer, whose place was a few miles from Blessings. And then there were two pigs. About weaning age and probably fifty pounds apiece.

"Joe, you and Bo put the pigs down."

"But Chief, we're just—"

"Now!" Lon said.

They put down the pigs. The moment the pigs' little hooves touched the floor, the squealing stopped. They bunched up and started running together, looking for a way out.

"Avery! Herd them toward that open cell down in the jail, and lock them up until we get this figured out."

"Yes, sir," Avery said, grateful that someone besides him had finally made a decision.

"Okay, now I want all three of you back in my office. Follow me," Lon said, and followed Avery and the pigs down the hall.

Bo and Joe were sobering up fast, and Buzz Higdon stomped every step he took behind them. They sat in the three chairs on the other side of the chief's desk, and when Joe opened his mouth, Lon pointed at Joe and shook his head.

Joe shut his mouth and slumped in the chair.

Lon started with the pig farmer. "Alright, Buzz Higdon, why are you in my station?"

Buzz pointed at the brothers with a shaky hand. "I had two weaning pigs stolen last night. I went by the sheriff's office this morning to report them, and then came into Blessings to pick up some groceries at the Piggly Wiggly for the missus. These two were passed out in their truck in the store parking lot, and when I got out of my own truck, I heard pigs a-squealin'. I looked in the backseat window and saw my pigs on the floorboard of their truck, so I called your office, and Deputy Ralph responded and ordered us all here."

Lon got on the intercom. "Avery, where's Deputy Ralph?"

"Working a domestic abuse call."

"Okay," Lon said, and then stood and walked around

to the front of his desk to where the Weaver brothers were sitting. They were staring at their boots.

Lon kicked the toe of Joe's left boot and Bo's right boot. "Look at me!" he said sharply.

They lifted their heads then leaned back so they could see his face.

"Thank you for your cooperation," Lon muttered.

They both nodded.

"Now. Which one of you would like to tell me why you had Buzz Higdon's pigs in your truck?"

"I will," Joe said. "Bo was passed out when they got in."

Lon frowned. "What do you mean, they got in?"

"Why, into our truck," Joe said. "We were on our way home last night, and I needed to pee, so I stopped on the road by Buzz's house. I got out of the truck to pee, then stepped in a mud hole, and fell down on my knees. 'Course I peed my pants before I could get up. It happens when I've had too much to drink."

Joe paused for breath.

Lon's arms were crossed over his chest, and he was biting the inside of his mouth to keep from grinning. "I'm listening," Lon said.

Joe nodded. "Anyway, once I'd done wet my britches, I didn't really want to sit back down in the seat in them, so I figured since we was so close to home that I would just strip down and drive without any drawers."

Bo's eyes widened. "I didn't know your butt was nekked," he muttered.

Joe punched him on the shoulder. "We're brothers. You've seen my business plenty of times. Now be quiet. I'm trying to explain the situation," Joe said.

Buzz looked at the chief and rolled his eyes.

Lon was staring at a spot on the wall just above Joe Weaver's head. "I'm losing my patience," he said. "Finish your story."

"Yes, Chief," Joe said. "Anyway, as I was saying… I started to take off my britches when I heard a rustling in the brush, and out comes these two pigs. I said, Bo, there's two pigs here, but he was too drunk to wake up. The pigs saw me and came running toward the truck like they'd just seen the Holy Grail."

Lon sighed. "Holy Grail? Really?"

Joe shrugged. "Or maybe they smelled the leftover bucket of fried chicken on the floorboard. I don't know. But they came right up to me. I figured they were lost, so I put them in the back with the chicken and shut the door, then I turned the truck around and was coming into town to report finding lost pigs. I guess I got too sleepy and fell asleep in the parking lot of the Piggly Wiggly."

"You would have passed the police station to get to the Piggly Wiggly lot," Lon said. "You'll have to do better than that."

"And I was almost as drunk as Bo," Joe said. "I'm pretty sure that by the time I got back to Blessings, I forgot what I'd been intending to do, and just parked out of the line of traffic."

Lon wiped a hand over his face, giving himself time to restrain a grin, and then glanced at Buzz. "Well, you heard their story. Do you want to press charges and come back to testify before the judge, or do you want to take your pigs and go home?"

Buzz leaned forward, fixing Joe with a cold hard stare. "Were you gonna sell them or eat them?"

"Probably sell 'em," Joe said, and then groaned when he realized what he'd said.

Buzz sighed. "I'm gonna take my pigs and go home." Buzz pointed at the brothers. "You two owe me. Big time. And you know it."

Their heads were bobbing up and down like fishing floats with a fish on the hook. "We were drunk, Buzz. We're really sorry. You're a good neighbor to us. We don't want any trouble."

"Neither do I," Buzz said. "However, I expect the both of you at my place within the hour. Bring a new roll of hog wire, half a dozen metal posts, and some fence clips. You're going to fix my hog pen."

"Yes, sir. As soon as we pick up the stuff from the lumberyard, we'll be right out," Bo said.

Joe frowned. "I'm broke."

"I'm not," Bo said.

"No, you're broke too," Joe said. "I rolled you for your wallet about half past midnight to pay our bar bill before we started home."

Bo stood up with a roar, swung a fist, and popped Joe in the nose. "Damn thief! Can't even trust my own brother."

Joe shoved Bo in the chest and sent him flying backward into the wall.

"That does it!" Lon said, and grabbed Joe by the back of the neck and Bo by the belt in his pants. He pushed Joe forward and dragged Bo backward toward the jail, yelling at Avery as he went.

Avery came running and opened the jail cells on either side of the pigs. Lon shoved Joe in the first and Bo in the third, while Avery locked the doors.

Bo rubbed the back of his head where he'd hit the

wall, not the least bit sorry that his brother was bleeding all over the floor of the jail.

"Dang it, Chief! How can we fix Buzz's hog pen if you go and lock us up?"

"You have family," Lon said. "You each get one call. They need to bring bail money and enough extra for Higdon's hog pen."

Joe groaned. "You're arresting us? Why?"

"You stole Buzz's pigs and admitted in front of me, the chief of police, that you were going to sell them, then started a fight in the office and bled all over my floor, that's why!"

Bo sat on the bunk and put his head in his hands. Joe kicked at the commode and then sat down on the bunk, his nose still dripping blood. The pigs grunted.

Lon walked out of the jail area with Avery behind him. "Gosh, Chief. I can't say we've ever had pigs in jail before."

"They're not in jail anymore. Get the key. I'm sending Buzz back to get his pigs."

"Yes, sir," Avery said, and headed back to the jail while Lon returned to his office.

Buzz Higdon was down on his hands and knees with a handful of wet paper towels, wiping up the blood beside the chief's desk.

"You didn't have to do that," Lon said.

Buzz shrugged. "I don't mind."

"Pull your truck up to the back door. Avery will help you get your pigs in your truck," Lon said.

"I sure appreciate this, Chief."

Lon grinned. "I didn't really do anything but watch them sink their own ship," he said.

Buzz chuckled. "Damn fools. They aren't mean. But they're stupid as all get out when they're drunk." He tossed the wet towels in the trash. "Thanks again, Chief."

"You're welcome," Lon said, then closed the door to his office and started laughing.

———

Hope was telling Mercy the story of her second birthday party and the white cake with pink buttercream icing their mother had made, painting a vivid word picture of Mercy as a toddler with both hands full of cake and frosting. She'd cried because Maria had tried to clean her up, and she didn't want to give up the cake she was holding.

Somewhere between Mercy's laughter and her mother's memory, Hope fell asleep. Mercy watched Hope's eyelids getting heavier, and when her words slurred, Mercy knew the pain pills were taking effect.

Now, watching her sleep gave Mercy the freedom to study her sister's face. Even though Hope had wounds and scrapes still in the healing stages, Mercy could see their resemblance. It was staggering and a little frightening to realize she had family, and she was understandably leery of giving away a piece of her heart that might not be returned.

The small grandmother clock in the corner of the room ticked away the minutes of Mercy's life as she watched the flutter of Hope's eyelids. When her breathing became erratic and her muscles started to twitch, Mercy wondered if she was dreaming of the wreck. When Hope suddenly flinched, Mercy reached for Hope's hand. "You're okay," she said softly.

Hope sighed, and the jerking stopped.

Still holding her sister's hand, Mercy closed her eyes. Just for a moment. Just while Hope slept.

Once the dinner dishes were done, Duke headed for the barn to unload some feed sacks, leaving Jack in the house with Hope. When he tiptoed down the hall to check on the sisters, he found the door ajar and peeked in.

The room felt chilly, and they had fallen asleep facing each other. He tiptoed in to cover them up and noticed they were holding hands. He couldn't imagine what the two must be feeling, but it had to be good. After making sure they would be warm, he closed the door behind him as he left.

It was almost six o'clock before Lon released Bo Weaver to his wife, Franny. Franny had three kids in tow and was pregnant with their fourth. It would be an understatement to say she was mad. Bo Weaver was subdued and apologetic, and she wasn't having any of it. She sent him to the car with their children, and then said her piece. "Chief Pittman, I am embarrassed and ashamed it happened at all, but it won't be happening again."

"That's good to hear, but don't promise something you may not be able to deliver," Lon said.

"Oh, I'll deliver on that just like I'll deliver this baby. Despite his lack of brains, Bo Weaver loves me, even enough to tell his brother to go to hell. He's already pissed that Joe stole his money while he was passed out. They'll make up because they're brothers.

But when I say they won't be drinking together again, that's what will happen. And I have no doubt Joe's wife, Theresa, is going to read him the riot act too. We don't have spare money lying around to bond people out of jail, never mind the fact they had Buzz Higdon's pigs in the truck. He's our neighbor, and I will never be able to look that man in the face again. So, we're leaving, and thank you again for not charging them with theft."

"That was all on your neighbor. He didn't want to press charges."

"Lordy be," Franny muttered, still shaking her head as she left the building.

Lon watched until they were out of sight then locked the front door and went to the back to tell Larry Bemis, the night dispatcher, that he was going off duty. "Hey, Larry!"

"Yeah, Chief?"

"I'm heading home. Call if you need me. You have two deputies on duty tonight, so here's hoping for a quiet one for a change."

"Yes, sir," Larry said as he popped a handful of M&M candies into his mouth. "You have a good one."

Lon got in the cruiser and started home. He was ready for this day to be over, but he still needed to stop at the Piggly Wiggly to buy some hamburger meat and buns. It was too cold outside to grill, but he was tired of eating out. He wasn't much of a cook, but homemade burgers sounded good tonight.

When he pulled into the parking lot of the Piggly Wiggly, he immediately thought of Mercy Dane and wondered how her day had fared. If asked, he would not have been able to explain what her presence here meant

A PIECE OF MY HEART

to him. Their one night together had been as accidental as Mercy walking in on the burglar. But it had truly been the best night of his life. And now she was in his life again, almost within reach. Before, he had a job he loved and a house he slept in. Now, he hoped to keep the job he loved, and maybe find his forever love along with it.

Hopefully, the transition in joining her new family had gone smoothly, although he wouldn't be surprised if there were fireworks somewhere. She didn't come across as someone who could be pushed around, and everyone in Blessings knew Duke Talbot was something of a know-it-all.

―⁓―

Mercy had no idea how life on a farm would play out, but it was certainly the quietest night she'd spent in years. Instead of getting ready to go to work at the Road Warrior Bar, she was in her sister's house doing the supper dishes.

Jack was helping Hope get settled in for the night, and Duke was in the home office discussing artificial insemination with a prospective buyer—an interesting aspect of farming she'd never considered.

Once she finished cleaning up the kitchen, she prowled through the cabinets, locating where things were kept, and then checked the pantry to see what was on hand for the baking she'd promised. Since some of the basics were missing, she began making a grocery list.

After a while, the muted voices down the hall and the background laughter on a television show no one was watching settled into Mercy's consciousness. She stopped what she was doing long enough to stretch the tense muscles between her shoulder blades, then laid the list aside and walked onto the back porch.

The quiet was startling, and even though there was a security light between the house and the barns, she wasn't used to so much darkness. City streets had lights, and businesses had night-lights, even when they were closed. Porch lights were left on in residential areas, and both cop and ambulance lights coming and going were always prevalent. Even though everything here was shockingly quiet, this kind of dark felt ominous, even isolating. She wondered how people got used to the absence of light and sound.

What few stars she saw were mere glimmers of light far above the growing cloud cover. The air smelled clean and damp. She thought it would rain before morning. As she listened, she heard a cow begin to bawl and the answering cry from a calf. Some mama had lost her baby. Poor mama. Poor baby. Even the animal world had issues dealing with loss.

A loose board on the porch squeaked as she walked to the north end and turned her face into the wind. What had been the pasture for a small herd of cattle she'd seen upon her arrival had, tonight, become a study of unrecognizable shapes and shadows.

Today had been life-changing and life-affirming, but she shook as a wave of exhaustion swept through her. She thought of the warm house behind her and the beautiful room awaiting her at the top of the stairs. It was time to go inside. But as she turned her back on the darkness, she was struck by a sudden surge of anxiety—a feeling that she needed to run from—and bolted into the house, frantically locking the door, just as she'd done every night at her apartment in Savannah.

Duke walked into the kitchen as she ran in through the utility room. "Everything okay?" he asked.

She nodded. "Just getting a breath of air. It's going to rain."

Duke frowned. "Not according to the weatherman."

"Whatever," she said, unwilling to get into another difference of opinion with the man. "I'm going to bed. What time does everyone get up?"

"Jack and I are usually out of the house by 8:00 a.m. in the winter."

"Then I'll help make breakfast. See you in the morning."

She was already out of the room before it dawned on him to bid her good night. "Sleep well," he called, and then heard footsteps going up the stairs.

He was going through the house locking up and turning on night-lights when he heard the first rumble of thunder, and by the time he got to his first floor bedroom, he could hear rain blowing against the windows.

Well, hell. It appeared, once again, she'd been right.

Chapter 11

MERCY TOOK A HOT SHOWER, BRUSHED THE TANGLES OUT OF her hair, and put on her old gray pajamas.

"Oh my God, this feels so good," she mumbled as she crawled into bed between soft flannel sheets.

She pulled up the covers and fell asleep to the sound of rain hammering upon the roof. She slept in fits and starts of things unseen, and dreamed of a tall, soft-spoken cop with black hair and kind eyes who brought her hot chocolate, and then stood watch in the doorway between her and the unknown.

Even though Lon had already cleaned up the kitchen, his house still smelled like hamburgers. It began to rain as he carried out the trash, so he ran the last few yards back into the house.

The rain was cold, but it wasn't supposed to freeze tonight, which was good. Slick roads usually led to accidents and stranded motorists. Hopefully, that would not be the case. He was longing for a night of uninterrupted sleep, so after locking up, he headed to his bedroom to shower. His job was busy, but his personal life was quiet—often empty. He hadn't had a steady relationship since his early twenties, and now here he was pushing thirty with no personal life at all. He turned on the television in his bedroom just for the company, then stripped and headed for the shower.

It was raining steadily by the time he went to bed, so he turned on the electric blanket, set his alarm for 6:00 a.m., then picked up his phone and sent Mercy a text.

Good night, Lucky.

Then he rolled onto his side and closed his eyes. Cradled by the warmth and comfort, he quickly fell asleep and dreamed of a beautiful woman with long legs and black hair, who flew without wings into his arms.

Back in Savannah at the Road Warrior Bar, the mood was as dark as the weather. Mercy Dane had been gone a week already, and her absence had left a huge and unexpected hole in their world.

When Big Boy came into the bar just after 10:00 p.m., he paused as he always did to scan the bar for Mercy. He'd been so drunk the night she left that he didn't remember her leaving with the stranger or hearing Moose talk about her not coming back. When he didn't see her, he yelled out, "Hey, Moose. Where's the looker?"

"If you mean Mercy, she's gone."

Big Boy frowned. "What the hell do you mean, she's gone?"

"She moved away to live with family," Moose said. "This isn't CNN, and I don't have any updates. Take a seat or get out."

Pissed that she was gone before he could even get a

piece of her, Big Boy took a seat at a table near the back and began to hassle Barb and Farrah instead.

—∿∿∿—

Ruby Dye heard the rumble of thunder a few minutes before rain began to blow against her windows. She muted the television, grabbed a jacket, and slipped onto the front porch.

The downpour blurred the streetlights in front of her house, while the wind blew rain up beneath the porch and onto the legs of her sweatpants. Even though she shivered against the chill, she loved the rain.

She sat down in the porch swing and pushed off with her toe, then giggled as the motion took her in and out of the blowing raindrops. A loud rumble of thunder rattled the glass in the windows behind her. "You don't scare me," she said, and then pulled her knees up beneath her chin and wrapped her arms around her legs.

The lights were already off in the house across the street, and as she sat, she watched two more houses on the block go dark. Tomorrow was a workday for her, but she just wasn't in the mood to go to bed. There were too many exciting things happening in her life, like having a secret admirer.

She had yet to mention it to the girls at the shop. In fact, she didn't want to talk about it with anyone. It was shocking and so special that she wanted to keep all the excitement to herself.

A police cruiser turned the corner and slowly drove toward her house. Knowing they were on patrol in her neighborhood made her feel safe. After the cruiser rolled on down the street, Ruby went back into the house, locking the door behind her.

She glanced at the candy dish on her dining room table as she went into the kitchen and shivered. What came next? Even more to the point, was she ready for it?

—〰—

Lon Pittman was dreaming of Mercy Dane when his alarm went off, and as his brother used to say, just when he was getting to the good part. He had to admit that she fascinated him on many levels and wondered if she saw him as anything other than a one-night stand—the cop who had tried to arrest her. Still, Lon wasn't the kind of man to quit on a notion, and he was of a notion to see what would happen if he asked her out.

So the dream was still on his mind as he walked in the back door of the station. He stopped in his office to check messages and then walked up front to greet the day dispatcher, Avery Ames. "Morning, Avery," Lon said.

Avery looked up then pointed to a large packet at the end of the counter. "Oh, morning, Chief. This came for you. I signed for it."

"Thanks," Lon said, and picked up the packet as he left.

He stopped in the break room long enough to pour himself a cup of coffee and grab a doughnut to take to his office. After a bite of doughnut and a quick sip of coffee, he opened the packet and quickly realized it was from the impound site where Hope Talbot's wrecked car had been towed. There was a brief note from a cop who'd removed the contents left inside the wreck, and an apology. The items should have been returned when the car was deemed totaled by the insurance company, but it had been overlooked.

Lon grinned. Now he had a valid excuse to go to the Talbot residence—to return Hope's personal belongings. The fact that he would be seeing Mercy again seemed like the universe had just given him the OK to follow his heart. Just to be on the safe side, he called Jack Talbot to let him know he was on the way. The call rang several times, and he was about to leave a voice mail when Jack answered. "Hello."

"Hello, Jack. Lon Pittman here."

"Hey, Chief, is everything okay?" Jack asked.

"Yes, everything is fine. I'm calling to give you a heads-up that I'm coming to your place with some of Hope's things from the wreck. The packet arrived this morning with a note that it had been overlooked earlier."

"Oh, that's great. We wondered about her purse… stuff like that."

"It appears all of that and more are in the package. So you might let her know. I'll need her to view the contents and sign off on them."

"Sure thing," Jack said. "See you soon."

Lon was smiling when he headed back up front. "Avery, I'll be at the Talbot farm for a bit. That packet you signed for has Hope Talbot's belongings from the wreck. I have to get her to sign off on receipt of the property."

"Yes, sir," Avery said. "Two deputies are on duty so everything should be covered."

Satisfied all was well, Lon got the packet, his coffee and doughnut, and headed for his cruiser. The dough-nut was gone before he cleared the city limits, and he finished off the coffee about a mile out of town, and he didn't remember swallowing a bit of it. The only thing on his mind was Mercy Dane.

———

Mercy was helping Hope get dressed when they heard Jack come into the house calling Hope's name.

"We're in here!" Mercy yelled, then they listened as he came running down the hall.

"He enters the house with such grace, doesn't he?" Hope said.

Mercy grinned as Jack came to a halt in the doorway. "Hey, honey, Chief Pittman just called. He's coming out with your things collected from the wreck. He got them this morning."

"Oh, that's great," Hope said. "I expected I would have to replace that stuff. I hope it's all there."

Mercy's heart skipped a beat. She hadn't seen his text from last night until she'd awakened this morning and was sorry she'd missed it. Now she was going to see him instead. This was a good day.

"Duke and I are checking fence lines until noon. Mercy, you've got this covered, right?"

Brought back to reality by the question, Mercy quickly agreed. "Absolutely, and I'm making dinner at noon."

"Much appreciated," Jack said, and then came in long enough to give Hope a quick kiss. "You look beautiful," he murmured softly.

"Except I don't," Hope muttered.

"All of what's bothering you will soon be gone," Mercy said.

Jack patted Mercy's arm in appreciation. "Thanks

again," he said, and left as loudly and abruptly as he had appeared.

Hope smoothed down the back of her hair and then began buttoning up the placket on her shirt. "So, Chief Pittman will probably be here soon," she said. "Would you mind making a fresh pot of coffee?"

"As soon as I get you settled in the living room," Mercy said.

"I'm as good as I'm going to look today. Let's do this," Hope said.

Mercy settled Hope in the living room, covering her with a well-worn quilt, soft and faded from many years of use. The past week had given Mercy plenty of time to settle in, and every day that passed, she felt more at home.

She started the coffee, made sure there was cream and sugar, and then checked the cookie jar. It was empty. She itched to get her fingers into some homemade cookie dough but still needed to shop. So, they would have coffee minus cookies, and she set three heavy mugs, the cream and sugar, teaspoons, and napkins onto a big serving tray.

"He's here!" Hope shouted.

Mercy's pulse jumped as she grabbed a towel to wipe her hands, then hurried back to the living room. As she heard him coming up the steps she regained her sense of calm. And then he knocked, and she opened the door. "Good morning. Come in."

Lon knew he was grinning like a fool, but he couldn't help it. "Good to see you again," he said softly, then focused on the woman in the recliner. "Hey, Hope, good to see you up and about. Thank you for seeing me so early this morning."

Hope waved him over to the sofa. "No problem. Come sit. I heard you have some things from the wreck?"

He took off his coat and laid it aside as he sat down beside her recliner. "The packet arrived this morning. I need you to look through the contents and then sign off on receipt of your property." He laid the packet in her lap and then glanced at Mercy. "So how do you like farm life?"

"I love being here with Hope," Mercy said. "And it's quiet."

Lon laughed.

Mercy watched a dimple come and go in his right cheek and tried not to stare.

Hope caught the byplay between them and smiled. The chief was flirting with her little sister. "Chief, would you like a cup of coffee?"

"I'd love one," Lon said.

"I'll get it," Mercy said.

"Do you need any help?" Lon asked.

"I've got this," Mercy said.

Lon watched her exit and then looked a bit embarrassed when Hope caught him staring.

He shrugged. "Sorry. She's, uh, she's so…"

Hope nodded. "And the best part is she doesn't know it."

Lon sighed and leaned back against the sofa as Hope began going through her things.

Mercy returned promptly with the tray and put it on the coffee table. "Help yourself," Mercy said, pointing at the mugs of hot, freshly brewed coffee.

"Looks great," he said as he picked up a mug, added a little sugar and cream, and stirred.

"Hope, do you want any coffee?" Mercy asked.

"In a minute. I want to go through this stuff first. Look! Can you believe everything is still in my purse? I was dreading having to replace my credit cards and driver's license. Even the money is still there."

"There's an itemized list," Lon said, and took a pen from his shirt pocket. "Check off the items as you find them, and then when you're satisfied with what's here, sign on the line at the bottom."

"Will do," Hope said, and began checking off the contents as she went.

Mercy pulled a chair near Hope, and as Hope located the list items, Mercy would check them off. Lon sat for a few moments watching the sisters, their heads together, so much alike and yet strangers. Then Mercy looked up and caught him staring. There was a moment of silence, and then a slight smile broke the somberness of Mercy's face.

Lon didn't know how long he sat there before he heard himself saying, "Next time you come to Blessings, maybe we could have coffee together, or another hot chocolate?"

Hope paused and looked up. The chief just made a pass at her sister.

Mercy hadn't answered. She kept looking at Lon so long he was afraid she would say no, and then after an anxious wait, she made his day. "Yes, that would be good, I think."

"Good. Just give me a call when you're headed into town."

"Let me know when you two are through setting up your first date," Hope drawled.

"Oh, hush," Mercy said.

Lon was ecstatic and trying not to act like a teenager who'd just scored a date for the prom. Mercy had less guile than any woman he'd ever known. "I appreciate the opportunity," Lon said.

She immediately frowned. "To do what?"

He blinked, and then threw back his head and laughed.

Hope grinned. "Just deal with it," she said. "She's driving Duke crazy. His bossy bravado has gotten him nowhere."

"I'm a cop," Lon said. "I like straightforward and honest. It saves a whole lot of time in this world if you get set on the right track from the start. So, I guess my answer to your question, Miss Dane, is I appreciate the opportunity to get to know you better."

Mercy's eyes narrowed slightly then she shrugged. "I just like to know where I stand."

You're standing right on my heart. You just don't know it yet, girl.

Lon sat quietly, drinking his coffee as Hope and Mercy finished going through the list. Then Hope signed off and put everything back in her purse as Lon pocketed the receipt.

"I am so happy to get this. Thank you for bringing it to me," Hope said.

"You're welcome," Lon said, then set his empty cup back on the tray. "I guess I better get back to town. Thank you for the coffee, and Mercy, I hope to be seeing you soon."

"First chance I get, I'm going to the Piggly Wiggly. I'll let you know when I'm headed that way."

"I'll be looking forward to that text," Lon said, and put on his coat as he stood.

"I'll see you out," Mercy said, and led the way to the front door.

"Take care of yourself, Hope," Lon said.

"I will. Lots of people helping make that happen," she said.

Lon paused at the door. "See you soon?"

Mercy nodded.

"Hot damn," he said softly, and then sauntered out. He didn't have the guts to look back, but if he had, he would have seen Mercy grinning.

She shut the door, and when she turned around, Hope arched an eyebrow. "The chief is one of Blessings' most eligible bachelors."

Mercy sniffed as she began gathering up the cups and napkins. "It's just coffee."

"Or hot chocolate. It might be hot chocolate," Hope said, and then frowned. "You can drive Jack's pickup anytime you need it."

"Thanks. I want to pick up some extra stuff to do a little baking for your family."

"They're your family too," Hope reminded her.

"I know, but I won't be here forever, and I want to help out while I can."

Hope's heart skipped a beat. "Are you planning to go back to Savannah? I thought maybe you would want to—"

"I can't live here with you guys indefinitely, but I'm not going back to Savannah. I'll find work in Blessings and a place to stay. I'll be close."

Hope sighed. "Okay. I'm not about to tell you what to do, but I am in no hurry to see you leave. You just got here."

Mercy gave Hope a quick kiss on the forehead. "I won't disappear, so quit worrying. I'm going to get started on dinner. Is meatloaf okay? I saw ground beef thawed out."

"It's perfect," Hope said. "Are you sure you don't mind cooking?"

"No. I like to cook. One of my foster mothers taught me how. She also taught me how to bake because she needed all the help she could get. You rest. Here's the TV remote. Yell if you need me."

Hope then turned on the television as Mercy carried the tray back to the kitchen. She fell asleep listening to Mercy singing as she worked.

Chapter 12

BY THE TIME NOON ROLLED AROUND, A BIG MEATLOAF WAS IN the warming oven along with a bowl of mashed potatoes and brown gravy. Mercy had green beans with bacon bits and a bowl of coleslaw for sides. She'd found some frozen blackberries in the freezer and made a fruit compote, then found enough flour and sugar to make some quick, biscuit-like shortcakes.

Duke and Jack came in to eat as Hope was folding napkins at the table, laughing at some story Mercy told about a drunk trucker locking himself out of his own sleeping cab in a rainstorm.

Jack only heard the tail end of the story as he went to the utility room to wash up.

Duke heard enough to voice his disapproval. "I would think a job that puts you in constant contact with drunks and itinerants would get old."

The smile on Mercy's face died and she immediately clammed up.

Hope glared. "She was just relating a funny incident and no one asked what you thought," she snapped.

Duke blinked. "Well, I didn't mean—"

"Let it go," Mercy said, and set coffee cups on the table.

Jack heard it all from the bathroom and frowned. "Hey, Duke! Can you come here a minute?"

"Be right there," Duke said. "What's up?" he asked as he stopped on the threshold.

Jack pulled him into the bathroom and shut the door. "Why do you keep doing that?" he hissed.

Duke frowned. "Doing what?"

"Belittling the state of her affairs. Mercy has done a damn good job of taking care of herself without begging for welfare to do it for her, and yet you remind her it's not a lofty enough position to suit you."

Duke didn't like to be challenged by his younger brother. "Maybe she needs someone to point out that there are better ways to live and better places to work."

Jack sighed. "What if she likes what she's doing?"

Duke shook his head. "Now that she's part of our family, she needs to elevate her level of expectation. We can't have—"

Jack jabbed a finger hard against Duke's chest. "She does not change for us. We love her as she is, you ass."

Duke glared. "I wouldn't marry someone like that."

Jack's mouth opened, but at first the words wouldn't come, and Duke didn't have sense enough to shut up. "I mean, I've given it some thought. It would be the perfect solution. The two of us, married to sisters. They wouldn't fuss about living under the same roof like two other women might, and I could—"

Jack held up a hand. "Stop talking. Just stop a minute. I can't believe I heard you correctly. Are you insinuating that you think you and Mercy would be a suitable match?"

Duke shrugged. "If she was willing to change some of her ways, I don't see a problem."

"You're an idiot," Jack said. "I didn't think you could be any more clueless, but I was wrong. You don't even like her."

"She's very beautiful," Duke said.

"She doesn't like you," Jack added.

"I'm sure if I pointed out the benefits of such a union, she would see the sense behind it," Duke said.

"You're supposed to love someone before you marry them, damn it."

"Love is overrated," Duke muttered.

"I beg to differ," Jack said. "I would give my life for Hope. That's how much she means to me. Now don't ever let me hear you talking like this again, and certainly don't let Hope hear you."

Duke frowned. "You're wrong," he said.

"And you're delusional. We're going out now to have dinner, and the only thing you're going to do with your mouth is put food in it and chew."

—⁂—

Hope didn't know what had passed between the brothers, but she knew Jack was upset as he silently pleaded his case with her not to flip out. She gave him a pointed stare and then arched her eyebrows as if to say, *What is wrong with your brother?* He just shrugged and started bragging about the food. "This looks amazing, Mercy, and tastes even better," he said as he took his first bite. "Oh wow, Hope. She made the green beans like Mom used to make…the kind with bacon bits in them."

"I know," Hope said. "You're a really good cook, little sister."

Mercy managed a smile, but she knew the brothers had been arguing about her. She just didn't know what to do about it.

Hope knew Mercy's feelings were hurt. In an effort

to change the subject, she mentioned that Lon Pittman had asked Mercy out on a date. She missed Duke's stunned reaction, but Jack didn't. He quickly picked up the conversation before Duke could say something he might later regret.

"Really?" Jack said. "That's great, Mercy. He's a nice guy…a really nice guy, and, well, the fact that you two knew each other already…couldn't be better."

Mercy shrugged. "We'd met, and it's just coffee."

"Or hot chocolate," Hope said, and then giggled.

Mercy laughed in spite of herself. "Yes, or hot chocolate. So does that make it a bigger deal if I have a choice?"

"So how did you and Lon happen to meet?" Hope asked.

Mercy shrugged. "We met a long time ago. I wasn't more than nineteen. I came home to my apartment and surprised a thief in the act of robbing me. He got away with all of the money I had saved, and the chief, who wasn't a chief then, had just moved in across the hall."

"Oh my God. Were you hurt?" Hope asked.

Mercy sighed, remembering again the panic. "No, just scared. The lock on my door was broken. I didn't have any money except what I was carrying. I didn't know what to do or where to go. Then this guy comes out of his apartment asking what was going on, and, well, one thing led to another, and I packed up my belongings in two suitcases and spent the night on his sofa. I left before morning and never saw him again until that day in the waiting room."

Hope was in tears. "I don't know what hurts my heart worse…knowing every time something bad came along, you had no one to help you through it, or the fact that

you two met again because I nearly died. There has to
be some kind of karma at work here, bringing you two
back together."

"It wasn't like that," Mercy said, and then knew she'd
just lied. It *was* like that—to her.

Duke was too dumbstruck to participate in the conversation. This information was putting kinks in his
grand plan. She and the chief had a history. All Duke did
was make her mad. "Pass the mashed potatoes, please,"
he said.

Mercy pushed the bowl across the table toward him
without meeting his gaze.

"Thank you," Duke said.

She nodded without looking up.

Duke sighed. Life hadn't been this complicated
before. He was happy Hope had found her missing
sister, but wished to God she'd been someone besides
this obstinate firebrand.

As the meal progressed, Mercy relaxed again. She
was beginning to figure out what made Duke Talbot tick.
Basically, he was the oldest child who'd been in charge
of taking care of business when he and Jack were growing up, and just because they were all finally grown,
Duke didn't know how to let go of being in control.

"If you want dessert, there's blackberry shortcake,"
Mercy said as she got up to refill Hope's coffee.

"What? Are you serious?" Jack asked. "I didn't
know there was anything on the premises that could
turn into shortcake."

"You're going to spoil them for me, and I won't be
able to hold up my end of the deal after you're gone,"
Hope said.

"Where are you going?" Duke asked.

Mercy shrugged. "Nowhere for now, but eventually I'll move into Blessings."

Duke sighed. *She's moving, and the police chief wants to date her*—which was another hint that he should let go of his fantasy.

"You have the option of eating it as is or with a scoop of vanilla ice cream," Mercy said.

"Ice cream for me," Hope said.

"And me," Jack added.

"What about you, Duke?" Mercy asked.

"Uh…yes…ice cream."

She served the shortcakes warm with the cold ice cream, then sat down with her own serving and dug in. "Good blackberries," she said. "Do they grow wild on the farm?"

Hope nodded. "Yes. I pick when they're in season, if I'm not working the late shifts. You need to pick berries early in the morning while it's still cool, before the snakes get out."

"I know," Mercy said. "One of my foster families lived in the country. They had lots of wild blackberries on their property, but they sold what we picked. We didn't usually eat any, except what we could sneak in our mouths while we were picking."

Jack frowned. "Did you have *any* good foster parents?"

Mercy shrugged. "I don't know what you call *good*. I know I didn't like any of them."

Hope was horrified. "Oh my God! Why not?"

"I don't know. It's not like every foster parent I had was abusive or mean, because they weren't. Some were okay, but I didn't feel like I mattered. I was just another name and number on a file. What I do know is that no one ever asked me what I thought or what I wanted, and if their lives changed or they didn't like us, we were packed up and sent elsewhere."

Hope was in tears. "I'm so sorry."

Mercy sighed. "You have no need to apologize. You didn't do it, and it's the nature of the beast. It's part of my past, that's all. And we were talking about blackberry shortcake, not all this downer stuff."

"That was a wonderful meal. I'll do dishes," Duke said abruptly.

"Okay," Mercy said. "Does anyone mind loaning me something to drive so I can go to the supermarket? I could go on my bike, but it's a rough ride for eggs."

Jack laughed. "You can drive my pickup, but if you're talking about groceries for the house, we pay for that."

"I promised Hope I would bake for her," Mercy said.

"Well, if I let you drive my pickup, do I get some of the baked goods?" Jack asked.

Mercy chuckled. "I'll make enough for everybody, but will you be around the house long enough to stay with Hope so I can go this afternoon?"

"Yes," Jack said. "I'm working on the books this afternoon, so I'll be in the house the rest of the day. I think I have another debit card in the office for the household account. I'll call the bank and tell them you're authorized to use it. I started a grocery list the other day, and I hate to grocery shop, so you'll be doing me a huge favor by picking up what's on it, as well as what else you need to make us fat."

"As a rule, our people didn't run to fat," Duke said.

Jack wadded up a paper napkin and threw it at the

back of his brother's head. "I was making a joke. What the hell made you say that?"

Duke shrugged. "Well, I was just sharing information...in case Mercy was interested in what we may or may not want to eat."

"If it's sweet, I want it," Jack said.

Mercy was trying not to stare at Duke but after the absurdity of his last statement, she was officially giving up trying to understand what made him tick. "Thank you for the information, Duke. I suppose that would be a valid thing for any cook to know."

"See? I knew it was something she would like to know," Duke muttered.

Mercy left the brothers still quarreling. She wasn't sure if that was normal family behavior or if they were really arguing, but it made her antsy. She went upstairs to change and then came down with her purse, picked up the debit card Jack had left on the counter beside the list, and within a few minutes, she was on her way out the door.

The day was clear, but the brisk wind in her face was cold. She had her leather jacket over her sweatshirt, and her jeans tucked into the tops of her boots. She jumped into Jack's blue truck, started it up, and put it in gear, then breathed a sigh of relief as she drove away. This trip made her feel like she was running away. She didn't want to seem ungrateful, but solitude suited her, and she'd had little of it since her arrival.

The grocery list was in her pocket, her purse with the debit card on the seat beside her, but she was thinking about Lon Pittman as she drove. He'd said to let him know when she was coming to Blessings, only he'd just made the offer a few hours earlier. She didn't know if he'd meant to be taken seriously so soon, but as she braked at the end of the driveway, she sent him a text before pulling onto the main road.

On my way to the Piggly Wiggly.

Then she laid the phone in the console and continued her journey. She hadn't gone far when she heard her phone signal a text, but the blacktop had too many twists and turns to look at anything but the road. Waiting to see what he said amped up her expectations and made the trip into town seem that much shorter.

She passed the city limit sign and then drove up Main Street, glancing at the police station as she passed, then at the Curl Up and Dye and Phillips' Pharmacy before turning into the Piggly Wiggly parking lot.

The moment she parked, she grabbed the phone and pulled up his text.

This day just keeps getting better. You. Me. Granny's Country Kitchen? Time?

Mercy smiled, glanced at the clock, and then sent another text.

3:00 p.m.

She was walking into the store when she received his answer.

Thank you for the opportunity.

She laughed beneath her breath as she grabbed a cart, and then did a little dance step as she headed down an aisle, searching for the things on her list. She began with the items Jack had listed—a large box of oatmeal, eggs, milk, laundry soap, and toilet paper. It took her a couple of minutes to find the aisle with cleaning supplies, and she went from there to canned vegetables and fruit. She saved the baking aisle for last, and one by one, began going down her list, picking up flour, two kinds of sugars, and the little papers for cupcakes. Then on to a couple of bags of chocolate chips, a bag of white chocolate chips, and a couple of packages of nuts. Hope's assortment of spices was suffering, so she added cinnamon and cloves, a small can of cream of tartar for making meringue, and bottles of vanilla and almond flavorings. She went from there to choosing canned fruits to make pie fillings, and at the last minute added a bag of sweetened coconut before heading to the checkout.

The clerk smiled at Mercy as she began emptying her cart onto the counter. "Afternoon. I'm Lorene."

"Hi," Mercy said.

"Did you find everything you needed?" the clerk asked as she began scanning Mercy's items.

"Yes, thank you," Mercy said.

When the clerk totaled it, Mercy scanned the debit card, then handed it to the clerk with her ID.

"You're using a card on a Talbot account?"

"Yes. Jack gave it to me to use for the family groceries. Hope is my sister, and I'm staying at the house with them for a while."

"Oh, you're the one on the motorcycle!" the clerk

cried as she handed back the card and Mercy's ID. "That was really something, finding your sister like that."

"Yes, ma'am, it was," Mercy said, and started putting sacks back into the basket to carry out to the truck.

"Oh, honey, there's no ma'am around here! Call me Lorene, and it's real nice to meet you."

"You too, Lorene. See you next time," she added, and headed out the exit pushing the cart full of sacks.

Chapter 13

THE COLD WIND HIT HER HEAD-ON AS SHE LEFT THE STORE, making her shiver. She wasted no time unloading the groceries into the backseat of the pickup, putting the perishable items in an ice chest, and then getting inside.

It was ten minutes to three.

Excitement upped her pulse rate as she drove out of the parking lot and headed further up the street to the cafe. From the number of cars parked on both sides of the street, it looked as if Granny's was doing a brisk business. She noticed a sign that stated parking was also available behind the cafe, so she took the turn that led to the larger lot. She found a place to park and then hastened her stride as she ran back to the street to the front entrance, anxious to get out of the wind.

The dining room was more than half full of what Mercy always called the idlers…the older retirees who no longer had to punch a time clock. They were two and three to a table, sharing coffee and conversation, and now and then, a piece of pie. But they all looked up when she walked in, and then looked again because she was a stranger, and then kept staring because she was so damn pretty.

Mercy was still looking around to see if Lon was there yet when the door opened behind her. She felt a cold rush of wind and then a hand slide around her waist. "I've come to claim my opportunity," he said in her ear.

Mercy's laugh was uninhibited and infectious as she turned to greet him, and every man, including Lon, fell a little bit in love. "You are the most outrageous police chief it has been my pleasure to know," she said.

"Good, then that means I'm at the top of your list. Let's grab a booth against that wall, okay? It's a little warmer there."

He cupped her elbow and led her to the booth, and the waitress was right behind them with menus and a smile. "Afternoon, Chief," she said.

"Hi, Della. This is Mercy Dane, Hope Talbot's sister. She likes hot chocolate. I'll have coffee, and they make really good coconut cream pies. I'm going to have a piece. How about you, Mercy?"

"Oh, I'll pass. I made blackberry shortcake at home, so I've already had my sweets for the day."

"Nice to meet you, Mercy, and I'll be right back with your orders," Della said.

Lon took off his Stetson and laid it in the booth beside him, then eyed Mercy without comment until she felt like a bug under glass.

"What?"

"I know. I'm staring and I'm sorry," Lon said. "You have two eyes, a nose, and a mouth, like everybody else. You have hair on your head and two ears to hear with. Your head sits on your neck just like mine, and yet I have never seen all of that put together quite as perfectly as it is on you. You were pretty when I first met you, but now, you are a work of art."

Mercy frowned. "So, all that rattling that just came out of your mouth was you saying you think I'm pretty?"

Lon grinned. "I also think you're smart and strong, and I admire you greatly as a person…and when we make love, you take my breath away."

Her eyes narrowed, and she had yet to crack a smile. "Are you flirting or stating a fact?"

His grin turned into a chuckle. "And that comment right there is why we're having this moment. You are the real deal, a straightforward woman with principles. I knew a woman like that once. She was the first woman I ever loved. Her name was Ethel Milam, my first grade teacher. The relationship was doomed from the start. I was only six, and she was dating the high school football coach."

Mercy giggled in spite of herself.

Lon grinned. "She broke my heart when she and the coach got married."

Mercy laughed. "Here comes your pie. Maybe now you'll stop talking crazy."

Della delivered the order, filled Lon's coffee cup, and set the thick mug of hot chocolate with marshmallow topping in front of Mercy with a wink. "It's hot, so blow on it a bit before you take a sip or you'll burn the hair right off your tongue," Della said.

"Yes, ma'am," Mercy said, and began eating the topping down to the drink, giving it time enough to cool, while Lon dug into the pie.

"This is my favorite pie, although I have never turned down a piece of pie in my life, regardless of the flavor."

"So, you like pie and you lock up the bad guys. Where did you grow up?" Mercy asked.

"Blessings. I never wanted to live anywhere else, so after I graduated from the police academy and was getting certified at the Council for Law Enforcement Education, which, by the way, was what I was doing when we met, I came back here to work."

"And your family?"

"My parents moved to Arizona after Dad retired. He has asthma. The weather is so much better for him there. My brother is a pilot. He works for an oil company flying the big shots around the world and ferrying workers back and forth from offshore drilling rigs."

Mercy watched the way his eyes lit up as he talked about his family, and she could tell they were close by the love she heard in his voice.

"So you always wanted to be in law enforcement?"

He nodded. "What about you?"

"I didn't want to be in law enforcement," she said.

It didn't take a genius to figure out Mercy didn't like talking about the past, so Lon changed the subject by offering her a bite of pie.

Surprised by the gesture, Mercy opened her mouth like a baby bird.

"Mmmm," she said as she chewed and swallowed. "That *is* good pie."

Lon forked another bite and carefully popped it in his mouth while trying not to think that her lips had just touched his fork. If he'd still been in middle school, he would have considered it as good as a kiss. But he wasn't a kid, and he was slowly coming to terms with the fact that he wanted far more from her than sharing a bite of pie. "What's your favorite kind of pie?" he asked.

"I think maybe pecan. Either that or key lime. Yes... key lime first, pecan second."

He grinned. "Options. I like options."

She was focused on a tiny piece of coconut caught at the edge of his lip. "You like opportunities too."

The comeback surprised him. "Yes, I do," he said, then felt the coconut on his lip and absently licked it away.

Mercy took a drink of her hot chocolate as she watched him finish off the pie. She decided Lon not only made love like he meant it, he had a great butt, a real pretty mouth, and he was funny and interesting. She was glad she'd said yes to the coffee and to the man.

After that, time passed far too swiftly. "I really should be getting home," Mercy said as she noticed the time. "Hope will think I'm lost again."

"I don't want this to be over yet, but I understand. This was fun. We have to do it again," Lon said.

Mercy finally smiled. "I would do this again too."

Lon signaled the waitress to bring their check, and while they were waiting, Ruby Dye came into the cafe on the arm of Peanut Butterman. When she saw Mercy, she smiled and waved. Mercy waved back.

"I see you know Ruby," Lon said.

"She was one of the first people to welcome me to Blessings," Mercy said.

"That sounds like the Ruby we all know and love," Lon said, and then looked over Mercy's shoulder at the trio of women walking toward them.

"Well, good afternoon, Lon! Being chief of police surely suits you. You look all handsome and official."

"Yes, official," the other two echoed, and gave Mercy a look without speaking to her.

"Thank you, ladies," Lon said. "Have you met Mercy yet?"

"Why, no, we have not had the pleasure," Tina Clark said as the trio shifted their focus to the stranger.

"Mercy, from left to right, this is Tina Clark, Molly Frederick, and Angel Herd. Tina's husband and Molly's husband are on the city council. Angel's husband is a local judge. Ladies...this is Mercy Dane. She's Hope Talbot's younger sister and a new resident of Blessings."

Tina smiled. "Oh yes! We heard about you! It is *such* a pleasure to meet you."

Molly wiggled her fingers, a gesture meant as a greeting. "How nice."

Angel smiled, but it never reached her eyes as she gave Mercy the once-over. "Bless your heart! How special to find family in such an unexpected way."

Mercy knew women like this. She felt the chill beneath their smiles and silly giggles. And she knew exactly what that "bless your heart" meant. Coming out of a Southern woman's mouth, the closest translation was probably "Kiss my ass."

"Yes, ma'am, and I do thank you for the blessing," she drawled and caught their glare.

By referring to Angel Herd as ma'am, Mercy had publically addressed the fact that Angel was older. Lon missed all of the subterfuge and smiled, assuming Mercy was being properly welcomed by three of Blessings' finest.

The moment they sat down in the booth behind him, he lost sight of them, but Mercy saw everything, including the looks of disapproval. She'd been disrespected most of her adult life by women like them. Three more weren't going to make a difference. But their presence had taken the glow off her time with Lon, and when she heard chatter on his two-way, she guessed their time was about to end.

Lon frowned. "Hey, Mercy, I need to call in. Give me a couple of minutes and I'll be right back."

"Okay," she said.

The moment he got up and walked out of the cafe, the women in the booth took advantage of his absence to dig their claws into Mercy's composure, raising their voices to make sure she heard every word they were saying.

"Disgraceful is what it is," Angel said. "Coming here and trying to step into respectability through Hope and Jack."

"I can only imagine what Hope must be thinking, finding out her long-lost sister belongs to a biker gang," Molly said.

"God only knows what kind of life she's led, but I wouldn't close my eyes with her under *my* roof," Tina said. "I can't imagine what Chief Pittman is thinking, being seen with someone like her. He has his reputation to consider, you know, being the chief and all."

Mercy lowered her head and pretended to be looking through her purse to hide sudden tears. She didn't see Ruby Dye's shock, or the glare she shot at the trio, and even if she had, it wouldn't repair the damage of what had been said about her.

Certain she was going to burst into tears at any moment, Mercy stood and walked toward the exit. She heard them laughing and couldn't get out of the cafe soon enough.

Lon was in his patrol car still talking to the dispatcher when he saw Mercy come out of Granny's. He waved, but she wouldn't look his way, and when she got into the truck and drove away, his heart skipped a beat.

What the hell?

He quickly ended his call and went back into Granny's to pay for their food.

The women in the booth chatted amiably, arguing the benefits of shrimp salad over Caesar salad with chicken strips, when he tossed some money on the table. He scanned the dining room, trying to figure out what could have possibly happened, when he saw Ruby wave him over. As he approached, he could tell by the look on her face she was upset. "Yes, ma'am?" Lon asked.

Ruby's cheeks were pink, and she looked fit to be tied as she pointed to the booth behind the one where he and Mercy had been sitting.

"If you are wondering why your girl left so abruptly, ask them. In less than two minutes, they insulted her in every possible way, insinuating she was from a biker gang, that she was ruining your reputation, and that she was surely dangerous to be around."

The color faded from Lon's face so fast Peanut Butterman thought the man might pass out. He wondered if those women realized they'd just made an enemy of the wrong man. As for Ruby, they were three of her regular customers, but she was so indignant on Mercy's behalf she didn't care if she ever saw them again.

Lon turned and walked back to where the women were seated. They'd heard enough of what Ruby told him to know he wouldn't be happy, but when they saw the look on his face, they froze. He looked at them long and hard and then walked out of the dining room without saying a word. He got into the patrol car and called Mercy's phone. It rang and rang, but she didn't answer. He leaned back in the seat and closed his eyes, so hurt for her that he couldn't think. All he could do was send a text.

Ruby told me what happened. I am so sorry. They
are hateful bitches who saw you as a beautiful
woman, something they will never be, and wanted
to hurt you. Please don't let what they said make
a difference in our friendship. Please. I like you,
Mercy Dane. A lot. I will call you tomorrow.

He started the car and was backing out of his space
when he noticed a car in handicapped parking without
a sticker. Then he saw one parked in front of a fire
hydrant, and another with an out of date tag. And he
knew who drove them.

~~~

The ladies in the booth were no longer as elated with
themselves after facing Lon Pittman and knowing they'd
been found out.

Tina shivered, and then tried to laugh it off. "What
did he expect, right?"

Molly shrugged. She wasn't sure, but they might have
overstepped themselves.

Angel was worried. A judge's wife never purposefully
committed a social faux pas. She glanced at Ruby and
then quickly looked away. They certainly hadn't thought
that through. Putting their hairdresser out of sorts with
them was a risky move too.

Their orders came, and they had just taken a few bites
when they saw Chief Pittman come back into Granny's. He
walked up to their booth with a daunting lack of expression.

"Mrs. Clark, you parked in a handicapped parking
area. Traffic court is next Tuesday." He tore off the ticket
from his book and dropped it in her lap.

Tina's mouth was agape.

"Mrs. Frederick, your license tag expired in November. Traffic court is next Tuesday."

Molly's eyes welled as he dropped the ticket in her lap, but she didn't speak.

"Mrs. Herd, you parked in front of a fire hydrant. Traffic court is next Tuesday. Your husband is presiding," he said, and dropped the ticket in her lap.

Angel moaned beneath her breath. "We're sorry, Chief. We—"

Lon turned his back and walked out.

"Oh my gawd," Tina muttered.

"My husband is going to kill me," Angel said.

Molly rolled her eyes. "It's going to take a blow job before mine gets over this."

They looked at each other, then at their food, then waved at the waitress to bring them their checks, while across the room Peanut leaned across the table and patted Ruby's hand.

"So, do we agree on the emcee for this year's Peachy Keen competition?" he asked.

Ruby nodded. "Yes. Asking Mike Dalton is perfect. He is young, handsome, and personable…and he's always so calm and organized at his health spa that the competition shouldn't rattle him at all."

Peanut grinned. "He calls it a gym, not a health spa."

"Whatever," Ruby said. "But we'll be calling it a health spa for the night of the event."

Peanut arched an eyebrow. "Remind me never to get on the wrong side of your sweet disposition."

Ruby sniffed. "There's no call for meanness."

"I admire passion."

Ruby blinked. "Thank you, Peanut."

He leaned forward. "Would you like more?"

She blinked again. "More?"

"Coffee. Would you like more coffee?"

She sighed. "I would like a refill, but I have a cut and color coming in about ten minutes. I need to get back to the shop."

"Sure thing," he said as he tossed some bills on the table and escorted her out.

Chapter 14

MERCY CRIED ALL THE WAY OUT OF TOWN. SHE COULDN'T remember the last time she'd let someone get under her skin. She was tougher than that. But after coming to Blessings, she'd let down her guard, thinking she would be safe with family at her back. Obviously, she couldn't have been more wrong.

When her phone rang, she knew who it would be. One glance at caller ID confirmed it, but she didn't answer. There was no way she would ever be able to look Lon in the face again.

Then her phone signaled a text. She pulled over to the side of the road and read it, then laid the phone aside, and cried some more. She was so humiliated by the incident that the thought of going back to Blessings made her sick.

Finally, she pulled herself together enough to drive home, and by the time she turned off the main road onto the driveway leading toward the house, she had put away the hurt, determined not to reveal anything about what had happened.

Hope met her at the door with a smile. "Did you have coffee?"

"Hot chocolate," Mercy said, and kept going to the kitchen with her arms full of sacks of groceries.

Hope followed. "Did you have a good time? Is he adorable or what?"

"He's adorable," Mercy said, and kept taking things out of the sacks.

Hope frowned. "You don't sound like he's adorable."

Mercy paused. "No, he is. Really. I like him."

"Then what's wrong?" Hope asked.

"Nothing. I'm just thinking about what I'm going to bake first."

Hope didn't believe her, but she also saw the jut to Mercy's jaw and knew she wasn't going to talk. Something had happened, and sooner or later she would find out.

"I'm going to get the last of the groceries," Mercy said. "Be right back."

"I'll finish putting this stuff away," Hope said.

The moment Mercy turned away, Hope could tell by the set of her shoulders that something was definitely wrong. It hurt to think Mercy didn't trust her enough to talk about it, but they were barely a week into this new relationship, and this was to be expected.

When Mercy came back with the last of the groceries, Hope had put the produce in the refrigerator. "I put some beans in to soak after you left. Maybe you could rinse them, and get them onto the stove. It will take at least an hour for them to cook, maybe more," Hope said.

"Will do," Mercy said as she emptied the last of the sacks and put the groceries away.

She dug through the pans in the cabinet until she found a good deep one in which to cook the beans and set it on the counter.

Hope got a large piece of smoked ham from the refrigerator and put it in the bottom of the pot as Mercy drained the water from the beans and then dumped them on top of the ham. She added fresh water, salt, pepper, and one small clove of garlic and brought the contents to a boil before she put on the lid and turned down the heat, leaving them to slow cook. "Those will be good for supper," Hope said.

Mercy nodded.

Hope sighed, then walked up behind her sister, wrapped her arms around her, and gave her a hug. Mercy froze. "I love you, Baby Girl," Hope whispered.

Tears blurred Mercy's vision. She patted Hope's hands and tried to walk away, but Hope wouldn't let go.

"What happened?"

Mercy shuddered, and Hope felt it.

"Who hurt you? And don't try telling me nobody, because I know better."

Mercy sighed. "It's nothing."

"Anything that shuts you down like this isn't nothing. If you hurt, I hurt, honey. That's how being sisters works."

Mercy took a deep breath and then swiped at the tears rolling down her cheeks. "Are you afraid of me?" Mercy asked.

Hope frowned. "What the hell are you talking about? Why would I be afraid of anything you do?"

Mercy shrugged.

Hope grabbed Mercy by the shoulders and spun her around. When she saw the tears, her eyes narrowed in anger. "Damn it all to hell, Mercy! I'm going to ask you something you can answer. Where was Lon when this happened?"

"Outside taking a call."

"Where were you?"

"Inside the cafe, waiting for him to come back."

"Someone said something to you."

Mercy sighed.

Hope squeezed her shoulders. "Honey, we're sisters. Talk to me."

Mercy started to shake, and when she finally did start talking, it was little more than a whisper. "They said I belonged to a biker gang. They said I would ruin Lon's reputation. They said I was using you and Jack to gain respectability. They said they would be afraid to close their eyes if we were sleeping under the same roof."

Hope gasped. "Are you serious? Someone actually said that shit to you? What did you do? What did you say?"

Mercy covered her face. "It's my fault. It's not like I haven't heard stuff like this before, but when I came here, I felt safe. I let down my guard."

Hope ripped Mercy's hands away from her face and wrapped her into her arms. "That's bullshit, and not your fault. Don't ever let me hear you say that again. And you should feel safe. You're supposed to feel safe where you live. I want to know who said this, and I want to know now."

The sympathy was too much. Mercy started to cry all over again. One huge sob after another ripped up her throat. She couldn't stop crying enough to speak.

Hope was livid. She couldn't hold Mercy tight enough to stop her trembling, and the sound of those sobs broke her heart. She was still holding her when Jack came into the kitchen.

The moment he saw them, he rushed forward and took them both in his arms. "What the hell happened here? Is Mercy hurt? Is she sick? What's wrong?"

"Someone said terrible things to her in town. I'm going to yank hair from their heads one strand at a time."

Jack frowned. "Who did that?"

"I'm waiting for names," Hope muttered. "Would you please bring me a wet washcloth?"

Jack bolted out of the kitchen and ran back with a warm, wet cloth. "Here, honey," he said.

Hope began wiping the cloth over Mercy's face as if she were a child, gently wiping away tears and telling her over and over that it would be okay.

"Come sit down," Jack said, and pulled out a chair at the kitchen table.

Mercy sat, embarrassed all over again that both Hope and Jack had seen her cry. "I'm sorry. I—"

"No!" Hope said. "You do not apologize again for anything."

Jack pulled out two more chairs, one for Hope and one for him.

"I want names," Hope said.

"I'm not sure I remember," Mercy mumbled.

"Concentrate," Hope said.

Mercy knew she wasn't going to let this go.

"How many were there?" Hope asked.

"Three. Lon introduced us, but I know bitches when I meet them. As soon as he went outside to take a call…" She shrugged.

"Names," Hope repeated.

Mercy's brow furrowed as she tried to remember. "Um…Gina. No, Tina, and another one was Angel, although she was anything but an angel."

A muscle jerked at the side of Hope's jaw. "Let me guess. By any chance was the other one Molly?"

Mercy nodded.

Hope's eyes narrowed in anger as she glanced at

Jack. "The same trio who tried to start something with me right before we got married." Hope cupped Mercy's chin and tilted it up until they were looking eye to eye. "Jack's church gave us a wedding shower. Those three women were there. Tina called me a foreigner because my skin was darker than theirs. Molly and Angel said something about Jack liking dark meat."

Mercy gasped.

"And they made the mistake of saying it where Jack could hear. He went to school with all three and lit into them without mincing words, then rounded up their husbands and told them to take their wives home and teach them some manners. They were no longer welcome at the event."

"What did the men do?" Mercy asked.

Jack shrugged. "I don't know what they said, but we received written apologies from all three of the women, and expensive wedding gifts, which Hope promptly sent back. Now we just make a point to walk on the other side of the street from each other."

Mercy drew a slow, shuddering breath, took the tissue Hope handed her, wiped her eyes, and blew her nose.

"Does Lon know?" Hope asked.

Mercy nodded. "I guess someone told him after I left. He called, but I couldn't answer. He sent a text, apologizing for what they'd said."

Jack put a hand on her shoulder. "You didn't talk to him about it?"

"No. I couldn't. I got in the truck and left."

"Bless your heart," Jack said. "Whatever they said to you—don't let it matter. We're family, and family sticks together, understand?"

"I'm beginning to," Mercy said softly, and wrapped her arms around Hope's neck.

Hope hugged her again. "Now, that's that. We're not going to talk about those witches again. So what are you going to bake first?"

Mercy was smiling through tears. "What do you want?"

"This is your call," Hope said. "I'm going to lie down for a bit and leave the whole kitchen to you. How's that?"

"Good," Mercy said, already thinking of recipes.

"I'll be in the office if you need me," Jack said, and kissed the top of Mercy's head.

A few moments later, Mercy was alone. She wiped her eyes one last time and got up. It was time to do something constructive.

Down the hall, Hope and Jack continued to talk about what had happened, and Hope was furious. The longer she thought about it, the more certain she became that they'd hurt Mercy as a way of getting back at her.

"You think so?" Jack asked.

"I wouldn't put it past them. I know it's been years since all that happened, but they are the kind of women who hold grudges. They saw an opportunity and took it."

"What do you think we should do?" Jack asked.

"I need to think on it a bit. Time will present the perfect opportunity, and when it does I am going to make them sorry," Hope said.

Jack hugged her. "You rock, honey, but you already know I think that, don't you?"

Hope nodded. "Thank you for being you."

"Is there something you want me to do?" Jack asked.

"I have to go back to Blessings tomorrow for a surgery follow-up. We need to make sure Mercy comes with us. Like getting back on a horse after you've been thrown, she needs to walk those streets and know that she's both welcome and safe."

"Agreed. Why don't you lie back and rest for a while. You've been up for several hours."

"I think I will," Hope said. "Keep an eye on Mercy in case I fall asleep, will you?"

"Of course, honey. You sleep. I've got this."

Hope fell asleep and missed the sweet aroma of baking cookies wafting through the rooms.

Duke came inside as Mercy was taking the first cookies from the sheet and transferring them to a cooling rack.

"Something sure smells good in here," Duke said.

Mercy was always at her best when she was baking and smiled as Duke sidled up beside her, obviously angling for a cookie. "Want one?" she asked.

"No, I want two."

She grinned. "Help yourself. There's more baking, and more to be baked."

"Chocolate chip. Mmmm," he said as he took a big bite. "Oh my word! Delicious."

Mercy's heart lifted. It felt good to succeed, even at something as small as a batch of fresh cookies. "Thank you."

"I'm going to take a couple with me to the office," Duke said.

Pleased they were a success, Mercy emptied the baking sheet and then set it in the sink before giving the brown beans a quick stir. She was already planning a pan of corn bread to go with the beans.

—ᴧᴧᴧ—

Lon worked in the office the rest of the afternoon and was still there when Tina Clark's husband came to the station. When Avery escorted him into the chief's office, Lon was not surprised to see him.

"Afternoon, Hank. Have a seat."

In his younger years, Hank Clark had been a quarterback for the Blessings High School football team. All of the muscles he'd had in school had turned to fat, and the frown he wore was gouged so deep into his soft flesh that the lines on his forehead looked like furrows in plowed ground.

"This isn't a social call," Hank muttered.

Lon shrugged. "That's okay. There's nothing social about the office of the chief of police. So what's on your mind?"

Hank shifted nervously. "You gave Tina a ticket!"

"Yes, I did. Did she tell you why?"

Hank waved a hand over the desk in a gesture of dismissal. "Oh, something about parking in the wrong place."

"A handicapped parking place. I believe you spoke on the seriousness of not letting people get away with this at the last city council meeting. Am I right?"

Hank cleared his throat and tugged at his necktie. "I suppose I did, but—"

"Surely you don't exempt yourself or your family from behaving in a proper, legal manner?"

"Why, no, of course not," Hank sputtered.

Lon nodded. "Will there be anything else?"

"No, I guess not," Hank said, and made a quick exit.

Lon went back to work.

About ten minutes later, Avery brought Ronnie Frederick to his office. Ronnie was as nervous and skinny as Hank was brusque and overweight. "Chief?"

Lon waved the man in. "Have a seat, Ronnie."

"This won't take long," Ronnie snapped as he rocked from the toes of his feet to the heels and back again. "You gave my Molly a citation! What on earth were you thinking?"

"Actually, you two don't pay much attention to your business. I was a little surprised we hadn't caught it before. We're almost into February, and the tag on Molly's car has been expired since last November."

Ronnie began popping his knuckles in rapid succession. "Oh, I know that, but—"

Lon frowned. "You knew? You knew it and still ignored the laws of the State of Georgia? Exactly how do you justify yourself, sir?"

Despite the cold day, Ronnie Frederick began to sweat. "No, of course not. That came out all wrong."

Lon glared.

Ronnie's cell rang. He grabbed his pocket as if that phone had just become the lifesaver he needed to get the hell out of the station before he made a bigger ass of himself than he'd already done. "I'll get that tag taken care of ASAP," Ronnie said.

"And you'll get that fine paid in traffic court as well," Lon snapped.

"Right! I'll do that. I need to take this call. Thank you for your time," Ronnie said and bolted.

A muscle jerked at the corner of Lon's eye as he turned back to his computer.

Less than an hour later, his desk phone rang. "Chief Pittman," he said as he answered.

"This is Wesley. Do you have a minute?"

"Hello, Judge. What can I do for you?" Lon asked.

"Angel just told me about that little citation you gave her today."

"The one about blocking a fire hydrant?" Lon asked.

He heard the judge take a deep breath and guessed he was about to try to make the citation disappear.

Wesley chuckled. "Oh hell, Lon. We both know it was just an oversight on her part. I don't really see any need in taking this to traffic court."

"I know you fined Melvin Wells, the only taxi driver in Blessings, for driving with a cracked windshield. That hardly compares with your wife's infraction. She parked in front of a fire hydrant, which is not only illegal, but could have resulted in the harm of others. She parked there only because it was closer to the door, when there were plenty of other parking places available."

There was a long moment of silence, and then Wesley cleared his throat again. "Can we be honest with each other?" he asked.

"I am honest," Lon said.

Wesley sighed. "What the fuck did the three of them do to get on your bad side?"

"What three?" Lon asked.

"Damn it, Lon. Angel and her two running buddies— that's what three."

"I only heard it secondhand so I won't comment. If you want to hear the ugly truth, talk to Ruby Dye or Peanut Butterman."

"Oh my God! Why?" Wesley asked.

"They witnessed it. Ruby told me. You ask her."

Wesley groaned. "Ruby Dye? Peanut Butterman? Are you serious?"

"Are you going to doubt their honor?"

"No, of course not, and I—"

"Good. I'll be in court next Tuesday. Just in case you need my testimony when they appear at your bench."

"Yes, well, of course," Wesley mumbled. "Thank you for your time."

"Certainly, Judge. Thank you for understanding the seriousness of this incident. Lives have been ruined by gossip and lies of this severity."

Wesley cursed beneath his breath as he hung up.

Lon disconnected, then turned back to his computer. He stared at the screen for what felt like forever, then saved what he'd been working on and logged out. He got his coat and his keys and headed up front. "Avery, I'll be out the rest of the afternoon. If you or Larry need me, you can reach me by cell phone."

"Okay, Chief. Have a nice night."

"You too," Lon said, and put on his coat as he headed for the back exit.

Chapter 15

WESLEY HERD WAS SICK TO HIS STOMACH. RUBY DYE CUT his hair and colored Angel's. Gossip ran rampant in the Curl Up and Dye. He knew because he heard plenty of it during his appointments. As for Butterman, it would be damn humiliating to talk to him about this. As judge, he needed to maintain his elevated status in court, and that would be difficult knowing the lawyer on the other side of the bench knew his wife was a bitch.

So Ruby it was. He'd call her, humble himself, and hope for the best. He made the call before he chickened out and then listened to it ringing several times before someone finally answered.

"Curl Up and Dye. This is Ruby."

"Hello, Ruby. This is Judge Herd. I wonder if I might have a word with you?"

Ruby grimaced. She knew exactly what that word was going to be about. "I have exactly five minutes before my next appointment so you'll have to make this quick."

"Are you alone? If you're not, I would ask that you take the call in private, so you feel comfortable speaking freely."

"If you're referring to the ass Angel made of herself in Granny's this afternoon, half the town already knows. I wasn't the only one to witness it. I'm just the only one who told Chief Pittman why his friend suddenly disappeared when he came looking for her. So, what do you want to know?"

Wesley groaned. "Just tell me what happened. Please."

"Happy to," Ruby said. "Do you know who Mercy Dane is?"

"No, I don't believe I do," Wesley said.

"She's the woman who rode a Harley from Savannah to Blessings on Christmas Day to donate blood to Hope Talbot so she wouldn't die."

Wesley's stomach roiled. Everyone in Blessings knew about that miracle ride, and that the woman had turned out to be Hope's long-lost sister. He just hadn't remembered her name. "Okay. I know who you're talking about now. What does she have to do with them?"

"Chief Pittman was having coffee with her this afternoon at Granny's when your wife and her two friends came in. I heard the chief introducing them to Mercy, which was a kind thing to do, since she's new in town. But instead of welcoming her, the moment the chief went outside to take a call, they insulted her beyond explanation. I can only assume they did it because they could."

"Well, hell, what did they say that was so bad it—"

"That they heard she belonged to a biker gang, that she was going to ruin Chief Pittman's reputation, that she'd come to stay with Hope and Jack Talbot for her own gain, and that she was dangerous."

All Ruby heard was a gasp and then total silence. "Are you still breathing?" she asked.

"Barely," Wesley mumbled.

"So that's what they did, and you can tell them from me that unless I hear they've done a complete about-face and made an apology that Mercy Dane has accepted, the three of them can find someone else to do their hair. They're not going to be welcome in my shop anymore."

"What about me?" Wesley asked.

"Unless you fine the lot of them to the extent of the law, including your wife, you can go find yourself another barber."

"But you're the only one in town," Wesley said.

"That has become your problem, not mine," Ruby said, and hung up.

Wesley blinked. No one hung up on him. He was a judge. Then he sighed. And he was going to be the judge who had to drive to Savannah for a damn haircut, thanks to Angel and her two cohorts. This was an appalling situation for sure. What they'd said was horrible. He'd never understood how women ticked.

He dropped his cell phone in his pocket and exited his office. He was going to have to go home for lunch and resist the urge to shake the shit out of his wife for causing so much trouble. She was nowhere close to an angel, despite the name.

By the time he got home, he was in a seething rage. He greeted their middle-aged housekeeper with a nod. "Hello, Lisa. Where's my wife?"

"I believe she and her friends are in the game room. I took some snacks and drinks to them about thirty minutes ago. I made beef stew. Just let me know when you're ready to eat."

"Thank you. Sounds good. Give me about fifteen minutes, and then serve it in the breakfast nook. I have a full afternoon of court so I can't linger."

"Yes, sir. Fifteen minutes," Lisa Cyrus said, and went toward the laundry as her boss walked down the hall.

Wesley heard the women talking before he got to the door. They weren't watching any movie, which was good. He'd have their full attention at once and braced himself for the war he was about to launch. He stormed into the room, intentionally letting the door slam against the wall before swinging shut on its own with a bang.

Angel screamed, and then saw it was Wesley, and started railing on him, her hand pressed against her heart as if he'd caused her mortal harm. "Good lord, Wesley! That is no way to enter a room. What's the matter with you?"

He gave each one of them a hard, angry stare, and in his loudest judgmental voice, lit into them without mincing words. "There have been many times when I've been irked at the three of you, but today absolutely takes the cake."

"Now see here, Wesley Herd. You're not my husband, and you don't talk to me like—"

"Shut up, Tina, and Molly, keep your mouth shut too, and hear me out. You three verbally attacked a woman today in Granny's with no compunction and no reason other than to be the total bitches that the three of you are. You are all the subject of today's gossip. I called Chief Pittman to inquire about the ticket my wife received and found out that having you stand before me in court is far from the least of my worries. When I asked what was really wrong, he advised me to call eyewitnesses, because his information was secondhand. So I find out, among others, Ruby Dye and Peanut Butterman witnessed all of it. Imagine my humiliation! Butterman is a man I deal with almost every day in my courtroom, and now to face him knowing what an embarrassing shit my wife is? I couldn't do it, so I called Ruby Dye. I should have called Butterman because Ruby was livid. She said what happened is all over town, and she has informed me that until you three make a proper and public apology to Mercy Dane, she's not taking appointments from any of us, and that includes me."

Angel's hand went straight to her hair. "She can't do that!"

"She can, and she has. You three make me sick."

Tina moaned. "I was getting a new color this week."

Molly was silent, too shocked to respond.

"I will be seeing all three of you in court on Tuesday. You're going to be fined to the limit of the law. Angel, consider the trip to Aruba canceled. I'm going to eat lunch. I don't want company. Sit here and figure out how you're going to make up for what you said. You shamed her in public. You will apologize the same way. And just for the record, you three disgust me."

He made his exit as loud and abrupt as his entrance had been. He ate lunch without tasting it and went back to work, still upset enough that he sat through one whole court case fantasizing about divorce.

~~~

It was closing in on five o'clock when Lon drove out of Blessings with a bouquet of flowers on the seat beside him and a sick feeling in the pit of his stomach. He'd told Mercy he'd call her tomorrow, but he knew he'd never get a wink of sleep tonight until he talked to her in person.

The sun was already behind the mountains. It would be dark within the hour, and from the looks of the clouds, a starless, moonless night, which pretty much fit the mood he was in.

He drove with an eye on the roadsides, knowing deer would be on the move after grazing and looking for a place to bed down for the night. He was just turning up the drive to the Talbot farm when his cell rang.

He cursed the timing and answered as he drove. "Chief Pittman."

"Chief, this is Larry. I'm sorry to bother you, but I got here to clock in for the night shift and found Avery asleep in one of the cells. He's burning up with fever, I think. What should I do?"

"Call an ambulance and have them take him to the ER, then call his ex-wife Georgia. Her number is his emergency call number."

"Okay, thanks."

"Keep me updated," Lon said. "I heard the flu is still going around."

"Will do," Larry said, and disconnected.

Lon frowned. Now he was going to spend the night trying to find another dispatcher to cover the day shift at the station. But in the meantime, Mercy came first.

He tapped the brakes as he turned and spooked a rabbit on the drive as it hopped into the brush, then kept on going. When he reached the house, the lights from downstairs were a warm and inviting sight against a darkening sky. He parked, grabbed the flowers, and headed toward the house, his heart pounding with every step.

Duke was in the office on the phone. Jack was in the bedroom talking to Hope. Mercy was in the kitchen taking a cast-iron skillet of corn bread from the oven when she heard a knock at the door.

She set the bread aside and headed to the living room. The television was on but muted, and it was already dark outside. She turned on the porch light as she opened the door and then froze.

"Please don't shut the door," Lon said, and held out the flowers.

Mercy's heart was hammering, and she couldn't think of a single word that would fit the circumstances, except *embarrassed*. She gestured for him to come in, then shut the door.

"These are for you," Lon said, and then laid them on the table by the door.

When she still didn't speak, he began to panic. Whatever he did in the next few seconds would either heal the chasm between them, or the relationship he wanted with her would be over before it actually began. "I am so sorry."

Mercy's eyes welled.

"Damn them to hell," he whispered, and wrapped his arms around her, pulling her close. "I'm so sorry that happened to you. Please don't shut me out. I want you in my life."

His words were the medicine she needed to let go of the pain. She shuddered as his arms tightened around her. Safe. He made her feel safe. He wanted her. She relaxed within his arms and slowly hugged him back.

It was exactly what Lon had been waiting for. He pulled back enough that he could cup her face, and before she could bolt, he kissed her. When she kissed him back, it was like oxygen to a drowning man.

The sound of footsteps at the far end of the hall ended their kiss, but it didn't cool the heat between them.

Mercy stood beneath his gaze, reading every emotion on his face. "Are we okay?" he asked.

"Yes. We're okay."

"Thank God," he muttered as he ran a finger down the curve of her cheek. "I have never been as angry in my life as I was today. And if it makes you sleep better tonight, you might like to know they suffered their own set of consequences after you left."

Mercy's eyes widened. "What did you do?"

"It was what else they did when they parked at Granny's that left them open for me. Parking in a handicapped zone. Parking in front of a fire hydrant. Driving with an expired license."

She almost smiled, imagining those haughty women brought down by their own mistakes. "You gave them tickets?"

"Just doing my job. They all have to appear in traffic court on Tuesday...and Angel's husband, Judge Herd, is presiding," Lon said.

Mercy sighed. He had stood up for her. His steadfast gaze and the twist of anger on his lips cooled the ugly burn of the slanderous words that had been heaped upon her head. "I want you in my life too," she whispered.

"Thank you, Lord," Lon said as Duke entered the room.

He frowned when he saw the flowers but said nothing about them. "Why, hello there, Chief. Are you here for supper?"

"I didn't come to eat," Lon said.

Jack and Hope came into the room behind him. "Hi, Lon. You're just in time for supper!" Jack said. "I'll set another place at the table."

"I didn't come to eat," Lon repeated.

Hope slid an arm around Mercy's waist. She saw the joy on her face and the glint in Lon's eyes and felt like dancing. "I know why you came. And now, you're invited to our table. It's just beans and corn bread, and fresh cookies for dessert. Mercy made everything. I think you should at least taste her cooking."

Mercy rolled her eyes. "For God's sake, Hope."

Lon glanced at Mercy. "Beans and corn bread?"

She sighed. "Yes. Would you like to stay for supper?"

"I thought you would never ask," he said.

Mercy grinned, but she was a little ill at ease as she turned to face the rest of the family. They watched her for a reaction, which made her nervous. She picked up the flowers. "I need to put these in water. Follow the crowd. We're all going to the same place."

Lon left his coat on the sofa and followed her.

Duke was the only one displeased with the company. He glanced at the flowers Mercy was putting in a vase, and this time didn't hold his tongue. "Is it someone's birthday?"

Lon wasn't talking. It wasn't his story to tell.

Neither Jack nor Hope wanted to bring down the mood by repeating the story.

Mercy kept putting flowers in water.

"Fine!" Duke said. "I only live here."

Mercy turned. "They're trying to spare me embarrassment. Three women in town called me every bad name in the book while I was in Granny's this afternoon. They waited until Lon had left, and it hurt my feelings. I cried all the way home. The flowers are a sweet gesture of trying to make me feel better. Would you please get the hot sauce out of the cabinet and the butter from the fridge? Supper is ready."

Duke was so shocked he couldn't think what to say, and quickly turned to get the things she asked for. He put them on the table and then helped her fill the bowls with beans and ham and set one at each place setting. When he went back for the last two, she was plating the corn bread.

"I'm sorry," he said softly.

Mercy nodded. "Thank you. We're good. Don't worry about it again."

Duke smiled. "Thank you for being so generous. I continue to say the wrong things to you, and you continue to forgive me."

"Family, right?" Mercy said.

Duke sighed. If she had him categorized as family, then he wasn't ever going to move past that in her eyes. "Yes, we're family," he said, and they carried the last of the food to the table and sat down.

"This looks and smells so good," Lon said.

"She's a really good cook," Hope said. "She puts all of us to shame."

Mercy wanted them to stop. "Well, you all look well-fed and healthy to me, so whoever was doing the cooking before had to be turning out some good stuff." And then she looked at Duke and grinned. "Although, the Talbots don't run to fat."

When they all laughed at what she'd said, Lon guessed it was an inside joke. He was delighted Mercy had become comfortable enough to tease them.

Then Hope dropped a bomb that wiped the smile from Mercy's face. "Jack is taking us to Blessings tomorrow. I have a post-surgery checkup, and then Mercy and I will go to the Curl Up and Dye. Jack has a cattleman's meeting in town, and we're going to redeem our free shampoo and style, compliments of Ruby Dye."

Mercy didn't want to go back to Blessings and chance running into those women, or more like them, and didn't hesitate to say so. "I'd rather stay here."

"No. We're going together. I already called her so she could work us into her schedule," Hope said. "I can't wait for you to meet the girls at the salon. Ruby has the coolest people working there. You'll see what I mean."

Mercy sighed. Now she was dreading the trip.

Lon knew her hesitation was because of those women. It made him angry all over again, thinking of the damage they'd done. "It'll be fine," he said.

Mercy saw a promise in Lon's steady gaze and sighed. "Okay, I'll go. The cop said it'll be fine."

Lon winked at her.

Hope now understood that first meeting between them years ago meant more than she first believed. There was a deeper relationship between them, and she was grateful.

"Time for dessert," Mercy said, and brought a plate of her cookies to the table.

Jack was up and refilling coffee cups when Lon's phone rang.

Lon glanced at caller ID and frowned. "Excuse me a minute. I need to take this," he said, and left the table.

"The life of a policeman," Duke said.

"It's an honorable profession," Mercy said.

Unwilling to comment again for fear they'd get into another argument, he shrugged.

A few minutes later, Lon came back. He had his coat

on and was moving fast. "I'm sorry, but duty calls. I have to get back to Blessings."

"Oh, I'm so sorry you have to leave. You didn't get cookies and coffee," Hope said.

Lon's gaze slid to Mercy. The disappointed look on her face was encouraging. At least it meant she liked him. "I'd happily take a couple of cookies to go," he said.

"I'll get them," Mercy said, and jumped up.

She put half a dozen cookies in a plastic bag. "I'll see you out," she said, and walked him to the door, then onto the porch.

"Is it a dangerous emergency...for you?" she asked.

He paused, reading a little bit of fear in her eyes, and adored her even more. "I don't think so.".

She handed him the cookies. "Will you do me a favor?" she asked.

He ran a finger down the curve of her cheek. "More than likely."

"Will you text me sometime tonight, just to let me know you're okay?"

He cupped the side of her face and brushed a gentle kiss across her lips. "Mmmm, you taste like cookies... and yes, I will do that."

Mercy's heart still pounded when he got into his cruiser. She watched until his taillights disappeared, and then she went back into the house and locked the door.

Chapter 16

DUKE AND JACK WERE CLEANING UP, AND HOPE STILL SAT AT the table as she walked in. "Well?" Hope said.

Mercy arched an eyebrow. "Well? That's a pretty deep subject."

Jack burst out laughing as Hope chuckled.

Duke eyed Mercy with new respect. She was funny when she relaxed.

Mercy slid into a chair beside her sister, and without thinking, reached out and clasped her hand. "One of my foster brothers was a smart-ass. I learned plenty of things from him, most of which I later discovered were illegal or immoral, but I was ten and thought he was funny."

"That's great," Hope said. "Did you ever stay in touch?"

"He's dead," Mercy said. "Heard it on the news one night. He'd already aged out of the system. Couldn't find a job. Didn't have any skills. Robbed a liquor store and died in the shoot-out."

"Oh my God," Duke said. "Don't you have even one happy moment in your life?"

Hope and Jack glared at Duke as if he'd just spit on the floor, but Mercy's answer not only humbled him but shut him up. "Yes. Two, actually. Finding out I had a sister, and then getting to meet her and finding out I had inherited brothers."

Duke felt like he'd just been sucker-punched. He

needed to say something but was ashamed of himself for provoking her.

"Thank you," Jack said.

"We are so blessed," Hope said.

"I feel blessed, but I'm tired," Mercy said. "If you all don't mind, I'd like to end this day on a good note. I had such a good time."

"We absolutely don't mind," Hope said, and hugged her close, then whispered in her ear as she kissed her cheek. "We love that you have Lon, and we love you. As for Duke, he's oblivious, but he means well."

Mercy returned her sister's embrace and added a quick kiss on the cheek. "Night, Hope," she said, and then left the room with tears in her eyes.

Hope walked across the kitchen and whacked Duke lightly on the back of his head. "Do you know what's inside your head?" she asked.

"My brain," he snapped.

"Then stop taking it out and playing with it all the time. Start using it for a change."

For once, Jack stayed out of it. Hope had defended her sister, and with good reason. His brother was an ace at ill-chosen words and the times he chose to use them.

~~~

Mercy could hear their voices as she began getting ready for bed. They were quarreling again, probably about her. She wondered if they'd argued like that before she came, and then let it go. She was no expert on family behavior, but she did know they loved each other, and she was beginning to understand that they loved *her*.

Long after she lay in bed unable to sleep, she could

still hear them moving about downstairs, locking up.
From the few words that she caught, she could tell they
were talking about what needed to be done tomorrow.
Her phone was in her hand as she rolled over on her side.

So this was what it meant to have family, she thought,
and closed her eyes.

Lon hadn't let on about the seriousness of the phone
call, but he was worried as he sped toward Blessings.
A missing child was a heart-stopper—even a teenager.

He drove with his lights on, and when he got closer
to Blessings, hit the siren as well. He reached the station
just as the frantic parents arrived. They met him at the
back door in tears. "Chief Pittman! You've got to help
us. Kelly ran away."

"Come inside," Lon said. "I'll need to get as much
info from you as I can before I send out a Be On the
Lookout to the surrounding counties."

They followed him into his office, stumbling and
weeping profusely.

Lon's stomach was in a knot. He had a bad feeling
about this, and the couple was hysterical.

"Okay... Paul, Betty, take a deep breath. If we're
going to find Kelly, you're going to have to help me."

Paul ran a hand over his thinning hair and took a deep
breath, trying to regain his composure.

"Just tell me how all this started," Lon asked.

"She has a boyfriend we don't approve of. We told
her she couldn't date him, and then we found out just
before noon today that she'd been sneaking around and
seeing him anyway," Paul said.

"We found out because she told us she's pregnant," Betty added, and then dissolved into tears all over again.

Lon could only imagine the chaos that had gone on in that house. "Okay, so how did you all receive the news?"

"Badly," Paul said. "We told her she would have to give the baby up for adoption, that she isn't through with school, and we aren't going to help raise that boy's kid."

Betty wailed. "We didn't think of anything but ourselves. We said all the wrong things. She cried and said she had expected better of us. She reminded us it would be her child too…our first great-grandchild, but we were both yelling and…oh my God, what have we done?"

"Great-grandchild? I thought she was your daughter. Who's the boyfriend?" Lon asked.

"Jimmy Dean Sawyer is the boyfriend, and Kelly belongs to our daughter, Paula. We haven't seen or heard from her since Kelly was a baby."

"Do you know where Jimmy Dean is? Did he run away with her?"

"No, he's at home with his parents. That's where we've been. We went out to his family home, thinking the boy would be gone. But he seemed shocked and said he didn't know she was going to tell us, or he would have been with her," Paul said.

"Then where do you think she went?" Lon asked.

"We don't know, but the last time we saw her was just after one thirty this afternoon," Betty said. "We went to town, and when we got back, her suitcase and some clothes were missing. The money she had saved for a prom dress is gone, and her car is gone too. She graduates this coming May," Paul said.

"Did you ask the boyfriend where she might go?"

"Yes, of course, but he said he doesn't know, and I think he's telling the truth. He was crying. He's as scared as we are. We've been to all of her friends here in town, and none of them even knew she was pregnant. She won't answer her phone. I don't know what else to do."

"I need the make, model, and license number of the car she's driving and how much money she took with her."

"I wrote down all the car details before we came here," Paul said. "I'd guess she has almost a thousand dollars saved."

"What's her given name?" he asked.

"Kelly Ann Rogers. She's seventeen years old. Her birthday is July 3. She's about five-foot-two and has long blonde hair. She was wearing jeans, a blue sweatshirt, blue Nikes, and her letter jacket."

"Okay, let me get this alert out to all the right people. We can't send an Amber alert because she's over sixteen and a runaway, not a missing person. Just wait here."

They fell into each other's arms as Lon headed up the hall to dispatch. "Hey, Larry. I need you to send a BOLO out on Kelly Rogers. This is the info."

"Will do," Larry said as he took the paper Lon handed him. "It's a bad deal, isn't it, Chief?"

Lon nodded. "I'm afraid it's going to be unless we get really lucky. She's been gone for hours."

He headed back to the office. "I need to ask you another question," Lon said.

"Anything," Betty replied.

"Where's Kelly's mother? Do they communicate? Do you and Paul hear from her?"

Betty threw up her hands. "Her mother? We never

heard from Paula after she left us hanging with her baby. We don't even know if she's alive or dead."

Lon frowned. "What's Kelly's cell phone number?"

As soon as they gave it to him, he called the state police, explained the situation, and asked them to trace the location of the calls made on that phone today, then requested a log of the calls made on it this past month as well.

"What do we do?" Betty asked as Lon put down the phone.

"Have you searched Kelly's room?" Lon asked.

"For what?" Paul said.

Lon shook his head. If he had to ask that, then they'd barely covered the basics. "We need to go back to your house. I need permission to search Kelly's room."

"You have it," Paul said. "But you won't find anything."

"You didn't know she was still seeing her boyfriend," Lon reminded him.

"Point taken," Paul said. "You can follow us back to the house."

"I know where it is," Lon said. "You two go home. I'll be right behind you. I need to tell my dispatcher where I'm going."

"Yes, sir," Paul said, and led his wife from the office and out the back door.

Lon gave Larry further instructions then left the station on his way to the Rogers's home. Paul was waiting for him on the doorstep. Betty was in the kitchen making coffee. Lon could smell it as they entered. "Where is Kelly's room?" Lon asked.

"I'll show you," Paul said, and led the way to another wing of the house. "This is it," he said as he held the door aside for Lon.

"Thank you," Lon said. "I'll just look around a bit. If I need you to answer any questions, I'll give you a shout."

Paul nodded and went to the kitchen to be with Betty.

As Lon began his search, he heard a house phone ring and then the sound of Betty's voice. He couldn't hear what was being said, but she was crying. He could only imagine how many times she would tell their story tonight. Friends just finding out would offer condolences and prayers because that's all they could do.

Then he closed the door. Almost from the start, it was obvious Kelly was preparing for graduation. She had a to-do list on her desk and a stack of college information beneath it. That must have been from before she found out she was pregnant. Too bad all the way around.

He searched dresser drawers, her closet, her bed, under the mattress—everywhere someone might think to hide something they didn't want found, but came up without a clue as to where Kelly would run.

Finally, he sat on the corner of her bed and looked at the room from a different perspective, hoping something new would pop up, and it did. There was a dull spot on the shiny hardwood floor just to the right of the closet. Curious, he got up to look and then realized it was visible only from the bed. It took him a few seconds to relocate what he'd seen, and once he did, he got down on his knees and felt around the edges of the planks. Within a few moments, one of the short ones moved slightly beneath his hand. Curious to see if it would come up, he got out his pocketknife and tried to get the blade beneath the wood. All of sudden, it popped up in his hand.

Lon set the board aside and rocked back on his heels,

then took out a flashlight and shined it down into the
space. At first he thought it was empty, and then he realized he was looking at a black drawstring bag. He pulled
it up and loosened the ties, then dumped the contents
onto the floor. There were at least a half dozen packets
of letters addressed to Kelly at a post office box like
those rented in the Box It Up store. He picked the one
with the oldest postmark, realized it had been mailed
about two years earlier, and then took the letter from
the envelope. He saw it had been written by a woman
named Paula Grimes and began to read.

"Oh man," he muttered.

Then he looked for the last one…a letter postmarked
only two weeks earlier. He scanned the contents of
that letter as well, and within seconds had a very good
idea where Kelly Rogers had gone. The only downside
was, with no return address to pinpoint her location, he
didn't know where Paula Grimes lived. But obviously,
Kelly did.

> *If things go bad, come to my house. I have a*
> *large home with four extra bedrooms and*
> *regret ever leaving you behind. I can't make*
> *up for the past seventeen years, but I can help*
> *you through what's happening now if the need*
> *arises, and will do it gladly with all the love I*
> *have to give you.*
>
> *Paula*

Lon tucked the letters inside his jacket as he left the
room. He debated about telling them what he'd found

when he walked into the kitchen, only to break up a fight. It appeared they were taking their fear and frustrations out on each other.

"Paul! Betty! What are you doing here? What purpose does shouting and screaming at each other serve? You need to be leaning on one another, not trying to tear each other apart."

Betty was livid. "He started it. He said it was my fault Kelly was gone, just like he said it was my fault when Paula ran away. We were living in Savannah at the time and had all those foster kids in the house. We took them in because we needed extra money, and he blamed me for not giving our own daughter enough attention."

"Only she fooled us!" Paul shouted. "She got back at us the best way possible. She left her bastard for us to raise—one more mouth to feed."

Lon couldn't believe what he heard. The rage on Paul's face made his skin crawl. "But you were getting money from the state to feed and care for the foster children, right?"

Paul realized what he'd said didn't quite hold true. "Yes, but the house was never quiet. After Paula ran away, we turned all those kids back to the state. I'd had enough. Add a squalling baby to three foster kids, and I knew I couldn't handle all that."

The tone of Paul's voice and the anger in his words was shocking. "Does Kelly know how you feel about having to raise her?" Lon asked.

Paul was startled by the question and suddenly became quiet.

"Yes, she knows," Betty said. "He was screaming it at her today when she told us about the baby. That's what the fight was really about."

"Damn it, Betty, shut up. You don't have to tell our business."

"Well, yes, she does, if it has to do with your missing granddaughter," Lon snapped. "So now we have a whole new story about why she's gone. You pretty much told her she wasn't wanted...not by her mother, and not by you two. What the hell did you expect her to do?"

Betty sat down at the kitchen table and buried her face in her hands. "I didn't say anything," Betty said. "I heard him say it, and I just sat there."

All of a sudden, Lon wasn't feeling the least bit sorry for them. He hated what Kelly was going through, but at least he had a place to start looking.

"I've seen all I came to see," he said. "I'm going back to the station. If I hear anything, you'll be the first to know."

"Wait, can't we go back with—"

Lon stopped and stared straight into Paul's face. "No, you can't come back to the station with me. I'm going to work the rest of the night, and I have no need to be interrupted by the discord between you. If there's news, I'll call."

They still argued as he left the house. Part of him wondered if they were secretly glad she was gone, and considered how much of what they felt was actually fear for her welfare, or guilt for what they'd said and done.

When he got into the car and started back to the station, he had Mercy on his mind. There had to be really wonderful people who chose to be foster parents, who took care of children with love in their hearts. But he had been given a dose of two who'd done it for the money. It made him sick to his stomach. He'd just seen firsthand part of the reason Mercy was so closed off.

He wanted to hear her voice and had promised to let her know he was okay. He was on Main Street a few blocks from the station when he parked. Instead of sending her a text, he called.

Chapter 17

MERCY WAS FAST ASLEEP WHEN HER CELL PHONE VIBRATED against her hand. She woke abruptly, saw who was calling, and quickly answered. "Hello?"

"Hey, honey. Just wanted to let you know all is well."

She rolled over and then sat up against the headboard and pulled the covers around her waist. "You don't sound like all is well."

He was surprised by her perception. "I could have worded that differently. I'm physically fine, but the situation isn't pretty."

"As long as you aren't in physical danger."

"I'm not, but I have a runaway teenager who could be. All I can say is, I just got a dose of what foster parents can be like."

"She was a foster child? Lots of fosters run away when they get older."

"Oddly enough, she was their granddaughter. They were also foster parents. All this time I thought she was theirs."

Mercy's heart skipped a beat. "I had a set of foster parents like that. They weren't mean to us physically, but we knew from the get-go that we were just a business."

At that moment, it dawned on Lon that since she'd been in the system in Savannah, which is where the Rogers family lived at the time Kelly was born, that she might have known them. "What were their names?" he asked.

"Uh…Roberts…no, Rogers! Mr. Paul and Miss Betty. They had a daughter named Paula. She ran away. And talk about coincidences…I ran into her about a year or so ago in Savannah. I still see her now and then. We even went to lunch together…sort of talked about old times, you know? I was surprised she remembered me because I was just a kid at the time, but she said except for being taller, I looked the same."

Lon's pulse kicked. "Do you know where she lives now?"

"If she lives in the same house, I know how to get there, but I don't know the address."

"Do you know where she works?"

"She works from home. She dresses nice, but I don't know what she does. Why?"

Lon's imagination went straight to prostitution, and then he felt guilty for assuming that. Still, that wouldn't be the environment Kelly Rogers needed, no matter how desperate she felt.

He thought about what he was going to ask, and then took a leap of faith. "Could you find the place?"

Mercy's eyes narrowed. "Like, now?"

"Yes, like now. If I turn all of this over to the Savannah police, it could put a desperate teenager into the same system that raised you. I hate to ask, but—"

"I'll do it. If Paula is still there, I can find it. But I can't help you if she's moved."

"Fair enough," Lon said. "Dress warm. It's chilly tonight. I'm on my way right now."

"I'll be ready," Mercy said.

She disconnected, then turned on the lights and began grabbing warm clothes. She could still hear the television downstairs, and heard Hope and Jack talking as she opened the door. She ran down the stairs and into the living room, carrying her leather jacket and a purse.

Hope heard her coming and looked over her shoulder. When she saw Mercy dressed, with a coat and her shoulder bag, she jumped up. "What's wrong?"

"I'm not sure," Mercy said. "I'd asked Lon to let me know he was okay after he left in such haste, and when he called back to tell me all was well, he mentioned something about dealing with a couple who used to be foster parents. One thing led to another, and then something I said set him off. I'm not sure what's happening, but I think a woman I know in Savannah might be connected to a missing teenager from Blessings. And the grandparents of the girl who's missing were once my foster parents."

"Good grief! What a convoluted scenario," Hope said, and then she frowned. "He's not taking you into a dangerous situation, is he?"

"I didn't get that from the conversation. I think he's trying to find the teenager before she gets caught in the system like we were."

"Oh, right!"

"You can ask him yourself," Mercy said. "He's on his way to pick me up."

"Why couldn't you just give him the address of the woman you know?" Jack asked.

Mercy sighed. "Because I don't know it, but I know how to get there."

"I see lights coming up the drive," Hope said.

"I'll be fine," Mercy said, and then grinned. "Don't wait up for me. I have a key."

A few moments later, they heard footsteps on the porch, and then a knock at the door.

Jack opened it.

Lon knew they were worried. He saw it on their faces. "You both know Kelly Rogers, right?"

Hope gasped. "That pretty little girl who works at Broyle's Dairy Queen? She's the one who's missing?"

Lon nodded. "Mercy knows Kelly's mother, who abandoned her newborn daughter and left her with her parents. I have good reason to believe that's where Kelly went. I found two years of letters from Paula, Kelly's birth mother, hidden in her room. They've been communicating all this time."

"Good Lord," Jack said. "I didn't know Paul and Betty were her grandparents. I thought they were older parents, you know?"

"We need to go," Lon said. "I promise, Mercy will be safe. I just need to find the mother's house, if for no other reason than to assure myself that's where Kelly went. If she's not there, then we have a bigger problem on our hands."

"Of course," Hope said, and leaned back, eyeing Mercy with something close to disbelief. "Isn't this something? It's a true example of how everything in life comes full circle. My wreck brought us back together, and your life in foster care may be instrumental in finding a runaway child. Just be careful."

"I'll take care of her," Lon said. "I'll bring her home as soon as I can verify Kelly's whereabouts. She'll either be there, or she won't."

Mercy went out the door and down the steps to the car, with Lon's hand in the middle of her back. He was the kind of man she'd dreamed of finding one day and hoped he felt the same way about her.

Hope felt anxious as she watched from the window until the taillights disappeared.

"She'll be fine," Jack said. "She's going back to her stomping grounds, honey. She took care of herself for a long time on her own. She's not alone anymore."

"You're right," Hope said, and then turned as Duke walked into the room.

"I thought I heard a car drive off."

"You did. The chief came to get Mercy. It's a long story. I'm going to get a cup of coffee. If you care to hear the details, follow me."

So he did.

Lon glanced sideways at Mercy. He'd wanted to spend time with her, but not like this.

"Are you worried?" he asked.

Mercy frowned. "About what?"

"I don't exactly know what kind of environment we're going into."

"But I do," Mercy said. "I was there before. Remember? It's a nice part of Savannah, and it's a house, not an apartment. I was only in the front part, but it's spacious, and the furniture is elegant."

"Really?"

She nodded. "I said I didn't know what she did for a living, but I could see into her office just off the living room. There was a wall of books, a couple of computers, a printer, and a scanner…all the things you would see in any business office."

Lon thought this might not be a bad deal after all. The more high-tech the world had become, the more people were able to work from home with minimal travel.

"We're going to be late coming home," Lon said.

"Good. Then I won't have to go to Blessings with Hope and Jack."

He frowned. "Well, that decision plays hell with the plans I had for my future."

"What do you mean?" Mercy asked.

Lon took a turn in the road before he answered. He could tell her the truth, or tell a lie, and he'd never been a man to lie to anyone. "I like you, and I'm not counting that wild and glorious night we spent together. It's still at the top of my 'Best Things Ever' list. But not wanting to go to Blessings doesn't work into the plan where I become so irresistible to you that you can't bear to be without me, because that's where I live and work."

Mercy eyed his familiar silhouette, his hands firmly gripping the steering wheel, remembering how they felt on her skin when they'd made love. She already looked forward to their long-distance texts and the fact that he'd cared about her safety. And she might not admit it to him yet, but that night they spent together was the touchstone for every man she'd met since. So far, none had measured up enough to keep. "Good. I like you too," she said.

He took a deep breath. "I *really* like you."

Her heart fluttered, almost missing a beat as she smiled. "I *really* like you too."

He looked away from the road for just a second, but it was long enough to see the smile. A wash of relief settled the tension he'd been feeling as he looked back at the strip of highway lit only by his headlights. He wished to God he could park somewhere and hold her in his arms. Instead, they were on the search for a broken child. "I could easily fall in love with you," he added.

She was silent for so long he got scared. He'd said too much too soon. Just when he started to apologize, she answered, "Besides sex, what would I need to do to make that happen?"

Lon was so relieved, he laughed out loud. "Just keep being you. We'll table the sex until you say the word."

"All I have to do is say *sex*, and you're on board?"

He reached across the seat and took her hand. "You are so beautiful. But I love your heart and your humor even more. I'll be on board with anything you choose, anytime, anywhere."

"I can live with that," she said.

"You mean you're not going to brag about my heroic traits and handsome face?"

She grinned. "No."

"How about the badge on my shirt and the gun on my hip?"

She laughed. "Not even that."

"So…besides sex, what do I have to do to get a compliment from you?"

"You already did it."

"Did what?"

"Cared that I was scared the night I was robbed. Cared whether or not I got home alive the day of Hope's wreck. Stood up for me when those women called me names. No one ever did things like that for me before."

Lon reached for her hand. "Knowing that hurts my heart. If you don't quit me, I can promise I'll never quit you."

She shivered. That promise sounded too good to be true. "I'll keep that in mind," she said softly.

And then his cell phone rang, and he had to turn her loose to answer. "This is Pittman."

"Didn't want to broadcast this," Larry said. "Neighbors called in a 'disturbing the peace' on the Rogers. Howard Ralph is the deputy on duty tonight, so he took the call, and when he showed up, Paul Rogers took a swing at him. Ralph put him in handcuffs and was taking him to the cruiser when Betty started arguing with Ralph, telling him Paul hadn't been hurting her and demanding Paul be released. And well, long story short, he brought both in and locked them up."

"Fine. They can spend the night in lockup and bond out like anyone else."

"What a mess. Stuff like this never happens when Avery is on duty."

"Yes, it does, and you're fine," Lon said. "I'll be back as soon as I verify this lead…and thanks for keeping this off the air."

"You're welcome," Larry said.

Lon disconnected and then glanced at Mercy.

Now that they were on the interstate, the traffic was heavier. She stared at the brake lights of the trucker ahead, and he could tell by the set of her jaw she'd heard enough to resurrect some bad memories. "You okay?" he asked.

"She's lucky she ran," Mercy said.

"Who's lucky?"

"That girl…Kelly. I wouldn't have done what Paula did. I would have never run off and left my baby."

"Did your mother run off and leave you?" he asked.

"I thought so until Hope found me."

"So what happened to her?"

"Our father murdered her."

Lon flinched. "Oh my God! Why?"

"She was a beautiful woman. He was jealous."

"I don't even know how to respond to such an atrocity," he muttered.

This time she was the one who reached across the seat and clasped his hand.

They rode the rest of the way in silence. It wasn't until they drove into the city limits of Savannah that he spoke. "Where do we go from here?"

Mercy leaned forward so she could read street signs and directed his route. Turn right. Turn left. First turn past this gas station. Take a left past an all-night Waffle House. When they took a turn that led into an opulent neighborhood, Lon was pleasantly surprised. "Paula Grimes lives in this area?"

"Yes. Nice, isn't it?"

Lon nodded. Nice didn't quite cover it.

They were in the antebellum neighborhood of Savannah. Elegant old mansions had big white columns stretching from the base of the verandah all the way to massive three-story balconies, like garter belts holding up the old girls' stockings.

Mercy suddenly leaned forward. "Turn here!" she said, pointing to another three-story house in a color his daddy would have called "titty pink." He was startled.

"The pink one?" She nodded. "Why would someone paint a mansion pink?"

"Because they can," Mercy said.

He grinned as he turned up into the driveway and

headed toward the house. "We're going to wake up the household."

When he parked and turned off the lights, Mercy reached for the door handle.

"You don't need to go to the door with me," he said.

Mercy paid no attention. "I'm the one who got you here. You might need me to get you in the door."

"Does she carry a gun?"

"I don't know," Mercy said. "But I wouldn't put it past her. She grew up in an environment as hard as mine. Obviously, she made better decisions than I did, or she wouldn't be living here."

"Don't be so hard on yourself. She's at least ten, maybe twelve years older than you are. So here goes nothing," he said, and took her by the hand.

They walked toward the house and then up the steps onto the verandah, which triggered motion detector lights that bathed the front in bright white light.

Lon looked over the door, saw the security camera and a tiny red light beneath it, and knew it was recording. He took a deep breath and rang the bell.

A few moments later, they heard a woman's voice over the intercom. "Identify yourself."

"Chief Lon Pittman of the Blessings Police Department, and this is—"

"Mercy? Mercy Dane? Is that you?"

"Yes, Paula, it's me. Chief Pittman really needs to speak with you."

"Be right down."

Lon arched an eyebrow at Mercy. "Thank you."

She shrugged. "I told you I could get you in the door."

They saw lights coming on inside the house as Paula

Grimes made her way toward the foyer. They heard the beeps as she disarmed the security system and then the click of a lock before she opened the door.

The cop in him noted a marked resemblance to her mother, Betty, only younger and prettier, with dyed red hair and a trim figure beneath a pink silk robe and slippers.

"This is a strange time for a visit," she said as she stepped aside for them to enter, then gave Mercy a hard look. "I am going to assume you have a really good reason for this?"

Lon immediately shifted the focus away from Mercy. "It's not her reason, it's mine, and I'm not going to waste words. I know all about the two years of communication between you and your daughter Kelly. Your parents have reported her missing. Officially, she's a runaway, but I need to know if she's in this house tonight. If she's not, no one is going to rest easy for worrying about her. Even me."

Paula's eyes narrowed. "What happens if she is? Would she have to go back to my parents' house?"

"Well, at the moment, they're both in jail for disturbing the peace and attacking one of my deputies. Is she here?"

All of a sudden, they heard footsteps, and then Kelly Rogers came into the foyer wrapped in a fuzzy pink robe and oversized slippers. "I'm here. Don't be mad at Paula."

Paula opened her arms. Kelly slid into the embrace like it was shelter from the storm within her life. "I told her she had to call them tomorrow," Paula said.

"Well, if she'd called them tonight, I likely wouldn't be here," Lon said.

Kelly started to cry. "That was my fault. I begged for one night of peace."

Paula held her daughter a little tighter.

"You two sure look alike," Mercy said.

Paula smiled. "Blood will tell. I know there's going to be a conversation here, so let's all go into the library. I think there's probably still some fire left in the fireplace."

Chapter 18

ONCE AGAIN, LON'S HAND WAS IN THE MIDDLE OF MERCY'S back as they followed Paula through the foyer, through an even wider arched doorway, and into a room filled floor to ceiling with books.

"Quite a collection," Lon remarked.

Paula shrugged. "Some are as old as the house. Please have a seat. Can I get you anything to drink? A brandy maybe, to warm you?"

"No, thank you," Mercy said.

"I'll pass," Lon added then turned his attention to Kelly. "I would like to hear, in your words, why you ran away today?"

Paula sat beside her daughter on a long, overstuffed sofa covered in butter-soft leather, and when Kelly wept, she pulled her close and held her hand. "You can do it," Paula said. "Just tell them what you told me."

Kelly nodded. "I've been dating a really nice boy, even though Paul and Betty told me not to. We did something else we were told not to do, and now I'm pregnant. We've already talked about getting married as soon as school is out. We're going to be together. He loves me as much as I love him, but when I told Paul and Betty I was pregnant, they went berserk. Paul raged about me turning into the same slut my mother was and said I was crazy if I thought they would raise another bastard. Betty yelled and cried, saying she was too old to raise another kid and had been looking forward to the day I was no longer their responsibility. I guess I lost it. I stood there watching them losing their minds and thought *I can't stay here until I graduate.* I was so scared that I actually thought they might hurt me. So when they left the house later, I packed some things and came here."

"Why didn't you leave a note?" Lon asked. "If you had, none of this would be happening."

"Because they don't know Paula and I had found each other. They don't know a thing about Paula or her life, and I didn't want to bring them back into her world when she'd spent so many years staying out of theirs."

"I have to ask," Lon said. "Why did you go off and leave your baby with your parents, knowing they were so erratic?"

Paula paled. "That's just it. I didn't leave her behind. I went to Nashville to find an apartment. Once upon a time, I had dreams of being a singer and planned to live and work there as I pursued that dream. I asked if they would keep her until I came back, and they said yes. They were in the process of getting rid of the foster kids they cared for. Mercy was one of the last to leave. In fact, she was still there when I left. I didn't know until we ran into each other a couple of years ago here in Savannah that my parents had told another story. All I knew was that when I came back less than a month later to get my baby and the rest of my things, they were gone. They had taken my child. I was twenty years old. I had no money, no prospects, just an old furnished apartment above a bar. I thought about going to the police, and then I thought about taking a four month-old baby into the unknown with me, and made a terrible decision. I went back to Nashville without looking for them. It was the worst decision I ever made. I was so happy when Kelly came looking for me."

Kelly leaned against her, as if gaining strength from her mother's presence. "I began the search because home was hell. I kept thinking whatever my mother was doing couldn't be worse than where I was."

Lon's frown deepened. "What was happening at home? Were you being beaten?"

The anger in Mercy's voice was obvious when she spoke up abruptly. "I'll bet I know why she left. Did you get the military punishments too?"

Kelly nodded and burst into tears.

"What do you mean by 'military punishments'?" Lon asked.

But this time when Mercy spoke, her voice was completely void of emotion. "Push-ups…fifty for anyone ten and under, one hundred for anyone older, running for miles at night with him on a bicycle beside us, going to school the next day with three or less hours of sleep, cleaning bathrooms with toothbrushes, and the ultimate punishment, solitary confinement."

Paula shuddered. "Solitary confinement was the closet in the basement, rats and all," she added.

Lon was shocked. "And your mother let it happen?"

"She was the one responsible for cleaning toilets with a toothbrush and solitary confinement," Paula said.

"So no one told a social worker?"

Paula shrugged. "I did. They told the social worker I was just angry because they wouldn't let me date. Then they asked the younger ones."

"And we were too scared to tell the truth," Mercy said.

"Are you going to make me go back to them?" Kelly asked.

"Oh, hell no," Lon said, and took the cell phone out of his pocket and immediately called the station.

"Hey, Chief, everything okay?" Larry asked.

"Yes. Kelly's fine. She's safe where she's at. I'm not going into details, but whatever you do, don't let the Rogers couple out of jail. I'll be back with time enough to deal with them myself. Talk to you soon."

"Will do," Larry said.

Lon glanced at Mercy. The white line around her mouth hurt his heart. "Bad memories?"

She nodded. "I was just a kid. I got over it."

Lon was sick to his stomach and afraid he'd say the wrong thing, so he squeezed her hand instead. "I'm so sorry."

"We're all sorry," Paula said. "Me, most of all. I knew what he was like, and I still ran away and left those foster kids behind without telling the police. And I ran away and left my own baby girl, not intentionally at first, but after I found the house empty, I let it go."

By that time, Paula Grimes was weeping.

Lon leaned forward, intent that Kelly understood the circumstances of her situation. "So your parents are in jail for now, but I can't promise a judge won't let them bond out."

"They're not my parents," Kelly said.

"They never adopted her," Paula said.

Kelly nodded. "They aren't my legal guardians either. Nothing was ever done through the courts. They're my grandparents, and this is my mother."

Lon shook his head. "This is going to take a lawyer to figure everything out, but can I trust Kelly to stay here and you to keep her safe?"

"Lord, yes," Paula said. "I'm not going anywhere. I've been a CPA for the last fifteen years with a damn good clientele and an office in my house open to the public. My husband died years ago. He didn't leave me rich, but I've been comfortable. My business put me here. I always was good with numbers. Just not so good at life."

"Then I'll be in touch. Kelly, I suggest you text your boyfriend tonight. I guarantee he's not asleep. He cried when he found out you were missing. At least let him know you're okay."

"Yes, sir, I will," Kelly said.

As Paula pulled her daughter close, she saw Mercy watching them and remembered something from their past. "Mercy, do you remember the night you asked me what it was like to have a mother?"

"No," Mercy said.

"Well, I do. I also remember what I was thinking when you asked me. I thought that of the two of us, you were the lucky one. Yes, you were shipped from house to house, and often going from bad to worse, but for you, there was always the hope that the next one might be better. For me, I was trapped. They were my parents, and I had nowhere else to go. I guess I'm telling you this now because I wanted to say it then and didn't. If you're holding onto any regrets from your youth, let them go. That was then, and this is now. Possibilities abound."

Mercy glanced at Lon then quickly looked away.

He was her possibility. Only time would tell how it all played out, but right now, he was her hope. He was the expectation for a happier life. He was the one who might actually learn to love her.

"Thank you for saying that," Mercy said. "I hope there are no hard feelings between us."

"Oh, honey, of course not," Paula said, and gave her a hug. "I told you when we ran into each other last year that seeing you grown up and living your life rid me of so much guilt."

"Good," Mercy said. "I was torn about telling. Almost felt like I was ratting you out or something, but I thought since we both knew why Kelly ran, you wouldn't hold it against me."

"Exactly," Paula said. "Chief Pittman, it was a pleasure to meet you, and I appreciate the way you went about this. I have several clients who are lawyers, and a couple who are cops. I'll call in the morning and find out the best way to go about filing charges against my parents for Kelly's abuse. When all of this mess finally goes to court, I will have representation."

"I don't know if it will matter, but I would be happy to testify against them, if it comes to a trial," Mercy said.

Paula took a deep shaky breath. "Even after I left you with them, knowing what they were like?"

"Even after," Mercy said, unaware she'd just taken a step closer to Lon as she said it.

"Don't worry about me, Chief Pittman. I'm going to be eighteen a month after the baby is born," Kelly said. "My place of residence will no longer be anyone's business but my own, right?"

Lon nodded. "You did your research, didn't you?"

"Yes."

Lon shook Paula's hand and smiled at Kelly. "We'll be leaving now, so you can get back to bed. I'll be in touch."

Paula walked them to the door, waiting on the threshold until they were in their car and driving away, before she locked the front door and reset the alarm.

Kelly was shaking. "I'm sorry, Paula. I messed this up."

Paula pulled her close. "Sweetheart, I am the master of messing up. We'll figure this out together. Just know you'll never sleep under their roof again. Now let's go back to bed. You have a text to send, and I have an eight o'clock appointment with a client."

She turned out the lights in the foyer and walked her daughter back up the stairs.

—◆◆◆—

"You were amazing," Lon said as he turned to the left at the end of the driveway and headed north.

"Thank you," Mercy said. "I was a little nervous, but it turned out okay."

"It sure did, honey. You made a good deputy. I might have to pin a badge on you next time."

She shook her head. "I don't want there to be a next time like this."

"Agreed," he said. "It's this way back to the interstate, right?"

She nodded.

He drove until he reached a main road that he recognized. Now he knew where he was, but before they started back home, he wanted to refuel. When he saw an all-night gas station up ahead, he pointed. "I'm going to stop there and refuel before we head home."

When she realized what part of the city they were in, she frowned.

"Just a warning. It's not the best part of Savannah, so pay attention to who's coming and going as you refuel."

"I will, and thank you."

"I'm going to make a quick trip to the ladies' room while you're pumping gas."

Lon moved to the right turn lane, drove off the street and up to the pumps, then parked and killed the engine. He noticed a trio of motorcycles parked in the shadows on the far side of the building and frowned, wondering why they'd chosen to park there instead of up front in the lights, then noticed the security cameras pointed only toward the pumps. And then it hit him. This would be the perfect scenario for a robbery, if they didn't want anyone to ID their rides.

And Mercy had gone inside.

He started to swipe the credit card to gas up and then stopped. Every instinct he had said trouble could be brewing. He needed to see if there was a back exit, and he needed to get Mercy back in his sight.

~~~

Mercy caught a glimpse of three men near the register as she looked for the restroom location. And then she saw the biker logo on the back of the biggest man's jacket and knew she was trapped.

It was Big Boy.

If she turned around and tried to walk out, he'd see her for sure. Maybe if she just kept walking, they'd be gone when she came out.

She hurried down a long narrow hall and into the

ladies' room, locking the door behind her, then used the bathroom in haste, not wanting to be there any longer than necessary. She washed her hands, glanced at her reflection, and then said a quick prayer that the bikers would be gone.

She was halfway up the hall when she heard the door to the men's room open. She pivoted quickly, and her heart sank. Big Boy was behind her with an ugly smile on his face and a knife in his hands. She didn't hesitate as she turned and ran, screaming while looking for some kind of weapon.

When she saw a display of big plastic jugs with handles, she knew what it was and knew it was heavy. Granulated de-icer. She reached, grabbing the handle on the jug as she ran past, and was almost at the end of the aisle when he got close enough to grab a fistful of her hair. He yanked, bringing her to a painful, skidding halt. Without missing a beat, she swung the jug up and then backward with all the force she could muster. It hit between his legs on the down swing, and hit so hard she heard something pop. The biker let out a shriek then grabbed his crotch with both hands as he dropped to his knees.

She saw movement from the corner of her eye and looked up. Lon ran into the store with his gun drawn, then she saw the other two bikers come running up behind Lon. One had a gun, the other a knife.

"Lon! Behind you!" she screamed, and then heard Big Boy trying to get to his feet, so she swung the jug against his head.

He went down as Lon pivoted and fired.

Chapter 19

AFTER LEARNING THE BACK EXIT WAS LOCKED, LON turned and ran to the front. The cash register was open and empty, and to his horror, he saw Mercy running and screaming through the glass storefront, and then the man she was running from. He ran inside just as the biker grabbed her by the hair. With all the shelving between them, he ran with his weapon drawn.

"Police! Let her go. Get down on the floor, or I'll shoot!" he yelled, but the man suddenly screamed, turned loose of her hair, and dropped out of sight.

Before he had time to find out what had happened, he heard footsteps running up behind him. He was in the act of turning around when Mercy screamed, "Behind you!"

He spun into a crouch, with his gun aimed, and saw one man with a knife and the other a handgun, both less than six yards away. "Police! Drop your weapons!" he shouted, but they didn't slow down.

With only a couple of yards left before they took him down, he shot the armed man in the leg and the other in the shoulder.

They dropped at his feet, screaming and moaning, as he quickly removed their weapons. He handcuffed the shoulder shot first and the leg wound second, before he stood and looked for Mercy, but he couldn't see her. "Mercy!"

"I'm here," she said as she stood. "Just making sure this loser doesn't get up and run."

He circled the end of the aisle, coming toward her on the run. He saw a man laid out on the floor as he took her in his arms and ran his hands on her shoulders, on her neck, on her face. "Are you alright? Did he hurt you?"

"Not enough to count," she muttered, and when Big Boy seemed to be regaining consciousness, she swung the jug of de-icer at his head one last time. He was out.

"Damn, remind me never to tick you off," Lon said, and gave her a swift, hard kiss. "Honey, there's a landline at the checkout. Use it to call 911 because it will register this address. Tell them there was an attempted robbery and a cop is on the scene. Tell the dispatcher there are three down, and at this time, the cop is searching for the missing clerk."

She ran toward the register as he raced past the counter into the office. It didn't take Mercy long to deliver the message, and when she heard Big Boy moaning, she grabbed a roll of duct tape from beneath the counter and ran back his way.

The moment Big Boy saw her coming, he curled up on his side and covered his crotch. "Don't hit me again. Don't hit me again."

"Shut up. Put your hands behind your back and grab your belt, or I will make you sorry."

"I'm already sorry I ever saw your damn face," he said, and rolled onto his belly and grabbed the back of his belt with both hands.

Mercy got down on one knee, pinning his head and shoulders to the floor, as she wrapped his wrists with gray duct tape until she was satisfied he couldn't break free.

"It's too tight!" he screamed. "Loosen it. My fingers are going numb."

"Then you better pray the cops get here fast because

I don't give a damn how miserable you are. You're a worthless piece of shit, and everything that's happened, you brought on yourself."

Big Boy groaned and dropped his head to the floor, wincing when it hit with a thud.

Mercy could hear Lon's footsteps moving around in the back and yelled out, "Are you okay? Did you find the clerk?"

"Yes and yes. Call back, and tell them the cop says to send one more ambulance."

Mercy hurried back to the phone, delivered the message, and then stood near the door waiting for the police. It wasn't more than a couple of minutes before she heard sirens, and then two police cars pulled up to the station in a skid and got out on the run with their guns drawn.

She held up her hands as they ran in. "I'm Mercy Dane. I'm the one who called this in. Two of the robbers are at your feet, and one more is taped up toward the back of the room beside the soda fountain. The cop is in the office. He just found the clerk and had me call for one more ambulance."

The cops scattered. One headed toward the office while the other one began getting names. Two more cop cars arrived and before long, Mercy stood behind the counter just to stay out of the way. When she saw a mobile news crew pull up in a van, she realized this was likely to end up on tomorrow's morning broadcast.

Lon came out of the back room with blood all over his hands and shirt. He picked up a roll of paper towels from beneath the counter and wiped himself off.

When she saw his hands shaking, she ran to him. "What happened?" she asked.

"They knifed the clerk. I don't know if he's going to make it."

She saw the tension on his face, wanted to hug him, but didn't understand this part of him enough to get too close. "I'm sorry."

His voice shook as he tossed the dirty towels in the trash. "And I'm sorry to say my first thought was I'm glad it was him and not you."

"Lon…stop," she said, and wrapped her arms around his waist, and then laid her cheek against his chest.

The feel of her body against him, the brush of that black silky hair against the back of his hands as she hugged him was like turning off a switch. The adrenaline rush moving him forward dropped as he pulled her close. At that moment, she completely forgot about the news crew and what they might be filming.

Lon was pulled away to assist until the front of the station was full of officers from the Savannah Police Department. One cop walked into the store to check out the ongoing activity and then focused on the beauty with the long dark hair standing behind the counter. "Do you work here?" he asked.

"No, I'm with the police chief from Blessings. He's the one in the corner talking to a detective. We stopped for gas. He was refueling when I came inside to use the bathroom. Before I knew it, all of this was going down."

"There's blood on the back of your jacket," he said.

She frowned as she felt for a cut on the back of her neck and felt a sting when she brushed across what must have been a scratch. "The sorry bastard must have scratched me when he grabbed me from behind."

Lon was on his way back inside when he overheard

the conversation. He hurried toward her. "Let me see," he said.

She lifted her hair and turned around. "Just his fingernails, I imagine," she said.

Lon waved down one of the EMTs, who cleaned the area with disinfectant and sprayed it with something that stopped the bleeding. "You're good to go," the EMT said, and went out behind the last gurney.

The last of the ambulances were loaded, and they hit the siren and lights as they drove away. Just when Lon thought they might be free to go, the detective he'd been talking to approached.

He sighed. Yet another witness statement. It was already nearing 2:00 a.m. There was no way they'd make it back to Blessings before morning. He called the precinct. "Larry, it's me. We've had a delay getting out of Savannah. How's everything going?"

"Fine. The Rogers finally quit shouting at each other and went to sleep. Did you find the girl?"

"Yes, we did. She's safe, and we'll figure it out in the days to come. Who's the arraigning judge tomorrow? Please tell me it's not Judge Herd."

"Let me check the schedule...uh, no, not Herd. It's Judge Parsons. Are you guys okay?"

"Actually, we stopped for gas before leaving the city and walked in on a robbery. We're fine, but the clerk is not, and I had to shoot two of the perps. By the time we're through here, it's going to be close to dawn. Just keep the coffee made, and we'll be there as soon as we can."

"Will do," Larry said, and hung up.

Dan Lowery, the same detective from the robbery division who had interviewed him, was talking to Mercy when Lon walked up. "You knew your assailant?" the detective asked.

"Sort of," Mercy said. "I know he goes by the name Big Boy. He frequents the Road Warrior Bar where I used to work. He was always harassing the waitresses."

"He grabbed her from behind," Lon said.

"And you two know each other?" Lowery asked.

Lon nodded. "I was working a runaway case—an underage teen from Blessings. Miss Dane had prior information from her years of living here that gave me the first much needed lead. We found the girl safe and sound, then tied up the loose ends of the trip, and were headed home when I stopped for gas. I'm wishing now I'd stopped somewhere else or paid attention to Mercy's claim. This isn't a safe part of town."

Detective Lowery nodded, kept taking notes, and asked questions until satisfied that he had all he needed. "You know where you can find me," Lon said as they parted company with the man, and then took Mercy's hand. "Are you ready to go home?"

"Yes."

They exited the station in full view of the news crew still on site. "Keep walking, and don't look up," Lon said as someone shouted, trying to get them to answer some questions.

Lon made it all the way to his cruiser and got them both inside just as the mobile news van left the scene. Glad that they were gone, he turned to clasp Mercy's hands. "Sweet lord, I have never been so scared. I promised you and everyone else I would keep you safe, and the first time you leave my sight, you're assaulted. Are you okay? Please tell me you are."

"I'm fine, really," Mercy said. "I was more mad than hurt. All he got was my hair, and he let go of that real fast when I hit him with eight pounds of granulated de-icer. He's not going to be straddling a bike anytime soon."

"Remind me not to ever tick you off," he said, and then groaned. "Dang it. I still haven't refueled." He brushed a finger down the side of her cheek and then opened the door.

Mercy felt the cold, but she didn't say it, and took comfort in knowing their time together still wasn't over.

Lon ran his card through pump four and then went back inside to ask one of the cops to turn it on. He swung sideways to the wind as he went back, more than ready to be gone.

When he finally got inside, he was shaking from the cold. He pulled a handful of wet wipes out of the dispenser and scrubbed the rest of the bloodstains and gas from his hands before he started the car.

The whole time, Mercy sat quietly, watching the expressions on his face. He looked at her from time to time, as if reassuring himself she was okay, and Mercy silently cursed the console between them, wishing she could slide closer.

When he finished, he rolled down the window, tossed the wipes into the trash can between the pumps, and quickly rolled it back up. "Are you okay? Ready to roll?"

She nodded, and turned up the heat.

"Thanks. That heat feels good."

"It does, doesn't it?"

He nodded. The silence drew out between them until he felt uneasy all over again and wondered if that glimpse into a cop's life had upset her. "Did the shooting freak you out?"

When she hesitated, Lon thought it would be an answer he didn't want to hear. Then her voice filled the silence. "The only part that upset me was when I thought they were going to kill you. All I could think was, well damn, just when I was getting used to having you around."

He laughed, but only so he wouldn't start crying. On a cold, Savannah night, he fell the rest of the way in love. "I lost track of you once. I'm not going to do that again," he said.

Mercy's eyes welled. "Just so you know, as good as this makes me feel, all of this forever stuff makes me wary. I've made promises to myself, but no one has ever made one to me and kept it."

Loving this woman was like hanging onto a slippery slope. Would she let him hang alone until he fell, or finally reach out and pull him in?

"I know you've had a hard life, but please don't see me as part of it. Except for one brief and glorious night with you, which, by the way, you ended, I've had no part in your past. But I want to be in your future. All I ask is that you give me a chance."

Mercy had dreamed of a man who would say pretty things to her and mean them. Everything in her was saying trust him, love him, believe every word. But all she could give him right now was her truth. "I'm giving you more than I've ever given anyone. I'm trying so hard to learn this life and how it works. I'm not going to quit you, cop. Just hold onto that, and let me get there on my own."

"I can do that," Lon said. "And when things get

weird, let me know. I'm already holding on to you as tightly as I dare. All you have to do is trust me. I won't let you down."

Lon could see the interstate signs and what exit to take to get them home now. "You've had enough excitement for one night. I know where we are now. Close your eyes and rest, baby."

"I can't sleep when someone else is driving," she said, and then made a liar of herself by reclining in the seat and closing her eyes.

There was a great big crack in the wall that kept her safe from the outside world, and her cop had cracked it with a smile, a kiss, and promises he'd already kept. She wanted to turn loose and just go for it. She wanted to believe he would love her as fiercely as she was falling in love with him.

"Sleep well, sweetheart," Lon said.

She fell asleep within minutes.

He smiled to himself. Even if she wouldn't admit it, she had to trust him, or she wouldn't have closed her eyes. Now the rest was up to him, and he had this. He'd known the moment he'd seen her in danger that he didn't want a life without her. All he had to do was wait for her to come to the same conclusion. As for now, he just kept driving. His first duty of this new day was to get her home, and he did.

It was nearly 3:00 a.m. when he turned off the black-top and headed up the drive to the Talbot farm. Mercy woke just as he was pulling to a stop. "You're home," he said softly. "I'm not going in and rouse everyone in the house. I'll hear about it soon enough that I didn't take very good care of you."

"I'm not going to wake them either, and stop saying that. I don't need anyone to take care of me. I've been in worse danger walking from work to home and back again. I did that for three years, in the rain, in the cold, and in miserable heat, and nobody knew I existed. I did not suddenly become helpless just because I learned I have family."

Lon sighed. "Point taken," he said, and then got out to walk her to the house.

She unlocked the front door, but instead of going inside, she followed her heart. She'd wanted to be in his arms ever since they'd started home, and she wasn't going to miss the opportunity. She wrapped her arms around his neck and leaned into his embrace.

"As soon as I can find a job and a place to live, I'm moving into Blessings. I already told Hope. I'm not by any means moving away from her, but I'll take care of myself."

Lon shoved his fingers through her hair, feeling the long silken strands tangling around his wrists as he pulled her close. "I will never argue with your right to choose, but I hope there comes a time in your life when you're willing to share it with me."

She sighed as he centered his mouth on her lips and then groaned when he cupped her hips and pulled her close. "Just a reminder," he said as he finally turned her loose.

"A reminder of what?" she asked.

"How it feels when we make love. Now go to bed before Duke and Jack feel the need to defend your honor."

She slipped inside, locking the door behind her, then tiptoed upstairs and into her room, being as quiet as possible.

The house was warm so she stripped where she stood,

pulled a nightgown over her head, and went to bed. Within minutes, she was fast asleep.

Hope had heard the car drive up, and then the door unlock, then Mercy going upstairs.

Thank you, Lord, for bringing her safely home.

Confident that all was right in her world, she rolled over and into Jack's arms. "You okay?" he mumbled.

"I'm fine," she whispered. "Just fine."

Chapter 20

LON SPENT FOUR HOURS ON THE SOFA IN HIS OFFICE before the alarm on his phone went off. He'd had some long nights on the job before, but none quite as harrowing.

He kicked off the blanket with a groan and got up, then went to the adjoining bathroom to freshen up for the day. He had a clean uniform on site, as well as an electric razor and toothbrush. Within a few minutes, he was as good as he was going to be today, and left his office, hoping someone had already made coffee and brought something in to eat.

After scoring a cherry Danish and a cup of coffee, he headed back to the jail. The Rogers were up and sniping at each, but in a normal tone of voice. But when they saw the police chief walk in, they were both on their feet and shouting. "Let us out! How dare you keep us in jail? We demand to see a lawyer."

He walked all the way up to the bars, eyeing them as he would animals in a cage, trying to figure out what made people like this tick. It wasn't until Betty Rogers turned on the tears and asked for news of their girl, Kelly, that he broke silence. "Mrs. Rogers."

She was still weeping and had started to pace. "Mrs. Rogers," he repeated. When she kept on wailing, he got in her face, with nothing but the bars between them. "Shut the hell up!"

She gasped.

Paul opened his mouth to protest, and Lon pointed a finger and shook his head. Paul dropped back down on the bunk, but the rage on his face said it all.

"Now. The jig is up. There's no one left to threaten. Kelly is safe, and that's all you get to know. When you do get your time with a lawyer, be aware that the district attorney in Savannah is quite likely to open an investigation into your years as foster parents and the alleged abuse the children suffered while under your care."

Paul leaped to his feet raging, while Betty was suddenly silent. "They're lying. Whatever they said is a lie. Was it Kelly? Is that how she repaid us? By accusing us of something terrible just because we refused to raise her bastard?"

Betty ducked her head and started to cry. "Oh, thank God," she moaned. "I've lived my life in mortal fear of this man. Whoever finally told on him has done me a huge favor…maybe even saved my life!"

Lon was startled by the admission, but he wasn't fooled. Especially when Paul Rogers leaped toward the bars that separated the two cells and screamed, "You bitch! You evil, conniving bitch! You're the one who made them scrub toilets with a toothbrush. You're the one who put them in solitary confinement."

Lon watched her turning from victim to a person capable of murder as she ran toward the bars and tried to scratch out her husband's eyes.

This situation had to be rectified and fast, so he opened a cell at the other end of the jail, and then went back up the hall. "Hey, buddy! You look pretty rough. Are you sure you're okay to work today?"

Avery nodded. "I'm just as miserable at home as I am up here, and I'm not contagious."

"It's your call, but let me know if you need to leave, okay?"

"What's up with all that screaming?" he asked.

"Mr. and Mrs. Rogers are not happy with each other. I need a deputy to the jail."

"Yes, sir, I'll dispatch the message."

"Tell them ASAP, or I'm going to need an undertaker instead," Lon said.

Three minutes later, Deputy Ralph arrived and came hurrying in through the back door with his hand on his weapon. He heard the commotion in the jail and came inside running.

"Chief?"

"Oh…hey, Howard. Thanks for getting here so quickly. As you can see, the Mr. and Mrs. aren't getting along so well. We're going in her cell to handcuff her, and then move her to the cell at the far end of the jail."

Howard Ralph wasn't as big as the chief, but what he lacked in size, he made up for in determination. "Then let's get it done."

The couple was so embroiled in their own war that both officers were inside Betty's cell before she knew it was open. When the chief grabbed one wrist and Howard grabbed the other, they had her face against a wall and cuffed her before she had time to object. But when they began moving her out, she objected, kicking and trying to dig in with her feet, and then finally collapsing, thinking they would stop. Instead, they hauled her upright and took her down the hall with the tops of her feet dragging along the floor.

"What are you doing?" she cried. "I don't want to be down here by myself."

"Turn around," Lon said, and when she didn't obey, he turned her anyway, faced her against the far wall, and removed the cuffs.

He and Howard were out before she turned around. She ran toward the door as it slammed in her face. Lon turned the lock. "Do you have a lawyer?" he asked.

"We can't afford a lawyer!" she said.

"I'll notify the court," he said, and walked back toward Paul's cell.

"Mr. Rogers, do you and Betty intend to share a lawyer?"

"Hell no!" he shouted. "The bitch is trying to get me locked up."

"Then do you have a lawyer?" Lon asked.

Paul Rogers slumped. "No."

"I'll notify the court," he repeated. "Breakfast is on the way. Have a seat. Food digests so much better when you're calm."

He and the deputy shut the door to the jail and headed up the hall. "Got some good Danish in the break room," Lon said.

Howard nodded. "Thanks, Chief. I believe I'll take one with me as I get back on patrol."

"Appreciate the help," Lon said, and took a left into his office and shut the door.

A few moments later, Avery came to the door. "Just got a call from the district attorney in Savannah. They're opening an investigation on the Rogers, and if there's enough evidence, charges will be filed against them."

"Good, because I already told them that would likely happen. Now I don't have to go back in and recant my statement. The DA knows we have them in jail, right?"

"Yes, and he's aware they'll bond out from whatever charges we have on them."

"Okay, then," he said. "Thanks for letting me know."

Avery went back to dispatch as Lon picked up the phone. He made a call to the courthouse telling them he had two prisoners requesting court-appointed attorneys, and then hung up. His responsibilities in this mess were nearly over.

———

Although Lon's office was in the hurricane's eye of life in Blessings, Granny's Country Kitchen was not. For as long as Lovey Cooper had owned the restaurant, Ruthie Whitman had been her baker. She made all the desserts, all the corn breads, all the biscuits, just like she was doing today.

Only Ruthie had been late to work because her car wouldn't start, and then when she finally arrived, she was an hour behind on morning baking. They were right in the middle of the breakfast rush when Ruthie slipped and fell. The timer on her last batch of biscuits had just gone off, and she was taking the hot pan from the convection oven when she went down.

The biscuits went up. The hot pan fell down, right on top of Ruthie's left arm as she landed on the other. She screamed. The snap was loud enough that Chester, the kid washing dishes, heard it break, and quickly ran to her aid. But Ruthie hadn't finished falling. The last body part to hit the floor was Ruthie's head, and now she was unconscious and bleeding.

Chester shoved the hot pan off her arm and yelled for the cook to call 911.

Lovey was manning the front register when she heard the commotion in the kitchen. She waved down a waitress to take over as she ran to see what was wrong. The entire dining area and the customers went silent. One of their own had been hurt.

They heard a siren, and then Peanut Butterman, who was having another breakfast meeting about the Peachy Keen Queen contest with Ruby Dye, because Mike Dalton wouldn't take the job of emcee, took it upon himself to go see what had happened.

He came back, white-faced and shaky. "It's Ruthie!" he said. "She took a bad fall. She has a serious burn on her left arm, broke her right arm, and hit her head. It's bleeding all over the place."

"I call this meeting canceled," Ruby said, and raced back to the kitchen to help her friend, Lovey.

Back in the dining area, George Franklin was the first to say what everyone else was thinking. "This is awful. What a disaster. Who's gonna make breakfast biscuits at Granny's?"

His wife Myra frowned. "Well, poor Ruthie. You're all worried about your belly when you should be worried about her. If you want biscuits, I reckon I can make you some."

George rolled his eyes. "I'll just say prayers for Ruthie."

The EMTs rolled Ruthie out through the back door as Chief Pittman came into the kitchen past them. Lovey was on her hands and knees, picking up the biscuits, with Ruby at her side.

Lon saw Ruthie on the gurney, then Ruby and Lovey

cleaning up the mess on the floor, and knew this was going to put a big kink in Lovey's world. He hurried over to where they were working, and squatted down beside them. "Lovey, I just heard the call go out when the ambulance was dispatched. What happened?"

"Ruthie fell," Lovey said, and then sat down on the floor with broken biscuits in her lap and started crying. "Ruthie's been with me from the first day I opened. I don't know how I'm going to get all this baking done without her."

"Is Ruthie going to be okay?" Lon asked.

"I think so, but I won't. I never was any good at baking."

The news that a baker was needed at Granny's gave Lon an idea. "I might know someone who could help you out. She's looking for a permanent job here in Blessings, but—"

"If she can do the job, it's likely to be a permanent one. Ruthie is pushing seventy. Who is it?"

"I'll make a call first. If she can come, you'll find out soon enough for yourself."

Ruby patted Lovey on the back as the chief left. "Come on, honey, let's finish cleaning all this up."

Mercy woke to the smell of fresh coffee and the low rumble of voices. She rolled over to check the time and groaned. She'd been asleep a little over four hours, but she'd gotten through a day on less. It wouldn't kill her.

She quickly showered and dressed in old jeans and an even older sweatshirt, then put on some tennis shoes, brushed the tangles out of her hair, and pulled it back with an elastic hair band as she went downstairs.

She noticed they had the television on in the kitchen and immediately thought of that news van, hoping whatever aired about the attempted robbery had nothing to do with them. "Morning, everybody," she said, and headed straight for the coffee.

"What time did you get home?" Duke asked.

"Well, gee, Daddy, I'm not sure. I didn't know there was a curfew."

Jack snorted. Duke glared.

"Is everything alright?" Hope asked.

Mercy grabbed a piece of toast and took it to the table with her coffee. "Finally, a sensible question I'd be happy to answer." She plopped down in a chair with a groan. "Everything went well with the runaway. We found her. She's safe. And I suspect the shit's going to hit the fan with Mr. and Mrs. Rogers."

"Why?" Hope asked.

"Please...don't any of you repeat what I'm about to say, but the reason Kelly ran away is because she was physically abused by her parents, actually her grandparents, and the same people were once a foster family to me. They did the same thing to all of us. They did it to their own daughter, Paula. It's a long, ugly story, but I don't think they'll ever be free to do it again."

"Good lord!" Jack said. "Who would have thought? Kelly was a baby when they moved here, and we all assumed she was theirs."

"Technically, they moved away from Savannah while caring for her, and when the daughter came home to get her baby, they were gone. Like I said, it's a long story."

"Wow. I see why you were so late," Hope said.

Mercy took a bite of toast and then pointed toward

the middle of the table. "Hey Duke, would you please pass the honey?"

He did as she asked, and then handed her a napkin. "Since you decided to eat sans plate, I thought you might need one."

She squeezed honey on the toast and then took another bite. "Much better. Now where were we? Oh yes, why we were late coming home."

"You mean there's more?" Hope asked.

"We were on our way out of Savannah when Lon stopped to refuel. I went inside to use the ladies room while he was getting gas, and to make a long story short, we walked in on a robbery in progress. The unfortunate part was that one of the thieves was a regular at the place where I used to work, and when I recognized him, he ran after me. Lucky for me, Lon had already seen what had happened and came in to save me. But the two other thieves came out of the office just as he ran in. One had a gun, the other a knife. Lon shot them."

Hope's hand was over her mouth because she was afraid to say what she was thinking.

Duke, however, was not. "What happened to you? I mean, you said that man was after you."

"Oh, I grabbed a big jug of that granulated de-icer from a shelf just before he grabbed me by the hair. I swung the jug backward into his balls. After that, he was toast." She grinned and took a big bite, chewed, and swallowed before finishing the story. "I had to whack him a couple more times on the head with it before he'd stay down, and once he settled, I rolled him on his belly, duct-taped his wrists together, and that ended that."

Hope laid her head down on the table and moaned.

Duke stared at Mercy as if she'd suddenly manifested horns.

Jack was in awe. "Damn, little sister. You rock! Is the chief okay?"

"Yes, but the clerk was stabbed and in bad condition when the ambulances came."

"Ambulances?" Duke asked.

"You weren't paying attention," Mercy said, took another bite of honey toast, and then held up one hand and began counting off fingers. "One for the clerk who was stabbed. One for each thief Lon shot. And then one for the guy who grabbed me. He'll be riding sidesaddle for months and seeing double. It was the best I could do with eight pounds of salt."

Hope raised her head, stared at her sister for a minute as if she were a stranger, and then threw her head back and laughed. "Oh my lord. Mama would have been so proud!"

"What? Why? What do you mean?" Mercy said.

"Oh, it was all before I was born, but the family always laughed about it when they got together and started reminiscing. The story was, when Mama was only fifteen years old, a boy took her out on a date then tried to mess with her. When she told him to stop, he didn't listen. She told him again, and he still ignored her. They said at that point, she doubled up her fist and broke his nose. While he was moaning and bleeding all over the place, she kicked him between the legs and pushed him out of his own car, leaving him stranded on some bayou road. Then she drove it back into town, parked it in front of the police station, and walked home. So then the kid comes into town beat all to hell. No way is he telling anyone a girl did it, so he says someone stole his car. Then the cops smell liquor on his breath, assume he got drunk and parked it there himself. He gets fined for underage drinking and for leaving it in a no-parking zone, and his daddy had to pay more to get it out of impound."

For the first time in Mercy's life, she felt a connection to the mother she couldn't remember. "I like knowing that," she said. "It makes me feel like I belong."

Hope reached for Mercy's hand. "Jack's right. You do rock, little sister, and you've always belonged. You just didn't know it."

Before she could ask about the trip into Blessings, Duke pointed at the television mounted on the wall behind the table and yelled, "Look! They're talking about that robbery now."

Jack grabbed the remote to up the volume, as they all turned to watch.

"That's Chief Pittman," Duke said as the camera swept the exterior of the station, catching Lon in a moment with Savannah cops.

The next shot was of Mercy inside the station in full view as she looked out the window. The journalist had identified her to the public and now extolled her virtues. She could gladly have done without this. And then it occurred to her that her friends at the Road Warrior Bar would find out she'd taken Big Boy down. She'd gotten even for all of them.

And then she keyed in on what the journalist was saying and sighed.

...took him down with an eight-pound jug of

granulated de-icer. Once in the groin, twice on the head, and then rolled him on his belly in a move any Savannah policeman would appreciate, and in lieu of handcuffs, duct-taped her assailant's wrists.

"Lord," Mercy muttered.

"You are freaking amazing," Jack said.

Hope was still in shock. Her lips parted as she watched the piece end with Lon and Mercy leaving the scene of the robbery together.

"So, are we still going to Blessings?" Mercy asked.

"You're not afraid that you'll run into those women again?" Jack asked.

"I didn't run the first time because they scared me. I left because I didn't want them to see me cry. And, after everyone sees that piece, I doubt I'll be challenged again. Besides, the cop says there won't be a next time."

"How can you be so sure?" Duke asked.

"Because Lon said, and he always keeps his word."

Duke snorted. "He's a nice guy, and I know you said you two had met, but that's hardly a personality assessment."

"That's not entirely true," Mercy said. "The first time we met, we were living across the hall from each other in a Savannah apartment building. I was nineteen and he was twenty-two."

"Are you serious?" Hope asked.

"As a heart attack," Mercy said, and stuffed the last bite of toast into her mouth and chewed.

"Did you date?" Hope asked.

"Ummm, not exactly, but I never forgot him, and that's the end of my story."

Then her phone began to ring. She recognized Moose's number and grinned. "It's my old boss from the bar. Probably saw the news."

"Go ahead and answer, sweetie, unless you need privacy."

"No privacy needed with Moose."

Duke's eyebrows arched at the name. Jack glared.

Mercy answered the phone. "Good morning, Moose. I'm here with my family, and I have you on speakerphone, is that okay?"

"It's fine with me. I just called because I saw the morning news! Are you alright? Scared the fire out of me, seeing you on the screen like that."

"I'm fine, and thank you for caring," she said.

"Aww, honey. You know we all care about you. We love you, and we miss you. Is everything okay there? If people aren't treating you right, I'll be happy to get Charlie and come bang some heads."

She smiled at the thought. "You leave that bat beneath the bar for someone who needs your help. You know me. I can take care of myself."

Moose laughed. "I know that for sure. Is everything good with you and your sister?"

"It couldn't be better," Mercy said.

"Hello, Moose! I'm Hope, Mercy's sister. I can tell you that having her back in my life is wonderful. I'm glad to know Mercy has such good friends."

"Well, now! Hello to you too, ma'am. Hope you're healing from the wreck."

"Yes, very well, thank you."

At that point, Mercy's phone signaled an incoming call, and she saw it was Lon. "Hey, Moose. Got another call I need to take. Tell everyone hi. First chance I get, I'll come back for a visit."

"If you do, bring cookies," he said. "We love you, girl. Have a great life."

Mercy hung up and took the phone off speakerphone. "It's Lon. I need to take this." She walked out of the room with the phone at her ear, leaving the trio in a burst of chatter. "Hello. So, you missed me so much you already had to call? Oh…and we made the morning news, so be prepared for all kinds of remarks. They had one shot with a great view of your butt."

Lon chuckled. "I wouldn't be calling this early because I hoped you were still sleeping, but this is sort of an emergency, and maybe that job you've been talking about."

"I'm listening," she said as she flopped down onto the sofa.

"The emergency is that the baker at Granny's Country Kitchen had a really bad fall about thirty minutes ago. She won't be coming back soon, and maybe not at all. Lovey Cooper, the lady who owns Granny's, is all upset because she doesn't have a baker. I don't know if it's anything you would—"

"Today? Does she want one today?" Mercy asked.

"She needs one now. If you do what she needs done, she'll hire you on the spot. I don't know what the pay is, but—"

"I'll be there in less than thirty minutes. Tell her I'm on my way."

She came up from the sofa and went back into the kitchen on the run. "I have a lead on a job in Blessings."

Hope groaned. "Already? I knew—"

"The baker at Granny's fell. She won't be coming back to work for a long time, maybe never, Lon said."

"Ruthie? Oh my lord, who'll make the biscuits?" Jack said. "Her biscuits were so good."

"My biscuits are good too," Mercy said. "Hope, I'm sorry, but you're going to have to do Ruby's without me."

She ran from the kitchen and then upstairs. A few minutes later, she came running back down. She was out the door before any of them thought, and then Hope remembered. "She forgot to get the truck keys."

At that moment, they heard the motorcycle start, and when they did, Hope was up. "She's going to ride that into town?" she cried, and rushed to the front door and opened it wide, just in time to see Mercy fly past the house, her ponytail flying out behind the silver helmet like a flag in the wind. "Oh, dear lord! Here I thought we were getting to know her and find out we haven't even scratched the surface."

"Something tells me she'll be fine," Jack said.

Duke shuddered. "I just missed that bullet, didn't I? Thank goodness I never asked her out. That relationship would never have worked."

Hope and Jack burst into laughter.

Chapter 21

LOVEY CLEANED UP THE FLOOR AROUND THE BAKING STA-tion. The kid who washed the dishes was back at the sink. The cook on day shift was still frying bacon and hash browns and cooking up eggs. They were down to less than twenty servings of biscuits when they all heard the roar of a motorcycle, and then the low, rumbling sound as it idled to a stop.

"What on earth?" Lovey said as she stopped mopping.

The steady chatter of diners was always present from anywhere in the cafe, so when the dining room suddenly went quiet, and footsteps could be heard coming toward the kitchen in a long, hurried stride, she turned to face the door.

She wasn't prepared for the beauty who walked in, or the biker jacket, or the helmet, but she knew immediately who she was. What she didn't know was why she was there. "Can I help you, honey?" Lovey said.

"No, ma'am. Your cop called me. My name is Mercy Dane. He said you needed help, and now I'm here."

The dishwasher dropped a cup. The day cook dropped a spatula.

Lovey dropped the mop. "But we needed a baker."

"Yes, ma'am. I can bake. Where do your employees leave their coats and stuff?"

Lovey pointed at a door.

Mercy was in and out in seconds, tying an apron around her waist as she walked.

"I understand the need for urgency. Just show me where everything is kept. I see you have a commercial mixer, which is good. It's a pain to stir that much dough on your own. Do you have a particular recipe you want me to use…you know…a standard for the cafe?"

Lovey groaned. "No. Ruthie had one in her head."

"No matter," Mercy said. "I have one of my own. I'll get started, but if you wouldn't mind staying close for a bit to show me where things are, we can get caught up a lot faster, okay?"

"Just for the record, did you just hire yourself, or are you on a trial run?" Lovey asked.

Mercy frowned. "Oh, no, ma'am. Lon said you'd need to try me out."

"Well, then," Lovey said. "Proceed. The situation can't get much worse. And you two…get back to work!"

The cook got a clean spatula, the kid swept up the broken cup, and Mercy started to measure flour then stopped. "Do you have self-rising and all-purpose, or just all-purpose flour?" she asked.

"All-purpose," Lovey said.

"Then would you please show me where the salt, baking powder, and baking soda are kept?"

"You use baking powder *and* soda?" Lovey asked.

"I do if you have buttermilk," Mercy asked.

Lovey pointed to the dry goods cabinet, and then the walk-in cooler.

"You bring me the buttermilk, please, and I'll get the other stuff," Mercy said, and flew around that kitchen as if she'd been raised there, unaware that her cop was on his way to Granny's.

He came in through the back door, saw Lovey in a

mild state of shock, and Mercy in charge. Satisfied that his job here was done, he slipped out.

Unaware Lon had come and gone, Mercy was focused on doing her best. She had measured up enough flour for the first batch and poured it in the mixer, then added the leavenings and the salt, then added the butter, and started it on low. She watched until she was satisfied it was cut into the flour the way she liked it, then added the buttermilk, and turned up the speed.

Lovey didn't know how they were going to taste, but she'd put together dough faster than Ruthie had done in forty years. When she stopped the mixer, she quickly transferred the dough to the floured breadboard and set to work.

"I need baking pans," Mercy said.

The kid came running with a stack of six and set them on the end of the worktable.

"Thanks, kid," Mercy said. "What's your name?"

"Chester Benton."

"I'll call you Chet. Sounds more manly. Is that okay?"

"Yes, ma'am," Chester said, and strutted his way back to the sink.

"What're you gonna call me," the day cook asked.

Mercy was greasing baking pans and didn't look up. "What's your name?" she asked.

"Elvis Kingston."

"Then I'll call you Elvis. Elvis was the king, and you can't mess with perfection, I always say."

Lovey had been watching without talking, but when Mercy popped her first pan of biscuits into the convection oven, Lovey laughed. "God in heaven, I hope those biscuits taste good enough to serve, because I like you, girl!"

"They'll be good enough to serve," Mercy said, and kept filling up biscuit pans until she ran out of dough.

They took the first pan out and put the other four into the oven at the same time, before Mercy paused to take a moment to breathe. She stood back, watching as Lovey took a biscuit and broke it in half, then handed half to Elvis and took a bite for herself.

"What about me?" Chet said.

"I'll share one with you," Mercy said, and pulled one apart in the middle, and handed half to Chet. She took a bite and sighed with satisfaction.

Lovey ate her half in two bites then wiped her hands on her apron. "Can you make pies and cakes? And corn bread?"

"Yes, ma'am," Mercy said.

"As good as these biscuits?"

"Well, I don't know if I'd say that. I was always told that my piecrust was the best, but I don't like to brag."

Lovey started to tease her, then realized Mercy was serious.

"How much do you expect a month for wages?" Lovey asked.

"What do you pay?" Mercy countered.

"I've been paying Ruthie same as Elvis…fifteen dollars an hour."

"I don't get that much," Chet muttered.

"That's because you don't do that much," Lovey said. "That's the fourth cup you've broken this week. Break another one, and it's coming out of that pitiful salary I pay you."

Chet blushed. "Yes, ma'am. I mean, no, ma'am. I mean—"

He stopped talking and went back to work.

"So?" Lovey asked.

"Yes, fifteen dollars is fine. I don't suppose you know of a place for rent here in town. Nothing over six hundred dollars," she said.

Lovey grinned. "Oh, you're gonna love small-town living. Houses rent for six hundred. Apartments for around four hundred, and those are plenty nice."

"I'll be needing a furnished apartment," Mercy said.

Elvis banged the spatula on the griddle and then cleared his throat. "Mr. Graham's garage apartment is empty, except I'm not sure he'll rent it out."

"You won't like that," Chet said.

"Why not?" Mercy asked.

Chet shrugged. "No one likes Mr. Graham."

"Why not?" Mercy asked again.

"I don't know. That's just what they say."

"If you don't know a truth about someone, the last thing you need to do is spread a lie," Mercy snapped. "So, Elvis, I'll be getting that address from you before I leave."

He nodded, then glared at Chet, who quickly turned around and went back to his job.

"So, I'm hired, right?" Mercy asked.

"You sure are. A true answer to a prayer. I need to tell Chief Pittman thank you."

"I'll be thanking him for sure," Mercy said. "Now what do you need next? More biscuits, or are you short on desserts? We have a few hours before noon. I might be able to get about a dozen or so fruit pies made before you start serving…if you have all the stuff."

"It's all here," Lovey said, and then two of the

waitresses came in.

"Hey, Lovey, the customers are freaking out over the biscuits."

Mercy grinned. "I'll be starting on those pies now. Just show me where everything is once, and I'll be good to go."

By noon, all of the regulars who frequented Granny's had heard about Ruthie's accident and Lovey's replacement. The customers came in with full intentions of rendering judgments and left as new converts to the baker at the local cafe.

Mercy took a few minutes to call Hope and tell her she had the job and wouldn't be off work until six. She sounded so happy that Hope couldn't be anything but happy for her, and told her to ride safely on her way home. Mercy was smiling when she disconnected, and then smiled even broader when she received a text from Lon.

Heard the biscuits were to die for. Congratulations. I'll be in for pie.

She sent a smiley face and went back to work.

Lon had fresh coconut cream pie at noon and peeked in at the kitchen as he left, gave her two thumbs up, and blew her a kiss.

Mercy still glowed from the satisfaction of a job well done when she finally got a break. It was just after 2:00 p.m. when she left Granny's, looking for the address Elvis had given her. His directions were good, because it was easily found.

She parked in the driveway between the house and the garage at the end of the drive, and then walked in a hurried stride to the front door. She didn't know what she was expecting, but it wasn't the man who answered her knock.

He wore a black velvet jacket and a crisp, white shirt buttoned up to the collar. There was a Bolo-style tie with a fire opal stone in a setting of oval-shaped silver, and his long white hair hung far past his shoulders. His face was almost devoid of wrinkles, and she couldn't have guessed his age in a million years.

"Mr. Graham, I'm Mercy Dane. Elvis Kingston told me you might have a furnished garage apartment for rent."

She didn't know that while she talked, Elliot Graham had checked her out in almost the same way she'd viewed him. Her stunning beauty was as unusual as her height. Her clothing was simple but clean. The fact that she'd arrived on a black Harley now parked in his drive fascinated him, as did the helmet she carried. "Yes, I do have an apartment. Would you like to see it?"

"I first need to know what it rents for. I'm on a pretty tight budget, having recently moved to Blessings. Right now, I'm staying at my sister's house, while she's healing. Her name is Hope Talbot."

His eyes widened and then pooled in quiet tears. "Your sister cared for my wife in her last days. She's been gone five years now, but Hope was a godsend to us."

"I'm sorry for your loss," Mercy said. "And I agree that Hope is special."

"You are special too. You're the Christmas gift that saved your sister's life."

Mercy resisted a strange urge to hug him. He was a

very unusual man, yet too quiet, only now she understood. He'd lost part of himself when his wife passed.
This was all that was left.

"I love thinking of it like that," Mercy said. "I hate to
rush you, but I don't have long to check it out. I just started
work today as a baker at Granny's Country Kitchen."

He gasped. "What happened to Ruthie?"

"She fell at work. I understand her injuries will take
a while to heal."

"Oh, I'm so sorry to hear this. She made the most
beautiful biscuits."

"I make beautiful biscuits too. That's why Lovey
hired me."

"Wait here."

He moved out of sight for a few seconds and then
came hurrying back with a key. "If it suits you, I will
rent it to you for four hundred dollars a month, utilities
included. I'll wait here for your verdict. Take your time.
I have nothing else to do."

Mercy restrained herself from running until she moved
out of his line of sight and then loped toward the garage.
The apartment above it was the same exterior as the
garage—a simple white frame building. She ran up the
steps, unlocked the door, and then said a quick prayer.

Please be okay. Please be okay. I need to be me again.

She opened the door, and the moment she walked in,
Mercy felt at home. The rooms were cold, but there was
a thermostat in the hall. When she turned on the switch,
she heard it hum. The floors were all hardwood in a dark
cherry stain with an area rug here and there. She moved
through the rooms, eyeing a small but cozy living room
done with a white leather sofa and two black recliners,

ornate side tables and a coffee table in the same cher-
rywood as the floors, and two paintings on the wall, both
signed *Elliot Graham*.

She smiled. He was an artist. She liked that.

The kitchen was charming. The stove and refrigerator
were standard sizes and stainless steel. The cabinets had
been painted dove gray, with a white and silver back-
splash, and there was a set of dishes inside the color of
onyx. She'd never seen black dishes before. One of the
drawers held stainless steel flatware in an ornate design,
and another drawer had basic tools for preparing a meal.
A set of pans and a couple of skillets made up the cook-
ware, and there was a nice black-and-silver microwave at
the end of the cabinet.

The utility room was small but had a washer and
dryer, and the single bathroom down the hall was also
in white and silver with a small built-in cabinet where
a half dozen matching white towels, hand towels, and
washcloths were kept. The bedroom took her breath
away. The bed was a four-poster with a matching dresser
and vanity and a single walk-in closet.

It was the nicest place she'd ever rented, and she
couldn't wait to move in. The first thing she would do in
that bedroom was make love to Lon. Beauty demanded
beauty, and what they did together when they had sex was
a beautiful thing.

"I'll be back," she said aloud. "You're wonderful, so
beautiful. You shelter me, and I'll make this a happy place."

In seconds she turned off the thermostat and was out
the door, locking it behind her. She ran all the way back
to the house and when she knocked, the door immediately swung open. "I love it. It's perfect. Do you need

first and last month's rent or—"

"Of course not. How do you know when your last month will come? The utilities run through my house, so they're already on."

"I didn't bring money into town because I had no idea I was going to do this until Elvis mentioned it, but I can give it to you in cash tomorrow. I'll put it through your mail slot on my way to work. You won't be up because I'll start work at 5:00 a.m."

"Then keep the key, so you can drop off some of your belongings as you stop by."

She couldn't believe this man. In a world where everyone always tried to one-up the next, or steal what didn't belong to them, he'd just trusted the key to a stranger.

"But you're not a stranger," Elliot said, and when Mercy's eyes suddenly widened, he realized he'd let another part of his secret slip. "Excuse me. I didn't mean to do that, but I think you're a fellow traveler I met in another lifetime. I'll enjoy having you as my renter."

"If that stove and refrigerator work properly, I will keep you in baked goods, sir. I love to bake."

He smiled. "Beauty, skill, warrior spirit, and a kind heart. I didn't think they made people like you anymore. It will be a treat to have fresh baked goods again."

"Thank you, sir. I won't let your expectations suffer."

"Call me Elliot."

She pointed to the mail slot in his door. "Four hundred dollars in that slot. 5:00 a.m."

He watched as she ran toward the Harley, mounted it in one smooth move, settled the helmet on her head, and rode out of the drive as quietly as a motorcycle could manage. Once on the streets, she hit her stride and flew like an arrow, straight down the street and out of sight; only then did Elliot Graham step back inside and close his door.

Mercy rode back to work and finished out the day the happiest she'd been in years. She had a job. She had a new place to live, she had a family, and she had Lon. Sex was the word. Their first time had been dynamite, and he'd had seven years to improve on his playbook.

Chapter 22

THE TRIO OF TALBOTS WAITED TO EAT SUPPER WITH MERCY when she got home. She was both touched by the act and a little anxious to tell them she was leaving. "You didn't have to wait," she said.

"We did it because we wanted to," Hope said. "So you're hired, I take it."

Mercy nodded.

"Are you happy?" Hope asked.

They watched Mercy's face light up in a way they'd never seen. "Yes! I'm in a kitchen, not a bar. I don't have to deal with the public, and I'm doing something I love to do all day long. I rented an apartment on my break. I need to ask a favor and have one of you drop off my things."

Hope sighed. "So fast. I'm going to miss seeing you all day, but it's pretty good timing. Another week at home, and the doctor is going to let me go back on the job part-time. I need to work up slowly to full strength, but once that happens, I'll be gone every day."

"That's wonderful," Mercy said. "I know how much you love your job. In fact, my landlord had nothing but high praise for you. He said you were an angel to him and his wife during her last days."

"What's his name?" Hope asked.

"Elliot Graham."

Duke gasped. "You saw Elliot Graham?"

"Yes. I knocked. He came to the door. Why?"

"Where's the apartment?" Hope asked.

"Over his garage."

"He rented that to you?" Jack asked.

Mercy frowned. "Look. Quit tiptoeing around what you're trying not to say, and spit it out. I'm hungry, and I have to pack tonight before I go to bed."

"His wife, Helena, was a big shot, an interior decorator from Savannah, and he was a nationally known artist. They retired to Blessings about ten years ago because Helena was born here. In fact, the house they lived in was the house where she grew up. She spent years doing it one room at a time. When they had finished, as a treat for their fiftieth anniversary, Elliott was taking her to Europe for a year. She didn't want to go off and leave their house unattended for all that time, but Elliot didn't want anyone else living in their home, so she redecorated the garage apartment for the house sitter and collapsed a couple of days later. Incurable brain cancer. She died a few months later in his arms. As far as I know, you're the first person to live there."

Mercy thought about the story. It explained a lot about Elliot. "Sad stuff happens in lives all the time, and you don't think much about it until it happens to you or someone you love. Then it becomes the most devastating time in your life."

"But this isn't a sad time. This is a good time for you," Hope said. "All three of us will take your things to your new place. The guys will carry up the bags and boxes, and I shall delight in making sure they get into the proper rooms. I won't unpack. I think that should be done by the resident, so you'll know where everything is. Will we get the key from him?"

"I have it," Mercy said, and slid it across the table to

Hope. "I have to slip the money for the first month's rent in his front door mail drop."

Jack's eyes widened. "He gave you the key to that apartment without you giving him any money first?"

Mercy nodded. "A very trusting man. Besides, he said something strange about us both being travelers on the same path, or something like that. Anyway, I have the cash. I need an envelope to put the money in, and I'll be good to go."

"Done!" Hope said. "So, we're having baked potato night. Big Idaho whites and lots of toppings. You can load it however you like. Jack, the toppings are in the fridge, and Duke will get the potatoes on the plates. You sit here and tell me how the day went, what you cooked, and did anyone complain?"

"I'll get the drinks for the table, and then we'll all share our day. This is one of the things about leaving here I will miss."

Hope was trying to smile through tears. "I will never issue an invitation. You will come and go at will because this house and the people in it are officially home and family. You have a key to the front door and the keys to our hearts."

Mercy clasped her hands together and then threw her arms out wide. In an unusual spurt of public joy, she did a perfect pirouette in biker boots right in the middle of the kitchen floor.

—∿∿—

Two days later, Mercy had finally unpacked, ready for company. She rode home after work with one thing on her mind.

The cop.

She ran up the stairs into her new home, still in awe that she lived in such beauty for such a small amount of money. Then she remembered what she'd been told about small town costs versus city living and knew she'd made a good decision.

She shed her clothes in her bedroom and crossed the hall to shower. She smelled like burger grease from the grill and fried shrimp. Today was all-you-can-eat shrimp until close. However, Mercy never had to stay for closing. Once her baking was done for the day, she clocked out. The only downside of the job was that as the only baker, it was 24-7. Riding home tonight it occurred to her that Lovey needed to think about hiring a couple more people to train with Mercy so she never got caught like this again.

However, there was way more on her mind tonight than the job. She came out of the shower, dried in a hurry, and made a mad dash across the hall to get her phone. She pulled up Lon's number, typed him a message, and then shivered as she hit Send.

Lon was on his way home when he saw three women hurrying along the sidewalk toward the park. It was nearly twilight, so why they would be carrying what appeared to be a long white banner was beyond him. When he recognized who they were, he pulled over and stopped, thinking, and rightly so, they were up to no good.

The women saw him and halted, their expressions a reflection of their moods.

"Ladies, might I ask what you three are doing?"

Tina sighed. "We're following Judge Herd's ruling."

Lon frowned. "And that would be?"

"Besides the money we all had to pay at court, we are required to make a public display of the apology we owe Miss Dane."

"Let me see," Lon said.

"But we're not there yet," Angel said. "It's heavy, and we just got it all rolled up so we could carry it."

"I still need to see it," he said.

"You don't trust us?" Molly asked.

"No, ma'am, I do not."

"Fine, but now you're going to make us late getting to the park. I don't want to be down there in the dark."

"Then you shouldn't have waited until the sun had set to do this. Show me."

With a lot of moaning and groaning and hateful little snaps at each other, the banner was finally unfurled.

He read it and nodded. "That'll work, but I don't think it'll get all that much notice at the park. I think you need to walk this up Main Street and string the banner across the empty lot between the shoe store and the travel agency."

"But that's all the way up Main."

"Walk or drive. Makes no never mind to me," he said.

They rolled it back up and headed to their cars. He watched them load it and then take off toward Main. He stood watching from a distance until he saw they were in the act of stringing it across the space before he left smiling at what the banner said.

Mercy Dane must be an angel. Saved her sister's life and Granny's biscuits.

We are so sorry. We were so mean.

This message approved by: Tina Clark, Molly Frederick, and Angel Herd.

Lon drove away. As far as he was concerned, it could hang until it rotted away.

He got home, grabbed a cold beer, and took it with him to the shower. By the time he'd washed the remnants of his day away, the beer was gone, and he was clean. He put on a pair of sweats, a long-sleeved T-shirt and some fur-lined moccasins, and was going to the kitchen when his cell signaled a text.

He stopped to read it, and then his heart thumped once so hard he almost lost his breath.

SEX

He grinned as he sent a text back and then went to grab a clean uniform and his work boots to take with him in case he had an emergency during the night and had to leave. He was as excited as he'd been as a kid packing for a sleepover with a friend, only better, and out the door in minutes, his heart racing with every step.

Mercy stood at the other end of the conversation, waiting for an answer. Then it occurred to her that he might not get that for hours if he was working some incident or case. She plopped down on the side of the bed butt-naked and sighed. This was going to be such a letdown if—

Ping, ping.

It was Lon. Her heart pounded as she pulled up the text. A slow grin, a heartfelt sigh, and then she closed her eyes and shivered.

Don't mind if I do.

Lights: Dim to none.

Music: Willie Nelson's classic—"Always on My Mind."

Action: Coming in the door.

Mercy heard his car drive up. Heard his footsteps running up the stairs and got hot all over. He wasn't wasting a minute. He knocked.

"It's open," she called out.

He opened the door, and for a moment, was little more than a silhouette against the street light behind him. "There is a password," Mercy said. "Come into my parlor."

"Said the spider to the fly?"

"Lock the door behind you."

Lon stepped across the threshold, tossed the stuff he was carrying on the sofa, and did as she asked.

He began taking off clothes where he stood, while waiting for his eyes to adjust to the dark, and then he saw her, a shadow in an unlit hall, and walked toward her. It didn't take long to see that she wasn't wearing a damn thing, not even a smile.

He stopped. "We've been here before," he said softly.

"But in a darker, sadder time."

"Then why don't we start over on the right foot…and the right name?"

He heard her sigh. "Hello. Thank you for coming to my aid. My name is Mercy Dane."

"How could I ignore a sweet woman's request? Nice to meet you, Mercy. My name is Lonnie Joe Pittman, but you can call me Lon. Is there anything I can do for you?"

Mercy shivered. "Just love me."

He wrapped his arms around her as he whispered in her ear. "I already do."

She pointed to the faint glow of blue light emanating from an open doorway. He swept her off her feet and carried her toward it, then into her bedroom, and laid her down on the bed.

She was shaking. "Are you cold?"

"Just remembering," she said.

He groaned. "Have mercy."

Mercy answered. "Please do."

And so it began. Two people needing what the other had to give. An awakening of kindred spirits chasing one goal. One minute led to another, and then another, until time ceased to have meaning.

Lon was lost in the heat, trapped within the clutch of lithe legs locked upon his back—of long fingers kneading, urging, searching. He could feel the muscles within her beginning to contract.

Mercy's breathing quickened as she rose up to meet each urgent thrust. Nothing was better. Nothing felt as good as that thick shaft buried within her warmth— the constant hammer of body against body. She felt it coming. Didn't want this to end, but couldn't stop. And then they exploded in a frisson of heat. As their bodies trembled, they rode the fire down in silence. The music switched off. Nothing to be said. Nothing to be heard but the shattered rhythm of their breathing.

For Lon this night of making love to Mercy was one of the best things he'd ever done. His heart was full, his body a slave to inertia. He wanted her to love him. He wanted her in his life forever. He wanted to have a family—grow old with her. She'd been cheated out of a childhood, but they had the rest of their lives to make things better. He wrapped his arms around her and rolled until they were face to face.

"You look beautiful in blue," he said.

"It's my favorite color. It's why I wore it for you," she said.

He eyed the blue lightbulb beneath the lamp shade. "How do you look in red?" he asked.

She never cracked a smile. "Too hot to handle."

Lon laughed, and then pulled her close. "You are for sure a hot mess," he whispered, and kissed the hollow at her throat. "So what do you have to say for yourself?"

He saw her eyes narrow, as if she were giving thought to her answer, and then she slid a hand down his belly, pausing just below his belly button, waiting to pull the trigger.

"Can we do that again?" she asked.

"Yes," he said, rolled her over on her back, and proceeded to show her that love was always better the second time around.

They made love and slept, made love and slept, until Mercy's alarm went off the next morning. The first thing she thought was "There's a man in my bed." She looked at him, remembering waking up all those years ago and leaving him sleeping. She would never do that again. She leaned over and gave him a kiss behind the ear, then ran a hand down his back, and cupped that cute, tight butt. "Lon, Lonnie Joe…sweetheart?"

"Hmmm?"

"Are you awake?"

"Yes," he muttered, his face still mashed into the pillow.

"Okay…just didn't want you to think I was running out on you again. But I have to get ready for work, so I'm headed to the shower."

"What time is it?"

"Four."

He rolled over and sat up, rubbing his face with both hands. "In the morning?"

She laughed. "Yes, and don't complain. The sex was heavenly. Worth losing sleep," she said, and got up.

"Oh. Speaking of heavenly," Lon said. "The three witches from Granny's hung a banner on Main Street in your honor last night. The judge ordered them to make a public apology, and they did."

"You're kidding. What does it say?"

"I'm not telling. I want you to see it for yourself as you ride to work."

"I can't wait," she drawled, and headed across the hall in a long, lanky stride.

Lon groaned at the full view of her backside. "Perfection, thy name is Mercy," he mumbled, and went to join her in the shower.

Fastest sex and shower in history, but they were both out the door in plenty of time for Mercy to clock in at Granny's and Lon to go home and shave. He took the clean uniform and dressed for work from there. But in the back of his mind, he already dreamed about the day that would no longer be necessary.

As for the banner, Mercy saw the white canvas strung across the empty lot facing Main, and as she rode closer, she saw the words and grinned.

"Saved my sister and Granny's biscuits," she read, and laughed as she turned and rode behind Granny's to park.

Lovey's car was already there. She heard Elvis's truck rolling up behind her and two of the waitresses arriving together. It was time to start another day.

Chapter 23

FOR THE FIRST TIME IN MERCY'S LIFE, SHE WAS completely happy. She had hope. She had a future, because she had the cop. He was what had been missing. Not just a man, but the man meant for her.

She loved him. So much. Even though she had yet to come right out and say it. But she would because he had so lovingly and freely said it to her. She went into Granny's with a bounce in her step, exuding joy. "Morning Elvis, morning Lovey, looking good, Chet. Let's make some biscuits."

Lovey looked up from her laptop and smiled. "Someone is sure happy today."

"That would be me," Mercy said as she strode past her with that steady stride and locked up her things. She came out of the break room tying a clean apron around her waist, adjusted the bib, and then reached for the baking pans.

Elvis banged the spatula on the side of the grill, his way of announcing he was about to speak. They all looked up. "You gonna be making them heavenly biscuits today?" Elvis asked.

Mercy grinned. They'd seen the banner! "Yes, thank you. I am."

Lovey shook her head. "I'm sorry I wasn't here the day that happened."

"No matter, Lovey. Ruby Dye must have stepped

in for you because the way I hear it, she pretty much cleaned house on my behalf."

Elvis banged the spatula one last time. "Next time you need to give someone a whipping at work, you tell me."

"Thanks to all of you for having my back," Mercy said, and then flour began to fly.

―᷈᷈᷈―

The ensuing months flew by in flour-filled, sugar-sprinkled days, and Mercy's prowess in the kitchen had become a well-known fact. After a conversation Mercy had with Moose one night, talking about her job and how much she loved it, Moose made sure to spread the word. After that, anytime someone mentioned her name, he told them she was no longer serving drinks, but baking full-time at a little place in Blessings called Granny's Country Kitchen.

Truckers were always on the lookout for a good place to eat, and when they heard that, they spread the word too. And as the word spread, truckers began to show up at Granny's, and there were a few times a week when customers actually had to wait to be seated.

The first trucker caused quite a stir when he tried to find a place to park his big rig. He'd come a long way for a good piece of pie and didn't quit until he found one. But after the truckers became commonplace, the city council cleared the zoning on a big graveled lot that had once been a used car business so it could be accepted parking for big-rig diners at Granny's. It was a block-long walk for the truckers, but none had voiced a complaint. And every time one came in to eat who had known Mercy from the Road Warrior Bar, they always yelled at her through the pass-through before they left, giving her two thumbs up for her biscuits or the dessert they'd eaten.

At Mercy's suggestion, Lovey had hired two part-time bakers and then trained them under Mercy so that on her two days off, there would be no danger of running out of cakes and pies, or the heavenly biscuits, as they'd become known after the banner had been hung. If Mercy was an angel, then it stood to reason why her baking was so good. Thus the phrase "heavenly biscuits" was born.

Mercy made sweets in the day and sweet love to Lon every night, and settled into Sunday dinners at the Talbot farm like she'd been doing it all her life, with the cop at her side.

And so it is with the way of people, memories of the shaming incident Mercy suffered had dimmed, and the women were slowly forgiven. Ruby was cutting the judge's hair again and taking appointments for Tina, Molly, and Angel. The uproar settled as spring came to Blessings.

———

It was a week before high school graduation when the weather brought a two-day bout of heavy rains. Roads flooded. Low-water bridges washed out, and travel in the area was limited.

Mercy had worked one of her days off last week so that one of the other bakers could go to a family wedding, and now that baker was working the following Friday for Mercy, giving her a well-earned three-day weekend.

She'd slept in past her usual 4:00 a.m. wake-up call and carried a load of laundry to the utility room when her phone rang. When caller ID told her it was Lon, she piled the laundry on top of the washer and answered with a smile. "Good morning to my favorite cop," Mercy said.

Lon grinned. There wasn't one thing about this woman that didn't make his heart sing. "And good morning to my favorite angel. Wanna take a ride with me?"

"Sure. Where are you going?"

"To check the two low-water bridges on the south and east roads leading out of town."

"Okay, I'll change shoes. Otherwise, I'm good to go."

"On my way to pick you up now," he said.

Mercy had planned to have lunch with Hope today, until Hope texted her last night and told her not to come. Because of the washed out roads, she had to work a double shift, since a half dozen nurses were unable to get to work. Mercy already knew the situation in and out of Blessings had become serious. She changed shoes, grabbed a jacket and her purse, and headed to the living room to watch for Lon, but when she looked out and saw her landlord in his wife's flower garden, she went onto the front door landing instead to say hello.

"Good morning, Elliot. Those roses are magnificent!"

He looked up, smiling as he waved. "Yes, they are." Then he remembered it was Friday and frowned. "Are you ill? You're not at work."

"No, I'm fine, but it's sweet of you to ask. I worked a Saturday last week for someone else, and now she's making it up to me. I'm going with Lon to check bridges," she said.

Elliot chuckled. He liked that those two were a couple, and he liked the good vibes of having love all around him once more. "Be careful."

"We will. Oh, there he comes," she said, running inside to get her jacket and purse. She locked up and then took the stairs two at a time with her long legs flying.

She waved again as they drove away and then leaned over the console and gave Lon a quick kiss before she buckled herself in. "You look particularly beautiful, today," Lon said.

Mercy smiled. "That's because I'm particularly happy."

"Good. How do you feel about being a June bride?"

She felt her forehead and then pinched her own arm. "Hmmm, I think I feel good about it."

He loved her corny sense of humor and grinned. "Anytime you want to set a date, I'm ready. I love you with all my heart. I want nothing more in life than to spend it with you."

Mercy reached across the console and held his hand. "I will confess I am at the point of looking at wedding dresses online. I haven't been putting you off. I've been struggling with *when*, not if."

"What do you mean?" he asked.

She smiled, thinking how every single thing about him was so perfect for her. "Do you remember when we first met?"

He nodded. "I was in CLEET training in Savannah."

"It was September," Mercy said. "I want our married life to begin on the same day you came to my rescue. I was so scared and so lost, and then you came out of your apartment. In the midst of the hell my life was in, you stepped in to help. It was the fifteenth of September. I don't know what day that falls on this year, but I want to get married on the fifteenth."

"Then we will," Lon said. "I'll write it on my calendar so that all of the perps and the drunks and the pig thieves will know to put their stupidity off while I'm busy getting married."

Mercy leaned back with a satisfied sigh. "Pig thieves. We live a dangerous life, don't we?"

"Not often, thank goodness, but now that we have the date to look forward to, time will drag. When it comes to you, Mercy, waiting is a hard thing to do."

Mercy nodded, but she had another fear. Now that she'd said the date aloud, she'd given the universe a shot at taking her down. She'd survived every bad thing in her life, and she liked to think this time was for her and her cop. She'd lived through so much, surely there was a downtime for sadness. Surely she'd paid her dues many times over for the privilege of stepping into a happy life. He winked, and she smiled, even as her stomach began to knot.

Then the drive became somber and startling with vivid evidence of water damage almost everywhere. A cattle guard had washed out at the entrance to a pasture, fencing down in several places. They were about a mile from the east bridge when Lon heard Avery's voice on the radio. "Dispatch to Pittman. Over."

Lon heard the panic in Avery's voice. "This is Pittman. Over."

"Switch to the other frequency, Chief."

Lon knew it must be bad as he switched and keyed in to let him know. "Pittman here."

"Okay. Now, we just got a call from the school. When one of their buses didn't show up this morning, they began making calls. While they were trying to find out what had happened, the bus driver on that route finally called in a panic. The east bridge washed out beneath them in the midst of crossing. Fifteen kids and a driver are in the river."

Lon's heart sank. "Who's been contacted?"

"County Search and Rescue and Blessings Fire and Rescue."

"I'm less than a mile from the location. I'll be on scene. Over and out."

He switched the police radio back to the dispatch channel and pushed the accelerator all the way to the floor.

Mercy's stomach was in knots. "Oh, Lon! Fifteen children. Oh my God, what can we do?"

"Hopefully, we'll figure that out when we get there," he said, and turned on the siren and lights.

A couple minutes later, they drove up on the scene, and it was a nightmare. The water was a rushing torrent of power and debris. The bus was in the river, hung up on a piece of the bridge, or it would have already washed downstream. The windows were all down, and they could see the horror-stricken faces of the children inside. The driver was barely visible, but seemed to be trying to keep them all calm and seated. Any sudden movement, and they'd be gone.

"Merciful God," Lon whispered.

"What do we do?" she asked.

"I have rescue ropes in the trunk, and that's it. If I can figure out a way to get them to the bus, the driver can tie them through the windows, and I'll tie the other end up on shore. If we get enough ropes tethered from shore to bus, we might be able to get everyone off before it gets swept away."

They jumped out of the police cruiser and ran to the

trunk. It didn't take long for Lon to see how limited his options were. He hoped to God the rescue squads got here fast. "There are four lengths of rope in here, and I'm pretty sure they're long enough, but I need some way to get one end of each of the four ropes to him."

Lon dragged coil after coil of rope onto the ground, while Mercy dug through the rest of the items in the trunk, looking for a miracle. As she pushed things around, she caught a glimpse of red all the way to the back of the trunk and realized it was a blanket. And when she leaned farther in, felt something rolled up inside. She couldn't pull it loose from where she stood, so she crawled into the trunk and shoved things aside.

Lon turned around and saw her in the trunk. "What on earth are you doing? You're going to hurt yourself."

She pulled until the blanket came free, and when she unrolled it, she gasped. It was a loaded spear gun with three extra spears. "Lon! Does this work?"

"I didn't even know that was in there," he said. "It must have belonged to our old chief. If this works, maybe I can shoot the rope to the bus. We might be able to stabilize it long enough to get everyone out."

She handed him the spear gun, and then got herself out of the trunk as he began tying each rope to a spear. But then he realized he couldn't tie a knot tight enough to keep it from slipping off the bare end of the spear when the spear left the gun.

Mercy saw the problem and crawled back into the trunk. "I saw duct tape somewhere in here," she said, and moments later found it between a fire extinguisher and a stack of all-weather ponchos. "Here!" she yelled and pitched it to him.

He caught the tape and rectified his problem by taping the knot and part of the rope onto each spear below each spear point. Then he grabbed a bullhorn from the trunk and ran to the river's edge with the gun, hoping the driver would hear enough to understand what he needed to make the kids do. "Hey! Can you hear me?"

The driver leaned out a window and waved.

Lon held up the spear gun and the rope. "Shooting them into the bus."

The bus driver nodded and waved.

"Thread it through two windows, and tie it off."

The driver gave him a thumbs-up.

"Everybody down. Kids under the seats."

The driver gave Lon another thumbs-up to reassure the chief that he'd heard and understood, and when he began moving the kids away from the windows, Lon loaded the first spear and waited until no kids were in sight, waited for the driver to give the okay and then disappear from view.

Lon's stomach knotted as he got ready to shoot the first one. "Please, God, let this work," he muttered. He eyed the bus, took aim, and fired. The spear flew across the floodwaters like an arrow from a bow and hit the bus about six inches above a window.

Moments later the driver appeared, leaned out the window on his back, reached up, tore away the duct tape, and pulled the rope off.

"Please, God, let this work," Mercy echoed.

"Hey, angel, say an extra prayer for me while you're at it."

They waited, watching as the driver threaded the rope out one window and then in the next, before tying it off inside. They heard sirens as Lon ran to a stand of trees along the bank and quickly tied off the other end of the rope.

Mercy was white-lipped and silent as she held ropes, spears, and duct tape, working hand in hand with Lon. Hearing the terrified shrieks of the children trapped inside was gut-wrenching. It was all she could do to stay focused.

Lon fired another spear from shore. It hit the bus again, and he waited as the driver tied off the river end to another section of windows before he ran with the shore end to tie it to a different tree farther down. He was ready to fire the third spear when the county search and rescue units began to arrive. By the time Lon had fired the last spear and tied it off, all the units were on site.

But there was another problem now. Once the children saw so many people to help them and still knowing they were just out of reach, they waved arms out the windows, screaming and crying, and the bus driver couldn't silence their fears.

Mercy sat on the ground with her back against a tree, her knees pulled up beneath her chin, and her face hidden against her knees. She could hear the babies screaming, "Mama, Mama," and crying "Daddy help me." Pleading over and over "Don't let me drown," while the men upriver came to terms with what they faced.

"We've got a chopper en route," the sheriff said. "If those ropes hold the bus, we might be able to get everyone off."

"How long?" Lon asked.

"I don't know."

Lon was sick to his stomach. He'd seen a lot of

devastation in the years since he'd gone into law
enforcement, but nothing got to him as fast or dug as
deep as when children were involved. He shoved a hand
through his hair and turned around, only to realize he
couldn't see Mercy. He started back toward his cruiser
when he spied her sitting by the shore.

He knew before he got there that she would be crying,
and when he stopped and knelt beside her, she looked
up. Her face was streaked with dirt and tears, but there
was a wild look in her eyes, like a trapped animal with
no way out. "Mercy? Honey? What's wrong?"

"Can you hear them?" she whispered.

"Hear what?"

She pointed to the bus. "The babies. They're crying.
They're scared, so scared. They're going to die, aren't
they, Lonnie? They're all going to die."

"No, we don't know that. We have to stay positive."
Then he heard the chopper and looked up. "There!
Look there! We've got a rescue chopper on site. You
say prayers while we get set up. If God is with us, we'll
airlift everyone out, including the driver, okay?"

She nodded, but when Lon turned and ran back to
join the others, she got up and ran toward the shore.

While the rescue took shape on-site, the news spread
in Blessings. Frantic parents in outlying farms to the
east knew their children were on the bus. The parents
of the children who had not been picked up counted
their blessings. Phone calls came in to the school, to the
Blessings police, to the county sheriff's office, all with
the same request. *Where is my child?*

A Savannah news crew flew the TV station's chopper
over some of the flooded areas to use as backfill footage

for the evening news. It was pure luck when they happened upon the rescue in progress, and immediately went live on air. Now they flew back and forth over the rescue area, catching everything on camera and relaying the information as it unfolded.

When the feed went national, viewers all over the country became caught up in the ongoing drama.

—⁓—

Tina Clark was in the Curl Up and Dye when Vera turned up the volume on the television so they could all hear. "What's happening?" Tina asked as she came out of the bathroom, pausing to pull out a debit card to pay for her appointment.

"A Blessings school bus was on the east end when floodwaters swept away the bridge."

Tina froze. "What? Where did they take the children? I think that's the bus my Callie would be on. She spent last night with the Fretwell girl."

Ruby came up behind Tina and put an arm around her waist. "They're in the act of rescuing them now," Ruby said.

Tina moved closer to the screen. "You mean they're in the river? They're still in that bus? My God, someone save my baby."

Ruby held her tighter. "Look, honey! See the chopper. They're bringing them out of the bus one at a time. Vera, how many did they say they'd taken off?"

"I think they said thirteen, and there are fifteen and the driver."

Tina went to her knees. "Help my baby. I need to help my baby." She moaned, and then started to shake.

"Call her husband," Ruby said. "Tell him to come get her. She's in no shape to drive."

Vesta ran to the phone while the rest watched.

———∿∿∿———

The back door of the bus was open. All of the children were safe on shore, and the chopper had come back for the driver. He stood in the doorway watching the harness swing in the wind as the chopper hovered over the bus one last time.

He looked behind him, scanning every seat to make sure there were no more children on board, and then turned and waited to make the grab, just as he'd done before. The harness was caught in the downwash from the rotors, swinging like the pendulum on a clock, and it took two tries before he finally caught it.

Everyone on shore had been holding their breath, and when he finally snagged it and pulled it inside the bus, their sighs of relief were clearly audible.

Mercy had watched the entire rescue in silence. She saw Lon in a way she'd never seen him before—on duty, calm, and competent. Even in the face of imminent failure, he had stayed focused on what had to be done, and now it was nearly over.

She watched the driver dangling high above the river as the chopper took off one last time. He looked up at the underside of the chopper and didn't glance back at the bus. He didn't see the little girl who came crawling out from beneath a seat and then stood in the open doorway, crying for someone to come get her, except the water rose by the hour. The river had yet to crest. And the bus had begun to rock.

At that point, Mercy looked away from the driver and saw the child silhouetted in the open door of the bus and screamed. "No, baby, no! Get back!"

Lon heard her scream and then looked to where she was pointing. His heart nearly stopped. "There's one more!" he shouted and ran toward shore.

All of the rescuers were horror-struck. Just when they thought they had averted a disaster.

The information was immediately relayed to the chopper pilot. He made the quick decision to turn around and fly back, lowering the driver close enough for him to grab her and take them both to shore.

When the driver saw her, his relief turned to agony, believing he had cost a little girl her life. And then the bus began to sway. It rocked to one side and then swayed to the other, and when it did, it ejected the girl from the bus.

Mercy screamed. She saw the panic-stricken look on the child's face just before she hit the water, and didn't think. She acted on instinct, the same way she'd lived her life—she took three running steps and dived into the flood.

Lon saw her go, and even as the water swallowed her, he ran, screaming, "No, Mercy!"

But she was already gone.

Chapter 24

THE NEWS CREW IN THE OVERHEAD CHOPPER CAUGHT IT ALL, from the child flying out of the bus, to the woman on shore going after her.

Tina Clark knew it was Callie from the moment the camera focused on her face. And just as her husband came through the door to get her, Tina watched their child disappear beneath the flood. At that point, she gave her up to God and fainted.

Hope was on duty at the third floor nurse's station, and like everyone else who could catch a moment, would run back to the television from time to time to watch the drama unfold.

She saw the little girl fall, and then suddenly, another camera had picked up on the woman running toward the river. Hope knew without seeing her face that it was Mercy, and when she dived into the water, Hope cried out. "No, Mercy."

But it was too late.

―――

Lon saw Mercy go under and started running, trying to keep her bobbing head in sight, and even as he ran, his heart was breaking. He didn't believe there was a chance in hell of either coming out of that water alive. Then all of a sudden, he heard men shouting on their two-ways, saying over and over they were alive.

The woman had the child in her arms and hung onto a logjam.

Lon was so overwhelmed he could barely breathe as he stopped to ask directions. "Where are they?"

The captain pointed. "About a hundred yards around that bend. She's hanging onto debris with the kid in her arms."

"Sweet Jesus," Lon muttered, and started running.

The moment he rounded the river bend, he saw them. Mercy clung to a tree trunk caught in a jam, holding the child. He ran to the shore, waving where he stood, until he knew Mercy saw him. He saw her lips move, but he couldn't hear what she'd said. And then the rescue chopper swept into view once more, flying above the river like a bat out of hell. Then it stopped in a hover position over the people below and dropped the harness.

Lon's heart pounded as he watched Mercy make a grab for it as the pilot sent it down. When she caught it on the first swing, Lon doubled up his fists and shouted with joy.

———

Mercy couldn't believe she was still alive. When she saw the little girl fall in, she didn't think, she just reacted, but the moment she hit the water, she knew that she would die. The force of the flood kept pushing her forward and pushing her down, and no matter how many times she tried to surface, the debris was so thick she couldn't push through.

No, no, no. Not now, please, not now.

Life had finally made sense, and now it was over? Then she heard a soft voice in her head.

Don't quit, Baby Girl. Don't quit.

She didn't know who it was, but she felt the love and power behind it, and while she was trying not to drown, a huge rush of water pushed her forward so fast that she popped into the air like a cork, and in the moment she was airborne, saw the little girl's body in the water. She reached out to grab her, knowing this would be her only chance, and caught a handful of her hair as they went under. When they popped up again, Mercy grabbed onto a passing limb, moving so fast in the water that holding onto that ride was like a surfboard in rough seas.

Seconds later, they were swept toward the left bank of the river to become part of the floating debris. Just as suddenly as they'd been swept away, the jolt of hitting the jam stopped all forward motion. They were caught between the shore and some rocks, still afloat, and this time above the racing, raging water.

The survivor in her wanted to believe the child was just unconscious. As she tried to untangle her, she heard a cough, and then a moan, and Mercy thought she felt the child's chest move.

She slung her over her shoulder and pounded her on the back, and when she heard another cough and then a retching sound, she was so elated that she screamed, and when she did, the child moaned again. Before she could rejoice, new panic set in. The debris jam was shifting. If it broke apart, they would die before they drowned. In a desperate move to keep their heads above water, Mercy shoved the child upon the trunk she was using for a float just seconds before a wall of water engulfed them. The water lifted Mercy up just enough that she was thrown on top of the child, and when the wave passed, she still held on.

The child was breathing because she could feel the slight rise and fall of her chest against the palm of her hand. She was so focused on keeping their heads above water and dodging the swift-moving debris that she almost didn't see Lon on the shore. But when she did, she also felt the crushing blow of separation. She was so in love that sometimes the simple sight of his face brought tears, and to think he might witness her die was a nightmare. He kept waving, but she couldn't let go of anything to wave back.

The little girl's body shook. The water was so damn cold. Mercy could no longer feel her own feet. *Please, God. Please help us.*

And then she looked downriver and saw a chopper coming toward them, flying fast and low—an answer to her prayer. "Look, baby. The chopper is going to take us out of the water!" But her eyes didn't open, and she was still limp in Mercy's arms. She hugged her close and kept talking. "They came back for you. You're going to be safe. They'll take you home to Mommy, okay?"

But the child didn't move, and when the chopper hovered over them, the force of the downdraft and the roar of the motor made it almost impossible for Mercy to hold on. The harness was lowered, and it took every ounce of strength Mercy had left to get the child fastened in it. Finally, she lifted her arm as a signal then watched as they raised the near-lifeless body out of the flood.

Mercy was so tired she couldn't think and couldn't stop shaking. Hypothermia? Not good. Where was that chopper? Where was Lon? She looked up, but the sky was just a blur. She looked toward shore, but the people didn't look like people anymore. They looked like ants.

She didn't realize until the water went over her head that she'd lost her grip, or that she had moved downstream with the flood-swept debris.

Lon saw her slide away from the log and screamed. He was already running, desperate to keep her in sight, saying her name over and over until it became his prayer and not her name.

Mercy. Please, Mercy. Dear God, have mercy.

The news crew in the sky above saw her go underwater and followed the current downriver to the point that it was obvious she wasn't coming up. The moment that became his reality, the on-scene reporter yelled, "Cut the feed," and the cameraman shut it down.

He could hear his boss yelling in his ear, "What the hell's wrong with you?"

The reporter had watched that drama play out from the time the woman first surfaced in the flood, to her grabbing the child, to watching from below as the rescue flew off. Seeing her give up to the power of the water was, for him, like a knife to the heart. "Wrong with me? What's wrong with you?" he screamed. "I watched that woman turn into a fucking Amazon. She saved herself and then saved that kid. I'm not going to sit here and watch her die just to boost our ratings, understand?"

The cameraman was just as rattled at what he'd seen. "What the hell was fair about that?" he said, and then covered his face and wept.

Hope stood in front of the television when Mercy began to float away. She started screaming, "Swim, baby, swim." But when Mercy sank beneath the water, Hope sank unconscious on the floor.

—◆◆◆—

Lon ran down shore as fast as he could move, praying with every inch of ground he left behind that God would spare her. Lon needed her to go on.

He ran through rock piles, and through trees when there was no shore, and kept looking toward the river, praying for just one sight of her face to let him know she was still alive, but he saw nothing. Still, he ran. He had no other place to go.

The rescue teams were in recovery mode. The chopper pilot had delivered Callie Clark to the ambulance on shore and was now on his way back to search the floodwaters. But this time there was a sick feeling in the pilot's gut that she was gone.

Lon had long since left the others behind and ran without seeing, pacing his stride to the hammer of his heartbeat, refusing to believe this had happened. Wishing with every breath in his body that he had never made that call. She would be safe back in Blessings if he had not, but it was too late to change fate now.

His legs shook, and he had no more breath left to run, and he still kept going until his legs gave way. He fell forward, catching himself on his hands and knees just before he would have hit face down. He pushed himself upright and then rocked back on his heels, his hands resting on his thighs, his breath little more than shaky gasps.

When he had enough breath in his lungs, he threw back his head and screamed. "Mercy! Merrrrcy!" Then dropped his head and closed his eyes. "Please don't do this."

The water roared beside him, foaming and bubbling like some damn witch's brew. And still, he waited without reason or result. "Mercy!" And still, no answer. He tried to move forward, but his legs wouldn't hold him, and so he shouted again, "Mercy!"

He looked across the raging flood, watching as the body of a dead cow swept past him, feet up. And then he covered his face. The pain in his chest was too great to cry. If he didn't die from it, he'd have to think about how to live without her.

His phone rang, but he couldn't answer, and then he realized they could be calling him to say she had been found. He couldn't get it fast enough. "Hello?"

"Chief, it's Avery. Is there anything you need?"

Lon disconnected and put the phone back in his pocket, waiting until the hurt turned to anger and the anger became rage. He stood and walked in circles, cursing God for what He'd done.

All of a sudden he heard a voice. *Be still*, the voice said, and so he was. He waited some more and then dropped his head and turned around. *Be still*, he heard again, and so he stopped and once again, turned around.

At first he thought it was the wind in the trees. And then he thought it was the roar of the water. When he heard the words *have faith*, the hair stood up on the back of his neck. He took a couple steps forward, and then a few more, and then he was running toward the sound of her voice calling his name.

The last thing Mercy remembered when she opened her eyes was that she had drowned, so now that she could see again, this must be death. But it looked nothing like what she had expected. She was belly down on a huge pile of boulders. She tried to get up, only to realize her legs were too weak to hold her, so she crawled instead—all the way off the boulders, through the graveled edge of the river, and into the tree line, only to wait with growing disappointment. Heaven was nothing as she had expected. When did the light come? Where were the angels? Why did she still hurt? Where was God?

"Help me," she cried, but her voice was barely audible, even to her ears.

It became apparent that if she were to get the rest of the way to heaven, she would have to take herself. She pushed herself up to a standing position and then winced at the pain in her ribs and in one leg. She stood for a few moments to see if her legs would hold her, and at first wasn't sure which way to go. Then she remembered she'd been swept downstream when she died, so maybe heaven was the other way.

She stood motionless until she believed her legs would carry her then began moving, but mostly staggered, falling and crawling until she could pull herself up once more. It was a lesson in pain.

She didn't know how long she'd been walking or how far she'd come, but her pace was slow, and it hurt to breathe. The first time she thought she heard someone shouting, she stopped, and in the distance she was certain someone had called her name. Was that God leading her to the Pearly Gates? She remembered one foster father always preaching hell and damnation to them, and then following it up with promises of heaven.

She heard her name again and tried to shout, but her throat was too sore, so she just kept moving. Within moments, she heard the voice again, and this time she stopped, stunned by the recognition. That was her cop! That was Lonnie! Was he dead too? If he was, she still wanted to go with him, and tried to move faster. It wasn't until she realized he was no longer calling her that she became afraid he'd left her behind, so she started running—calling for help. Calling over and over, until her voice finally gained strength, but her body was failing. That's when she screamed out his name.

And then she saw him, standing so still upon the shore, and looking at the river with his head cocked to one side. When she realized he wasn't gone, but was waiting, she wept. Ever faithful.

"Lonnie," she screamed, and then fell to her knees. Her legs wouldn't move, and it hurt to breathe. "Help!"

She saw him turn toward the sound of her voice, and then he walked forward, moving faster and faster until he was running.

Mercy sighed. He'd come for her. She wanted to run toward him, but the ground was beginning to move as fast as the river, spinning her around and around until she lay down, unable to go any farther.

Lonnie found her just inside the tree line and was at her side in seconds, checking for a pulse, for broken bones, for obvious injuries. "Mercy, oh my God, my darling! Can you hear me? Can you talk?"

She reached out in the direction of his voice, felt his arm, and grabbed it. "Did you die too?" she whispered.

He pulled her into his arms and sobbed. "Thank you, Lord. No. I'm not dead, baby, and neither are you. Just hang onto me, and don't let go. I'll get us both back home."

Epilogue

<small>SCHOOL ENDED.</small>

Tina Clark sent flowers while Mercy was still in the hospital. A large attached greeting card came with a fervent message inside:

> *We owe our daughter's life to your heroic actions. You do not owe the hospital a dime. We gladly pay the debt, and more, if needed. I wish it were as easy to rid myself of guilt for how I hurt you. I wish you a long and blessed life with no more floods and no more storms.*

Mercy took the flowers home in a vase and the message home in her heart. Some beginnings were rockier than others, but this one was finally smoothing out.

She went back to work exactly a week to the day she had died. She still didn't know how she came up from the bottom of a river or how she wound up on the rocks. Hope said it was their Mama's doing, and it just wasn't Mercy's time to die. Mercy didn't care how it happened, just that it had. She needed at least a lifetime of loving and babies and growing old with Lon to make up for the rocky start.

The leaves had begun to turn on the day Lon and Mercy were wed. Lon had gone through all the trappings of wedding showers and bachelor parties he could handle. He wanted a ring on her finger and his bride by his side.

As it neared the time, Lon walked out behind the preacher, and took his place at the altar. The church was packed and silent. The suspense was maddening as he waited for his first sight of Mercy's face, while everyone else waited to see the dress. In their minds, she was so beautiful that whatever she wore would certainly take on the majesty of a royal wedding. Lon waited for what would be his last sight of Mercy Dane. Within the hour, she would be not only a Pittman, but his wife.

When the organist hit the loud opening chord, Lon sighed. Finally. He turned and looked up the aisle at Callie Clark. Bonded by their near-death experiences, she was the only flower girl Mercy would choose.

Callie was so excited to be a flower girl with a basket full of white rose petals that she literally bounced on her toes. When she started down the aisle toward the altar, she looked like a tiny sprite in a fern-green dress, dancing among the roses.

Hope journeyed down the aisle as the matron of honor, escorted by Lon's brother, Cole.

His parents were in the audience, and Duke and Jack served as the ushers. Once the wedding began, their jobs were done, and they now stood at the back of the church, watching people in the wedding procession. Duke privately decided that the side of the church he'd seated looked more orderly than Jack's, which satisfied his perception of himself as infallible.

All of a sudden, the music ended. There was a soft rustling of feet toward the doorway, and everyone knew the bride had arrived. The organist struck the chord on the organ as vehemently as if she'd just uttered a scream. As she did, everyone turned to the woman in the doorway, and the giant of a man standing with her.

At first glance, to the guests it appeared as if a real angel was standing in the light, when it was Mercy dressed in white beneath the skylight, and surely, no angel had come to a ceremony in such a tight-fitting dress. It fit her like a second skin, from the high neck to the long sleeves, to the mermaid-style skirt. White over white, satin to lace, red lips against sun-kissed skin, and black hair framing a face of immeasurable beauty, and all Lon could think was "She's mine."

The man at her side was the only loving father figure she'd known, and for the first time in his life, Carson Beal, otherwise known as Moose, had tucked himself into a tuxedo and a ruffled shirt just to walk her down the aisle.

The guests gasped, and then oohed and aahed, as Mercy moved toward the altar, but she didn't hear them. She was looking at the cop. The forever hero who loved her before he ever knew her name. Once she locked into his gaze and knew her dream had become their reality, the last vestiges of the voiceless child within her were swept away.

As the pastor began the ceremony and asked the traditional question of who was giving the bride away, the whole town of Blessings shouted out loud, "We do!"

Mercy blinked as Lon laughed. He'd have the whole town to answer to if, God forbid, he ever made her mad. The sound of his laughter made Mercy shiver, and as the ceremony continued, she repeated her vows and did all of the things it took to get herself as married to this man as the law would allow. She still couldn't believe it was happening until he slipped the ring on her finger.

She looked straight into his eyes, into the forever he had promised, and couldn't wait for it to begin. She tuned back in to what was happening just as she heard the preacher say, "Lonnie Joe Pittman, you may finally kiss your bride."

And so he did.

The reception afterward was a study in perfectly orchestrated joy. The cake was cut, and bites of the sugary confection were exchanged, and then a kiss. "Mercy, my Mercy, you are sweeter than the cake," Lon said.

Mercy smiled. Joy abounded.

Ruby Dye had eaten her piece of cake and nibbled a couple of nuts and a mint, then called it done. She dabbed at a tear, thinking of one more happy-ever-after for Blessings, and wondered what was up for her.

When they called all of the single women for a try at catching the bridal bouquet, Ruby went with them because that's what she always did...accepting her situation in life and living it with pride. Tradition said the one to catch it would surely be the next bride. Ruby saw three widows, and counting her, three divorcees, besides all of the never married women at the church.

"Are you ready?" Mercy called out.

"Let 'er rip," Lovey yelled.

Mercy turned her back, gave the bouquet a windup before flinging it high and wide, straight into Ruby Dye's arms.

Ruby stared at the bouquet in shock as everyone crowded around her, teasing and congratulating her all at the same time. Then she felt a hand on her waist and a whisper in her ear. "All in good time."

She gasped and turned around, certain she would finally see him, and all she saw were dozens of women. "Did you see him?" she cried. "The man who whispered in my ear."

"I didn't see any man. There was no man here. That's wishful thinking!" they all said.

Ruby glanced around the room, looking at one face and then another, seeing all of the familiar people she knew, and no one seemed in any way focused on her. She clutched the bouquet to her breasts as she moved back to her table, gathered her things, and went home. All the way there, she kept thinking—

What did this mean? Who was doing this? Was she the target of a would-be romance, or was it something more—something sinister?

Only time would tell.

saving

Jake

THOMAS WOLFE ONCE WROTE, "YOU CAN NEVER GO HOME again." Jacob Lorde never took the word of a stranger. He was on the way home, marking the passing of every mile with a war-weary soul. He needed a place to heal and Blessings, Georgia, the place where he grew up, was calling him.

He'd come back briefly over a year ago to bury his father, and the calm and peace of the place had stayed with him long after he'd returned to his unit. Only a couple of months later, an IED on one patrol too many earned him a long stint in the hospital and brought his time with the army to an end.

Now he was coming home to try and bury the soldier he'd been.

He wanted to be done with war.

He needed peace.

He needed the emotional security that comes with knowing where he belonged.

He needed that like he needed air to breathe, so when

the Greyhound bus in which he was riding came around the curve and he saw the city-limit sign of Blessings gleaming in the early morning sunlight, his eyes blurred with sudden tears. He took the sunglasses from the pocket of his uniform and slipped them on, then held his breath as the bus began to stop.

The brakes squeaked. They needed oil.

Jake stood slowly, easing the stiffness in a still-healing leg, walked down the aisle, and then out into a sweet Georgia morning. He took a deep breath, smelling pine trees on the mountains around him and the scent of smoke from someone's fireplace.

He was home.

The driver pulled his duffel bag from the luggage rack beneath the bus, shook his hand, and got back on board. The rest of the trip home was on Jake.

———

Ruby Dye had just opened The Curl Up and Dye when the Greyhound bus rolled through Blessings, belching black smoke from the exhaust. Because the bus came through Blessings on a regular basis, she never paid it any attention, but today it began slowing down. When it stopped, she moved closer to the window, waiting to see who got off, but the only person she saw was the driver who circled the bus to remove luggage from the carrier beneath.

A few moments later, the bus drove away in a small cloud of the same black smoke. It was then Ruby saw the man in uniform reaching down to get his duffel bag. From this distance she couldn't tell who it was, but he was limping slightly as he walked away.

"Welcome home, soldier," she said softly, and then went back to work.

―〜〜―

Jake paused on the sidewalk and took a deep breath as the early morning air filled his lungs. Enveloped by the silence, he exhaled slowly as the weariness of the bus ride fell away. Shifting the duffel bag to rest easier on his shoulder, he headed south. Unless he caught a ride somewhere between here and home, he had a six-mile hike ahead of him, but after sitting for so long, he didn't care.

As he walked through town, it was somewhat comforting to see everything pretty much looked the same. Granny's Country Kitchen still appeared to be the main place to eat. He thought about stopping there for breakfast, but food wasn't as urgent a need as it was to see home.

He continued south down Main, noticing one thing had changed. The old barbershop was closed. There was a sign in the window that read: Haircuts Available at The Curl Up and Dye. He smiled, remembering Ruby Dye and the girls at her shop.

When he noticed a school bus heading out of town, he guessed the driver was beginning his route and thought of all the boys and girls hurrying around in their homes right now, getting ready for school, still innocent of what life could do to their dreams.

Traffic was picking up by the time he reached Ralph's, the small quick stop at the edge of town. He'd already had the utilities turned on at the house a month earlier, had cable set up so he'd have television service, and had the house cleaned at that time as well. But there wasn't any food, and picking up a few things here would be enough to tide him over while he settled in. The bell over the doorway jingled as he walked in, which made everyone in the store turn and look.

Jake knew the army uniform he was wearing and the military duffel bag marked him as a vet and wondered if there was anyone inside who might give him a ride.

Ralph Sinclair, who had always reminded Jake of Santa Claus because of his white hair and beard, was behind the counter. "Jake! I heard you might be coming home. It's good to see you!"

"Hi, Ralph. It's good to be here," Jake said.

He set his duffel bag against the counter, picked up a small shopping basket, and started moving down the aisles. He was reaching for a squeeze bottle of mustard when he heard someone call out his name. When he turned to look and saw Truman Slade standing at the end of the aisle, the first thought that went through his head was, *Well, hell*. Probably the only enemy he had in the entire state, and he was not only out of prison, but back in Blessings. A muscle jerked in his jaw as he forced himself not to react.

Truman Slade was two hundred and twenty-three pounds of pure mean, exacerbated by the years he'd spent in prison thanks to Jake Lorde's testimony against him. Truman didn't give a damn that all of that had happened when Jake was still in high school. All he knew was the kid's statement at his trial sent him to prison for eight years. The years and Truman's lifestyle had not been kind to him. Even when he was young, his short legs and big, round face, plus a distinct underbite, had given him a bulldog look. Now he had the big belly to go with it.

The moment he'd seen Jake Lorde walk in the door, his first thought had been *time for payback*. He walked up to where Jake was standing, pushed himself into Jake's personal space, and waited for him to react. He so wanted to whip his ass.

To Truman's dismay, Jake didn't acknowledge his presence. Instead, he calmly reached over Truman's head for a loaf of bread, which accentuated how short Truman really was, and how tall Jake had grown. As he did, his elbow grazed the tip of Truman's nose, which made Truman flinch. Jake was acting as if Truman were invisible. When he turned around and moved a few steps down and put a box of granola in the basket with the bread and mustard, Truman followed.

"Still afraid of your own shadow?" Truman whispered, then made a gun with his hand and pointed it at Jake.

Jake stared at Truman until he flushed a dark, angry red and shoved both hands in his pockets. Jake walked back to his duffel bag, pulled a big handgun from a side pocket, gave Truman another look, and then slapped it down on the counter in front of Ralph.

"Hey, Ralph, do you know where I could get ammo for this?"

Truman heard Ralph talking, but he couldn't focus on the words, thinking of that look Jake had given him. It was just beginning to dawn on Truman that war had changed Jake Lorde in a dangerous way. By the time he tuned back in on what was being said, Jake had shoved the handgun back into his bag and was at the deli, waiting to get some lunch meat and cheese sliced to take home.

Truman was leaning against the counter with a smirk on his face, and when Jake approached with his shopping basket to pay, Truman purposefully slid his shoe in front of Jake, intending to force him to step aside. Instead, Jake took the next step right on top of Truman's shoe and then stopped.

Truman inhaled sharply. The bastard was standing on his foot! He started to push Jake off, and then something told him not to lay a hand on the man. By his own actions, he was momentarily pinned to the floor.

Jake paid, picked up the groceries, shouldered his duffel bag, and left the store.

Truman groaned beneath his breath when the pressure on his foot was released and then hobbled out the door and drove toward town. He needed to put distance between him and Jake Lorde to recoup his swagger.

As for Jake, his head was pounding as he walked out of the store. The blood raced through his veins the same way it had done at the end of a deadly exchange of gunfire. Even though the morning air was cool, he could almost feel the desert heat. Despite his inability to focus, instinct kept him moving toward home.

Laurel Payne was on her way into Blessings to an early morning cleaning job. She would have to drop her daughter, Bonnie, off at a friend's house in town until it was time for them to walk to school. There were always difficulties arising from being a single parent, and having good friends to help her out like this made her life a little easier.

She was less than a mile from town when she saw the soldier walking on the side of the road. Her heart skipped a beat. The sight of a man in uniform was still a painful reminder of her own husband, Adam, who'd come home from a war without a single wound and then shot and killed himself only a few months later.

As for the traveler, she knew who he was even before she got close enough to see his face. She knew because she'd been the one who'd cleaned his father's house weeks earlier. He was not a stranger. He was a few years older, but she'd known him all her life.

When she passed him, the first thing she thought was that the neighborly thing to do would be to give him a ride home, but she didn't want to reawaken the sleeping demons in her life by befriending anyone who reminded her of Adam. Then she glanced in the rearview mirror, saw the slight limp in his stride, and her heart sank. Despite her reservations about getting involved, she hit the brakes.

"Mommy, what are we doing?" Bonnie asked as Laurel made a U-turn in the road.

"I'm going to give Mr. Lorde a ride home," she said.

Bonnie frowned. "But Mr. Lorde went to heaven already. Did he come back?"

Laurel sighed. "No, honey. That man we just passed is his son."

"Oh," Bonnie said, but her curiosity was piqued.

Jake saw the old pickup coming toward him but paid it little mind because it was going the wrong way to do him any good. When it came closer, he noticed a young woman and a child inside, but didn't recognize them. He nodded politely as they passed and kept on walking.

When he was a little farther down the road, he heard the vehicle braking, then turning around, and his first instinct was to brace for another confrontation. When the pickup caught up with him and stopped, he didn't know what to expect.

Laurel rolled down the window and managed a brief smile.

"Jake Lorde?"

"Yeah?"

"I'm Laurel Payne, your neighbor down the road. Get in and I'll take you home."

Jake breathed an easy sigh of relief. "Thanks," he said, and put his things in the truck bed. He saw the little girl in the backseat as he opened the door and winked at her as he got in.

Bonnie was immediately charmed, partly because he reminded her of her father, whom she missed, and partly because he belonged to Mr. Lorde, whom she had adored.

Laurel waited until he settled before she accelerated.

"Welcome home," she said shyly, and kept her eyes on the road.

"Thank you," Jake said, trying to figure out who she was, and then it hit him. "You were Laurel Joyner, right?"

She nodded.

"You said it's Payne now. By any chance did you marry Adam Payne? I knew him in high school."

"Yes, I did," she said.

"My daddy is dead," Bonnie announced.

Laurel sighed. "That's my daughter, Bonnie. She's a first-grader this year."

"Hello, Bonnie. I'm sorry about your daddy, and I'm sorry for your loss," he told Laurel.

"Thank you," Laurel said, but when she wasn't forthcoming with any further information, Jake didn't push the issue.

A few minutes later they drove up on the mailbox at the end of his driveway. Laurel slowed down, and when she turned off the road and headed up the driveway, the ruts were so deep that they bounced in the seats all the way to the house.

"Sorry," she said.

"Looks like you just pointed out the first repair I need to put on my list," Jake said.

She pulled up to the fence surrounding the yard, put the truck in park, and started to get out.

"No, don't get out. I can get it all," Jake said. "I really appreciate the ride and hope I didn't make you late to wherever you were going."

"We're fine with the time," Laurel said. "Have a nice day, and again, welcome home."

"Thank you," Jake said.

Laurel waited while he gathered all of his things from the back of her truck and then headed for the front door. As soon as he was clear of her truck, she began backing up to turn around.

When Jake turned to watch her hasty exit, he saw her little girl on her knees in the backseat watching him. She waved.

He waved back and then they were gone and he had

no other excuses to delay the inevitable. He reached above the door for the key, unlocked it, and went inside. He set his duffel bag against the wall and then headed to the kitchen with the groceries.

His footsteps echoed on the old hardwood floors, and despite the cleaning, the rooms smelled musty. He set the groceries on the counter and then opened the two windows in the kitchen to start airing the house. The house might get chilly, but he was choosing fresh air rather than airless, musty rooms.

Opening the cabinet doors as he put up food was like turning back time. His mother's dishes were still stacked in the same places they had been when he was growing up. A couple of coffee cups were missing, probably broken from years of use. When he opened a drawer to the left of the sink and found the notepads and pens they'd used to make lists and saw his father's writing on the top page of one pad, a moment of anger swept over him. His father's grocery list was still here, but he wasn't.

He picked up the one on top to begin a new list of things he was going to need, then took it with him as he walked through the rooms, making notes of what he needed to buy.

He knew for sure he needed toilet paper, bath powder, and toothpaste for the bathroom. Laundry soap, stain remover, and cleaning supplies for the utility room. Light bulbs for the house, and everything it took to restock a kitchen.

He was passing a window when he saw the school bus go by the house. He glanced at the clock and smiled. Fifteen minutes to eight—the same time he'd always caught the bus. He continued through the house, checking off things needing repairs. The showerhead was leaking and he'd noticed loose boards on the front porch when he'd stepped on it.

Several times he thought he heard footsteps in the house and would turn, expecting to see his father walk into the room with a big welcome-home grin on his face, and then remember. He made a note to get a Wi-Fi connection at the house and to set up his email.

It was moving toward noon when he finally closed all of the windows and turned on the central heat to warm up the house, then grabbed the keys to his dad's pickup from a small nail inside one of the upper cabinets and headed toward the barn. It's where he'd left the truck after the funeral.

A trio of pigeons roosting in the rafters flew off when he entered. The red Chevrolet truck was a little dusty but otherwise intact. Jake unlocked it with the remote and then looked inside. It was just as he'd left it. He backtracked to the last granary where he'd hidden the battery and put it back in the vehicle. He checked the oil, the transmission fluid, and the air pressure in the tires before he was satisfied, and then started it up and drove it to the house and parked beneath the carport.

He was back in the kitchen making a sandwich when he thought of Laurel Payne again and wondered where she'd been going so early, then wondered what she did for a living. It had to be tough being a single parent.

He sat down in the living room to eat and turned on the television to catch local news, only to realize he didn't recognize any of the journalists reporting. So some things had changed after all.

The food he'd made was tasteless, but his hunger had

been satisfied, and that was all that mattered. He was thinking about going into town and setting up his banking, then checking in with the post office to let them know he was home and to resume delivery.

But then he fell asleep and went back to war.

The explosion from the IED sounded like the end of the world, and when Jake came to, he thought he was dead. The pain from his wounds had yet to register, and he was trying desperately to stand. He couldn't hear, he couldn't see for the smoke and dust, and he couldn't feel his legs. This was a blistering disappointment. He thought heaven would be prettier than this.

Someone yelled at him. DeSosa! He was telling him not to die, but the way he felt, he wasn't making any promises. It wasn't until the ground began vibrating beneath him and the air was spinning above his head that he started yelling for help. That was a chopper, and he didn't want to be left behind.

Jake woke up in a sweat, his heart pounding and tears in his eyes.

"Son of a... Ah, God," he muttered, and bolted off the sofa as if he'd been launched, trying to get as far away from the dream as possible.

He yanked the front door open and strode onto the porch, taking in the fresh air in gulps. The sweat on his forehead began to cool as the tears dried on his cheeks, and he began to pace. The loose boards squeaked, reminding him of a job still undone. Furious from the dream and frustrated because the war still haunted his life, he went straight to the toolshed for a hammer and nails, then back to the house.

Every time the hammer made contact with a nail, it

took everything he had not to duck, because it sounded like gunshots. He was so focused on getting rid of the nightmare that he didn't see Laurel Payne driving home, but she saw him.

———≈≈≈———

Laurel was already exhausted and she still had four loads of laundry to do and supper to cook for her and Bonnie. She'd actually forgotten about seeing Jacob Lorde this morning until she drove past the house and saw him on his hands and knees on the porch. She saw the hammer in his hand and remembered the loose boards when she'd been there last month to clean the house. It was obvious he wasn't wasting any time putting it to rights.

But when she consciously noticed how broad his shoulders were, she looked away. She didn't care what he looked like. He didn't matter in her world and never would. She had a daughter to raise, and she wanted nothing to do with another war vet.

Her head was hurting by the time she got home, and climbing those steep steps into their double-wide trailer seemed like insult adding to her injury. Once inside, she breathed a sigh of relief at being in her own home, not someone else's, and headed for her bedroom.

The first thing she did was take down her hair. It was thick and a slightly curly auburn that hung well below her shoulders, and sometimes having it up all day gave her a headache. As soon as it was down, the release of tension in her body was palpable. She quickly changed her clothes and got to work.

By the time the school bus stopped to let Bonnie off,

Laurel was taking the last batch of cookies from the oven. She had the third load of clothes in the washing machine, a load in the dryer, and vegetable soup simmered on the back burner.

The sound of Bonnie's footsteps coming up the steps of their trailer was Laurel's signal for an emotional shift. Whatever was bothering her did not belong on her little girl's radar. She turned toward the door with a smile. Seconds later, Bonnie came inside in a rush, talking nonstop.

"Mama, I got a happy face on my new words, and Lewis threw up on my shoe at lunch. Mrs. Hamilton washed it off but it still smells funny. I think it got on my sock, too. Milly was mean to me at recess but I told her she was acting like a baby. Then she cried, which proved I was right. Can I have a cookie? How long till supper?"

Laurel grinned. "Come here and give me a kiss. I missed you today."

Bonnie threw her arms around her mother's neck and kissed Laurel's cheek as she reached for a cookie.

Laurel grinned when she saw the second cookie in Laurel's other hand and stopped her long enough to get the stinky tennis shoes and socks off Laurel's feet.

"Change out of your school clothes before you go feed Lavonne, and put on socks with your old shoes. It's chilly out today."

"I will," Bonnie said. "Can Lavonne have a cookie, too?"

"No. Chickens don't need to eat sugar. Just her regular feed, okay?"

"Okay, Mama," Bonnie said, and ran barefoot to

her room, her little feet making *splat, splat* sounds as she went.

In minutes she was out the back door and running toward the little chicken coop. Her daddy had built it for Lavonne, and she thought of him every time she went to feed her pet, but it was getting harder to remember what he looked like. That scared her a little, but she was afraid to talk to Mama about it. She heard Mama crying sometimes at night. It was hard being Mama's big girl when she still felt little and scared.

When she unlocked the gate to the fence around the coop and Lavonne came running, it made the sad thoughts go away. Lavonne was her buddy and had the prettiest black feathers ever. Mama said she was from a family of chickens called Australorps, but Bonnie disagreed. Lavonne was from the family of Paynes.

The chicken's constant clucks sounded a lot like Bonnie's chatter as Bonnie scooped up feed and put it in the feeder inside the coop. When she left the chicken yard to get fresh water, Lavonne was right beside her, clucking and occasionally pausing to peck the ground.

"What was that?" Bonnie asked. "Did you get a bug? Good job!" Then she suddenly squatted and pointed her finger in the grass. "Oooh, look, Lavonne, there's another one!"

Lavonne was on it in seconds, then wandered off a few feet while Bonnie carried fresh water back to the coop and filled the watering station. As soon as she was through with all that, she pulled a fresh hunk off the bale of straw and loosened it. She was getting ready to put it in Lavonne's nest when she saw the egg.

She squealed and dropped the straw then came out of the chicken coop on the run, screaming, "Mommy, Mommy."

When Laurel heard Bonnie's scream her heart stopped. She dropped the armload of wet clothes back into the washer and went out the back door on the run.

"What's wrong?" she cried as Bonnie ran into her arms.

Bonnie held out the egg in two hands as if it were pure gold.

"Look, Mama, look! Lavonne laid an egg. Does that mean she's all grown up now?"

Laurel was so weak with relief it took a moment to answer.

"Well, my goodness, I guess it does. Way to go, Lavonne," Laurel said.

Bonnie giggled.

"We're both growing up, aren't we, Mama? Here, you take the egg. I'm going to play with Lavonne some more."

Laurel sighed as she watched Bonnie running back to the coop. Yes. Her little girl was growing up. She turned around to go back to the house, carrying the proof of Lavonne's launch into hen-hood, and the farther she went, the angrier she became at Adam. By the time she reached the back steps, she was crying.

"Oh, Adam, just look at what you're missing. Why did you have to go and blow your damn head off? We need you. Life wasn't supposed to be like this."

Chapter 2

TRUMAN SLADE DROVE UP TO HIS HOUSE, A PLACE HE'D been renting for almost a year that was a couple miles outside of Blessings. He wished he'd had the foresight to pick up some barbecue before he'd left town. It was almost sundown, and with no lights burning from inside the house, it appeared uninhabited, which suited Truman just fine. He liked flying under the radar.

The night air was cold, making him hurry as he moved toward the house and unlocked the door. He locked it behind him and then went through the house turning on lights, then ignited the fire in the fireplace. It didn't burn real wood, but the fake logs behind the propane flames made it look real pretty. The stove popped as the flame caught, and then he turned on the TV for company before heading to the kitchen.

A quick search through the cabinets and then the refrigerator confirmed what he already knew. There were no leftovers of any kind anywhere. Forced to make do with what was there, he ate peanut butter and crackers for supper, washing them down with reheated coffee, and blamed his forgetfulness on Jacob Lorde's return to Blessings.

Truman had been back in town for some time now and deceived himself into believing people had forgotten his past transgressions, but that would no longer be possible now that the man who'd sent him to prison would be a physical reminder.

This place wasn't big enough for both of them, but he wasn't sure how he could bring that to a successful resolution without winding up back in jail.

———

Ruby Dye was carrying trash to the alley behind The Curl Up and Dye while the twins, Vesta and Vera Conklin, were sweeping the floor and folding towels, getting everything ready for the next day.

Mabel Jean, the manicurist, was about to lock the front door when LilyAnn Dalton from Phillips' Pharmacy came hurrying inside with a big smile on her face.

"Oh, you're locking up," she said. "I won't keep you, but I just heard news Ruby will want to know."

"What news?" Ruby asked as she came in from outside.

"Jacob Lorde is home!" LilyAnn said.

Ruby smiled. "So that's who I saw getting off the bus this morning. Is he staying for good?" she asked.

"That's what I heard," LilyAnn said. "Remember he was here for his daddy's funeral, and then he went back to his unit? So, they said he suffered some pretty severe injuries not long after that. Anyway, he's out of the army on an honorable discharge."

Ruby frowned. "He's out there all by himself. We need to get some of the ladies at church to make some food. We can take it to him tomorrow evening. Like a welcome-home visit."

LilyAnn grinned.

"I'm in for macaroni and cheese casserole," she said. "I'll bring it by the shop tomorrow before you close, and I'll volunteer my Ford Explorer to make deliveries if others will go with me."

"That's wonderful," Ruby said. "I'll go, and I'll get at least one more to go with us."

LilyAnn waved good-bye and left as abruptly as she'd appeared.

"Well, now," Vesta said. "I remember him as a really nice-looking young man."

Vera frowned.

"Isn't he the one who testified against Truman Slade while he was still in high school?"

Ruby nodded.

"I'd forgotten about that, but now that you mention it, he sure did."

Vera's frown deepened.

"That no-account Slade lives outside of town. I wonder if he'll try to bother Jake?"

Ruby shrugged.

"Truman Slade went to prison. Jake Lorde went to war. My money is on Jake no matter what occurs. Now, as far as I'm concerned, this day is over. Let's go home."

"I vote for that," Mabel Jean said.

A few minutes later they were gone.

Laurel put the last glass in the dishwasher and started the cycle, then went to get the final load of laundry from the dryer. Since it was all towels and washcloths, she carried them to her bedroom to fold later. She could hear Bonnie playing in her room as she passed the door and smiled. It sounded as if she was playing school and using her stuffed toys for students. Bonnie was always the teacher, and Panda Bear was her worst student. He suffered a lot of time-outs.

Laurel tossed the towels on the bed, then went to get Bonnie ready for bed. As she walked in, Bonnie was putting Panda Bear in time-out again.

Laurel grinned.

"It's bedtime, honey," she said lightly.

Bonnie frowned. "Oh, Mommy, not yet. Panda was naughty."

"Well, you go brush your teeth and put on your nightgown. By the time you're finished, his time-out will be over, okay?"

"Okay," Bonnie said, and then shook her finger at the bear as she walked out of the room, as if to say *you better behave*.

Laurel could imagine Bonnie's teacher doing the same thing at school. Teaching was one job she could never do. She wouldn't last a day with a room full of six-year-olds.

Bonnie had squirted a little toothpaste on the end of her finger and was writing on the mirror when Laurel walked in.

"Bonnie Carol! Why on earth are you doing that?"

Bonnie looked startled.

"But, Mommy, when Daddy used to shave it made the mirror get all foggy, and he would write *Hello* to me on the glass. I just wanted to write *Hello* back to Daddy…in case he came to see me while I was asleep."

There was a knot in Laurel's throat, but she made herself smile.

"You are right! I forgot he used to do that. So, finish writing your word and then wash your hands. It's time to get in bed."

"Okay," Bonnie said, and added the last L and O, then washed and dried her hands.

Laurel waited in the doorway, then followed Bonnie across the hall to her room. Bonnie skipped over to where she'd left Panda and tossed him on her pillow.

"I'm gonna sleep with Panda tonight so he won't feel bad for getting in trouble today."

"Good idea," Laurel said, still struggling not to burst into tears. She sat on the side of Bonnie's bed to hear her prayers.

"Okay God, here's the deal," Bonnie said.

Laurel rolled her eyes. Now she didn't know whether to laugh or cry as her daughter continued. "I wrote Daddy a note on the mirror. Tell him it's here so he can some see it. Also, bless Mommy, who works very hard. Bless Daddy, who is in heaven. Bless Lavonne for laying her first egg. And bless Mr. Lorde's son. I think he is lonesome. Amen."

Laurel was so stunned to hear Jake Lorde added to the prayer list that she didn't know what to say, so she said nothing. Instead, she pulled the covers over Bonnie's shoulders, tucked in the naughty Panda, and kissed her good night.

"I love you very much," Laurel whispered.

"I love you, too, Mommy. Don't forget to leave—"

"I know, I know," Laurel said. "I'm leaving the night-light on."

Bonnie sighed. "Thank you, Mommy. You and Lavonne are just about the best friends I have."

Laurel patted her daughter's shoulder.

"Thank you for putting me in such fine company,"

Laurel said, and then reached over and turned on the angel night-light plugged in near the headboard and tip-toed out of the room.

She went into her bedroom with tears rolling down her cheeks, folded the towels on her bed, and put them away, then took a quick shower and put on her pajamas. She paused in the hall outside Bonnie's door, making sure she was asleep, and then walked through the house, making sure both doors were locked.

She didn't have to be at work tomorrow until 10:00 a.m. That meant she could make a decent breakfast for Bonnie before she caught the bus. She closed her eyes, whispered a quick "thank you" prayer for getting through another day, and then thought of what Bonnie said about Jake Lorde being lonely, and impulsively added a quick prayer for him to be well in mind and body. The moment she said it, she felt guilty. It was the same prayer she'd prayed for Adam, and it hadn't worked.

A little uneasy that she'd somehow marked Jake Lorde's future as iffy, she turned over, pulled the covers over her shoulders, and cried herself to sleep.

Jake's rest was never sound, and sleeping in a new place exacerbated the process. He had been gone so long that the sounds of the old farmhouse were unfamiliar again.

The pop at the window behind him was nothing but a limb from the azalea bush blowing in the wind. The creak on the floorboard in the hall was just the house settling, and the drip he kept hearing was the shower-head in the bathroom. He knew the sounds when he was awake, but when they filtered through his sleep into the nightmare he was having, they sounded like an enemy ambush.

He could see them moving through the shadows, heard the clink of metal against metal, and knew he needed to run, but his feet wouldn't move. He tried to shout a warning to the others, but he couldn't make a sound. He could hear someone crying and was afraid to turn around and look, for fear he'd see yet another one of his buddies dying. And then the world exploded.

He woke up to realize he was the one in tears and rolled out of bed, anxious to leave the nightmare behind. He glanced at the clock. It was a little after 6:00 a.m. He hadn't intended to get up so early, but no way in hell was he going back to bed after that dream, so he got dressed and went to the kitchen to make coffee. While it was brewing, he got one of his dad's work coats out of the closet. When the coffee was done, he put on the coat and took a cup of coffee to the back porch swing. He eased down onto the swing and then took a quick sip. It was still too hot to drink, so he pushed off in the swing, while he gazed across the back of the property, waiting for sunrise.

He thought about Laurel Payne and wondered if they were up yet, and if Bonnie was getting ready to catch the bus. If he closed his eyes, he could almost imagine his mother in the kitchen behind him, making biscuits and frying bacon, while making his dad's lunch for the day. He would have been getting dressed and smelling all those wonderful scents drifting down the hall toward his bedroom, secure in the knowledge that all was right with his world.

He wished his parents were still living. He could

use a little pep talk along the theme of "this too shall pass." God, he hoped even a little bit of that could be true. He couldn't imagine living out the rest of his life in this violent state of mind.

And so he sat on the swing until his cup was empty and sunrise was just a breath away. At that point, he stood, walked off the porch and into the middle of the yard.

The sky was already lighter in the east. The moon was still in the same place in the sky, but swiftly fading from sight. While he was waiting for sunrise, a flock of geese took off from the pond, resuming their winter flight south. He watched until they had flown out of sight, thinking how quickly they'd left their past behind. If only it were that easy for him.

He turned toward the east just as Mother Nature swept the horizon with a light brushstroke of gold, followed by a faint overlay of pink. Just after the pink turned to purple and the gold turned orange, a tiny portion of the sun was suddenly visible.

Once again, tears blurred Jake's vision. There were too many days from his past when he had believed he would never see a sunrise from this location again.

"Thank you, God," he said softly, and lifted his head, standing witness to the new day in much the same manner as he'd stood at attention during morning inspection.

When the sun was finally a valid orb too bright for further viewing, Jake went back in the house. He hung the old coat on a hook by the door and refilled his coffee cup before pouring himself a bowl of cereal.

Breakfast was served.

———〰———

Ruby Dye was at The Curl Up and Dye early, verifying the number of ladies who were making food for Jake Lorde. She needed to make sure they knew to bring it to the shop by four this afternoon.

Rachel Goodhope, who ran the Blessings Bed-and-Breakfast, offered food and a helping hand to Ruby to carry it in, so they were all set. Ruby checked to see if there was a phone number for the Lorde property, but couldn't find one. They would have to hope Jake Lorde was at home when they arrived.

———〰———

With the extra time to make breakfast this morning, Laurel made pancakes for Bonnie. The treat was unexpected and so exciting that Bonnie almost made herself late because she talked so much through the meal. She was on her way to the bus stop when the big yellow bus came around the bend.

"Don't run!" Laurel shouted as Bonnie started to sprint. "He'll wait on you."

Bonnie slowed down, and sure enough the driver stopped, honked the horn at Laurel, and waved. Laurel waved back and then waited until she saw Bonnie take a seat inside the bus before she relaxed. She'd just put her daughter into the hands of the Blessings school system and wanted her back in the same shape in which she'd sent her. Maybe a little dirtier, and hopefully a bit smarter, but safe. She took her time cleaning the kitchen and then changed her clothes and headed to work.

Today she only had two houses to clean. One

belonged to P. Nutt Butterman, Esquire, and the other was at the Blessings Bed-and-Breakfast. She cleaned rooms while Rachel Goodhope, who owned the B and B, did laundry and all the baking. She only worked at the B and B when Rachel called because they didn't always have overnight guests.

She made herself a sandwich and packed it in her lunch bag with a banana and a cookie and, at nine thirty in the morning, headed out the door.

The radio was on in the truck, and she was humming along with the song when she drove past the Lorde place and saw Jake at the barn. He was working on broken rails in the corral, and once again, she was impressed that he was being productive.

She started to honk and wave and then didn't. No need encouraging him in any way. She was not on the market. But to her disgust, he was still on her mind when she drove past the city-limit sign and into Blessings.

—⁓—

Jake heard the vehicle coming before he saw it and immediately recognized Laurel's old pickup. He kept working as he watched her pass. As soon as he nailed the last loose board on the corral, he put up his tools and headed for the house. He had business in town and wanted it over with.

—⁓—

Truman Slade didn't punch a time card or bother himself with a regular job. He got a disability check from the welfare department for an injury to his back from when he was in prison. Truman considered not having to work was fair compensation for having been beaten within an inch of his life. He had a couple of pins in his spine as a result.

The way he looked at it, if he hadn't been convicted, he wouldn't have been hurt. He blamed the state for his troubles and considered it his due. It was how his daddy had lived, and his mama had never complained.

He and his brother, Hoover, had been named after presidents. It had been his mother's hope that they would therefore aspire to higher goals than the ones their father had never set, but it hadn't worked. Both Truman and Hoover had spent most of their adult lives in and out of prisons. Truman was out. Hoover was still in. Truman thought about doing better, but not hard enough to change his life to make it happen.

Laurel liked Mr. Butterman's house. She liked cleaning it. She had known him all her life and when she was little thought his name was funny. She used to wonder who would name their child P. Nutt, but his parents had. Now it said something about how he walked through life to have taken a crazy name and turned it into an asset. She also loved the big shade trees at both ends of the house. They reminded her of sentinels guarding the property.

Today Mr. Butterman had left a note asking her to clean out the refrigerator before she left and apologized ahead of time for anything growing its own beard. Laurel giggled when she read the note. She'd seen his leftovers before.

She got to work on the house first, changing sheets

on his bed, cleaning the bathrooms, dusting, and then running the vacuum over the carpets before running a dust mop on the hardwood flooring. She left the kitchen for last.

She began by cleaning the stove and countertops, then opened the refrigerator and began removing all of the covered bowls and carryout containers. Once it was empty, she quickly scrubbed down the shelves and drawers, then closed the door and threw away cartons, emptying the little dabs of leftovers Peanut seemed obligated to keep but never ate.

By the time she was through, it was almost 1:00 p.m. She had to be at Rachel's Bed-and-Breakfast by one thirty. She pocketed the check Butterman had left for her and ate her lunch as she drove to Rachel's. By the time she arrived, she was ready to start all over again.

Jake had a grocery list in his pocket and a cashier's check to open an account at the bank as he drove into Blessings. The familiar sights were reassuring. Seeing a farmer's cab-over John Deere tractor rolling down Main was commonplace, but it still made Jake smile, especially when he saw the Great Dane sitting beside the driver, calmly looking out the windows as they passed. Jake laughed. It was obvious it wasn't the big dog's first tractor ride.

He was still smiling when he parked in front of the bank and went inside. He saw the president, Carl Buckley, sitting in his office with a customer. Two of the tellers were with customers, but the lady at the customer service desk recognized Jake and stood up.

"Jake Lorde! It is so good to see you," she said.

Jake smiled. Hattie Morris had been one of his mother's good friends.

"Hello, Mrs. Morris."

"How can I help you?" she asked.

He took the cashier's check from his wallet and handed it to her.

"I want to open a checking account."

"Certainly! Just have a seat here at my desk." Jake sat, stretching his long legs out in front of him and eyeing the autumn decorations as he waited for her to be seated. "So are you home for good?" she asked.

"Yes, ma'am, and glad to be here."

"That's wonderful. I drive by your home every time I go see my grandchildren, and it will be good someone is in residence there again. We all miss your father. He was a good man."

"Yes, ma'am. I miss him, too," Jake said, and then sat quietly as she went to work setting up the new account, ordering checks, explaining their debit card system and the app for online banking features.

Jake left the bank, heading to the post office to reestablish rural mail delivery at the farm, and once again he was on the receiving end of a big welcome home. By the time he headed to the grocery store, he was feeling good about his decision to return to Blessings.

He pulled up in the parking lot and, as he was getting out, saw Lon Pittman leaving in his police cruiser. When he saw the young man sitting in the backseat with an unhappy expression on his face, he guessed someone might be getting a life lesson on the perils of shoplifting, then flashed on witnessing Truman Slade beat up the cashier at a gas station before he robbed it. He frowned, still disgusted this memory had the ability to bother him, and headed for the store.

He paused just inside the Piggly Wiggly to get a basket, pulled out his list, and started down an aisle. It had been a long time since he'd had a chance to enjoy something as mundane as buying groceries, and he went at it with gusto, even adding candy and snacks that weren't on the list. He was shopping through the canned goods aisles when he heard someone say his name. He looked up and saw Lovey Cooper, the owner of Granny's Country Kitchen, coming toward him.

"Jake Lorde! Is that you?" Lovey said.

He smiled. "Yes, ma'am. It's me."

She eyed the groceries and then him. "Looks like you're setting up housekeeping. Are you home for good?"

"Yes, ma'am, and happy to be here."

She beamed. "Well, that's wonderful news. Next time you come into my place, your first meal is on me. I'll make sure all my servers know ahead of time."

"That's really kind of you," Jake said.

"Just thanking you for your service," Lovey said. "Say, are you going to be home this evening?"

"Yes, ma'am. Why?"

"I happen to know there are some ladies making you some welcome-home food. They were worrying about how to notify you they were coming."

"Oh, they don't have to do that," he said.

Lovey rolled her eyes. "Now you know better than to turn down some good, home-cooked food, right?"

He laughed. "Yes, ma'am. I guess I do."

"Then that's that. I'll let them know you'll be home,

and you don't bother cooking any of that food you're buying for a while. Save it all for another day."

"I will do that," he said.

Even after she walked away, the news that he was going to be on the receiving end of more heartfelt wishes and home cooking made him smile.

He was standing at the checkout lane later when he remembered the ruts in his driveway. He'd meant to put the blade on his dad's tractor and grade the road smooth, but he didn't even know if the tractor would start.

After he paid, he hurried to the parking lot to load his purchases and then headed out of town. If the tractor would fire up, he'd smooth the road before company arrived.

Chapter 3

RUBY DYE, RACHEL GOODHOPE, AND LILYANN DALTON were in high spirits as they drove out of Blessings. When Ruby got Lovey's phone call and found out Jake had been notified they were coming, she was relieved. It would have been a mess trying to deliver all this food if he'd been gone.

LilyAnn was driving and talking about how excited her husband, Mike, was about the upcoming arrival of their baby, chattering on about the colors they'd chosen for the nursery and what all she'd received at the baby shower they'd given for her at church.

Rachel was talking about how their business was growing and the early bookings they already had for the bed-and-breakfast. She was excited for the fact that there were only a few nights still open between Thanksgiving and Christmas. She was bragging about what a smart move she'd made by hiring Laurel Payne to come twice a week and do the heavy cleaning in the rooms, so that Rachel had more time to devote to holiday decorations and baking for the constant turnover of guests.

Ruby wasn't paying much attention. She'd chosen to sit in the back and hold the three-layer coconut cake Rachel made, thinking about Jake Lorde and what it must have been like for him to come back to that empty house. Then her attention shifted as LilyAnn turned off the blacktop to the road leading to the house.

"Oh, look! The driveway looks like it's just been graded," she said.

"Hold on to that cake just in case," Rachel cried.

She glanced back at Ruby and then gave a sigh of relief. She was competently steadying the cake with both hands. When the car finally stopped, they breathed a bit easier.

LilyAnn got out, then opened the back door and took the cake from Ruby so she could exit the vehicle. Rachel went around to the back and opened the hatch to the array of covered dishes. Ruby was on her way to the house with the cake when Jake came out the front door, smiling.

Ruby started talking, even as she was waving a hello.

"Good evening, Jake!" Ruby said. "I'm glad Lovey ran into you to give you a heads up. We brought food — the best kind of welcome-home gifts."

"This is so kind of you," Jake said. "What can I do to help?"

"Come carry this ham," Rachel yelled.

He ran to her aid and the four of them entered his house, loaded down with all they could carry. By the time they finished, there were at least a dozen different dishes on his kitchen counter — from salads to desserts and everything in between.

"This is amazing!" Jake said as he peeked beneath the lids and foil-covered dishes. "And it all smells wonderful. I can't thank you enough."

Ruby handed him a list.

"These are the names and addresses of the women who donated, and I made a note of what they sent, so you can thank them personally."

"Thanks," Jake said. "I'll get some thank-you cards in the mail soon. I promise."

Rachel was used to being the center of attention around good-looking men. She had an eye for them too, but a recent brush with infidelity had taught her that looking was one thing, but never to take that next step again. And Jake Lorde was obviously not in the market, because the only vibe she was getting from him was related to good manners.

LilyAnn was hovering, pointing out things that would need to be reheated and how to do it, things that would freeze better than others, because her mothering instincts were on constant overload. She was completely comfortable with Jake because they'd grown up together, so they had a history in common. When Jake congratulated her and Mike on the baby on the way, she beamed.

"We own the gym on Main Street. It's the only workout place in town," LilyAnn said. "Mike told me to tell you, if you're interested, that your first visit is on him… if you ever feel the need to go sweat in public, that is."

Jake grinned. This evening was far different from his arrival yesterday. He knew without asking that Ruby was the one who'd organized this. He remembered that about her from his father's funeral. He hadn't even known Blessings had a bed-and-breakfast until Ruby introduced Rachel Goodhope, but she was nice. She'd made sure to let him know that the dining room at the B and B would be open to the public on Thanksgiving, which was good to know for the people like him who had nowhere else to go.

"We're going to leave now," Ruby said. "Enjoy your supper, and if you need anything, all you have to do is ask."

Jake followed them to the door, giving each a quick hug and a thank-you for what they'd done, and then he stood on the porch and waved as they drove away.

As he was standing there, the school bus went by on its way into town. Jake thought of Laurel's little girl, Bonnie, riding that bus and guessed Laurel would be scurrying around now, tending to her family. He glanced in that direction and then chided himself that they were too far away to see, went back inside, and closed the door.

After the chatter of three women, the silence of his house surrounded him like a warm blanket on a cold night. It was the peace he'd sought. The healing he needed. He turned on the lights and then went to the kitchen and began filling a plate with whatever took his fancy. He poured a cup of coffee and started to sit down in the kitchen to eat, then changed his mind and carried it to the living room. He wanted a little conversation with his meal, but he didn't want to have to participate, so he turned on TV and kicked back to watch as he ate.

The mood inside Laurel's trailer was far from peaceful and a long way from quiet, but it was home. Bonnie was changing out of her school clothes and hurrying out to feed Lavonne before it got dark, and Laurel had white beans and a ham hock heating while she tried to scrub a ketchup stain off of one of Bonnie's white socks. It was business as usual at her house.

She was in the middle of scrubbing at the stain when she flashed on the scene of finding Adam's body and how hard she'd scrubbed before she'd gotten the blood off the carpet in her bedroom. The memory was jarring and, as she looked down at the sock and noticed the stain was gone, she wished she could wipe away the one from her memory as well.

Then Bonnie came running into the house from doing her chores, bringing life and a cold gust of air with her, and Laurel turned loose of the sadness. "Mama, it's not school tomorrow, right?"

"That's right. Tomorrow is Saturday, why?" Laurel asked.

"I told Lavonne that I'd make her a new nest. I just wanted to make sure."

Laurel smiled. "So Lavonne is getting a new nest?"

"Well, just new straw and grass and stuff like that. She likes the box nest on the wall. She said it keeps the cold air off her feet when she sleeps."

Laurel was used to listening to Bonnie's chatter, but the mention of cold air reminded her that she did need to winterize the little coop, so she and Bonnie would both be hanging out with Lavonne tomorrow.

Jake spent a good portion of the evening dividing the food into smaller portions, saving some of it to eat for the next few days and putting the rest in the old chest freezer in the utility room. Tomorrow was Saturday, but he didn't have a schedule. It was quite the luxury not to have to report for duty on base or clock in at some business. Having this much freedom was the trade-off for experiencing it alone. He couldn't help but wish his dad were still here. There were so many things they could have done together—so many things Jake could have done for him. But such was life, and Jake figured he'd lived through being blown up for a reason, so he would figure it out on his own.

He went to bed with a hopeful attitude and a full belly, and then he fell asleep and dreamed, and in the dream he bled and died.

He woke up bathed in sweat and shaking, then glanced at the clock and groaned. Only 4:00 a.m. It was too early to stay up, but if he went back to bed, he'd never fall asleep. And he didn't want to take any sleeping pills. They kept him locked into the nightmares longer. He thought of the three-layer coconut cake, put on a pair of sweatpants, and went barefoot to the kitchen. Turning on the kitchen light chased away the lingering memories of the nightmare. Cutting a big piece of the cake and pouring a glass of milk to go with it was powerful medicine.

He sat in silence, savoring each bite and remembering the nights he'd done this with his mother. She'd had insomnia, and he'd had a hollow leg, as his daddy used to say. As a kid, Jake couldn't remember ever being completely full, and a nighttime raid for a snack had been commonplace. He'd had the best conversations about his life at this table with her.

He took a bite of cake and lifted it in a toast.

"To you, my sweet mama. Thank you for the lessons."

After that, he went back to bed and slept without dreaming until sunlight coming through the cracks in the blinds woke him up.

He spent the morning setting up his email and Wi-Fi and then caught up on waiting messages. Most of them were from buddies. Some were still in uniform while others, like him, were no longer in service.

—∿∿—

Laurel had winterized the chicken coop by pushing some hay bales around the outside for windbreaks while Bonnie put fresh hay in Lavonne's nest. The fact that they'd gathered another egg had been a huge source of excitement, and Bonnie had carried it into the house and put it in the refrigerator while Laurel finished up outside.

She was on her way inside when she met Bonnie coming out. "Where are you going?" Laurel asked.

"Just outside to play," Bonnie said.

"Okay, but stay close to the house."

If Laurel had paid more attention, she would have noticed Bonnie didn't answer as she ran past her mother. She wanted to go visit Mr. Lorde's son like she used to visit Mr. Lorde.

—∿∿—

The day was cool, but the sky was clear. Jake had tired of being inside and got on his dad's tractor and dragged up a couple of fallen trees from the woods. He was sawing up the logs into two-foot lengths before splitting them into firewood when he saw a shadow on the ground behind him. He turned around, a little surprised by the visitor, and quickly let off the throttle and killed the chain saw.

Bonnie Payne was sitting on an upended bucket. "Hi!" she said when the engine stopped running.

He grinned. "Hi. Does your mother know where you are?"

"My mama lets me play in the creek."

"You are a ways from the creek," Jake said.

"I know, but I came to see your daddy all the time."

That surprised Jake a little. His dad had become a little cranky in his old age, but he must have had a soft spot for his youngest neighbor. "What did you and my dad do when you came to visit?"

She shrugged. "Mostly, I just watched him work. I used to watch Daddy work, but that was before he made himself die."

Shock rolled through Jake so fast it made the hair rise on the back of his neck. "Your dad killed himself?"

She nodded. "Mama had to clean up the bedroom afterward. Mama cleans houses for people in Blessings so she knows how to do it."

Jake was speechless. Laurel must have been the one to find him. Now he understood what the cold vibe he felt from her was all about.

"I'm sorry," Jake said.

Bonnie sighed. "Me too."

Jake glanced at the time. He didn't want her in trouble, and he didn't want to be in trouble with Laurel, either. "I think you need to get back before your mother starts to worry, don't you?"

Bonnie shrugged and then launched herself off the stump. "Mr. Lorde used to give me a treat before I left."

"What did he give you?" Jake asked.

She pointed toward the orchard. "Sometimes an apple from those trees."

"It's too late for apples now. They're all gone. How about a stick of gum?" he asked as he pulled a pack from his pocket.

She held out her hand. "Yes, please."

He let her pull a stick from the pack and then waited while she peeled off the paper and popped it in her mouth. She handed him the wrapper and waved as she ran toward the creek.

He watched until she was completely out of sight and then wondered if he should call and let Laurel know she was here, only to realize he didn't know her number.

He started the chain saw and resumed what he'd been doing, but he couldn't get the image of Laurel finding her husband's body out of his head, imagining her shock and the horror of cleaning up blood from the bed where they'd slept—imagining the grief and, eventually, her anger—because anger always followed death for the ones who'd been left behind.

—⁓—

Laurel was just about to go down to the creek to check on Bonnie when she saw her emerge from the tree line and come skipping toward the house. Bonnie saw her mother and waved.

Laurel waved back and then continued on her way to the cellar to store the last jars of jelly she'd made the other day. When she came up, she walked toward the chicken coop where Bonnie was playing with Lavonne. She could hear Bonnie talking to the hen as if she were one of her school friends. If life had been different, Bonnie would have had a sibling by now—someone else to play with besides a chicken. Then Laurel saw Bonnie was chewing gum and frowned. She never bought gum because it was bad for her teeth.

"Bonnie, where did you get that gum?" she asked.

"From Mr. Lorde."

Laurel's heart skipped a beat, and when she spoke, panic tinged her voice. "You went all the way up to the Lorde property?"

Bonnie looked up then nodded. "Yes, you always let me go see Mr. Lorde."

Laurel's voice rose an octave. "But he's not there anymore, and his son is. I didn't tell you it was okay to go there."

Bonnie was confused and it showed. "But, Mama, he's nice just like Mr. Lorde, and he's like my daddy."

"He's nothing like your father, and you don't know anything about him. I'm telling you now, you are not allowed to do that again, do you hear me?"

Bonnie's chin trembled and her eyes welled with tears. "He's lonesome, Mama. If I can't go visit, who will be his friend?"

"He has his own friends. You do not go back to that place again. Promise me."

Tears rolled as her shoulders slumped. "I promise," she whispered, then took the gum out of her mouth, dug a little hole with her fingers, and buried it as solemnly as if she'd buried the man who'd given it to her.

"Come into the house now," Laurel said. "I'll make lunch."

"I'm not hungry," Bonnie said.

"Come into the house anyway," Laurel said and held out her hand.

Bonnie got up, but wouldn't hold her mother's hand and walked into the trailer house on her own. Even though Laurel knew she'd hurt Bonnie's feelings, she was convinced she was in the right. She followed her daughter inside, locking the door behind her as she went.

About the Author

Sharon Sala is a member of the Romance Writers of America, as well as the Oklahoma Chapter of RWA. She has over ninety-five books in print, published in five genres—romance, young adult, Western, general fiction, and women's fiction. First published in 1991, she is an eight-time RITA finalist, winner of the Janet Dailey Award, four-time RT Career Achievement Award winner, five-time winner of the National Readers' Choice Award, five-time winner of the Colorado Romance Writers Award of Excellence, and winner of the Heart of Excellence, as well as the Booksellers Best Award. Her novels are *New York Times* and *USA Today* bestsellers and get great reviews from *Publishers Weekly*. Writing changed her life, her world, and her fate. She lives in Oklahoma, the state where she was born.

A SKY FULL OF STARS

Love dazzles in this tender, emotional
Shaughnessy Brothers book from Samantha Chase

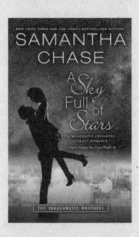

Brilliant astrophysicist Dr. Owen Shaughnessy feels more
connected to the cosmos than to people. He's great with
calculations, but when he leads a team of scientists to study
a famous meteor shower, he doesn't factor in his free-
spirited artist assistant Brooke Matthews.

Polar opposites in personality, the friction between
them threatens to derail the project. But the beauty and
mystery of the night sky draw Owen and Brooke together—
and she's going to surprise him in ways the stars never could.

"A delight for readers...a classic love story."

—RT Book Reviews, 4 Stars for *This Is Our Song*

For more Samantha Chase, visit:
www.sourcebooks.com

A NEW LEASH ON LOVE

First in the fresh, poignant Rescue Me series
from award-winning debut author Debbie Burns

When Craig Williams must take his daughters' adorable
new puppy to a shelter after the holidays, it's just another
painful episode in the fall-out of a miserable divorce.
Getting grief from the fiery woman running the shelter is
the least of his problems.

For Megan Anderson, it's hard enough to run an
underfunded no-kill animal shelter without taking on the
problems of a handsome man with a troublesome puppy.
But as Craig and Megan are drawn closer together, they
realize the magic of unconditional love can do anything—
maybe even heal a broken heart.

For more Debbie Burns, visit:
www.sourcebooks.com

BACK TO YOUR LOVE

A successful businessman reignites an old flame in
the first Brothers of TDT book
from Kianna Alexander

As a hardworking businessman and aspiring politician in his
Southern hometown, Xavier Whitted has a lot on his plate.
A weekend at the beach for his best friend's wedding is
exactly what he needs—until he runs into the woman who
broke his heart ten years ago.

Imani Grant is more beautiful, confident, and intelligent
than ever, and their connection is still sizzling. But Imani
harbors a secret that could destroy their blossoming careers.
She knows she should keep her distance, but Xavier is
determined to win back her heart—consequences be damned.

"Sexy and unforgettable."

**—USA Today Happy Ever After
for *This Tender Melody***

For more Kianna Alexander, visit:
www.sourcebooks.com

SWEET SOUTHERN TROUBLE

An ambitious Southern belle, a reclusive
NFL bachelor, and a fake engagement...
What could go wrong?

Kindergarten aide Marabelle Fairchild is a gal who gets
things done. Feeling unappreciated at her school, she
determines to score with the next big fundraiser. What she
doesn't expect? A smokin' hot football coach to throw her
off her game...

NFL coach Nick Frasier is Raleigh's most eligible
bachelor, but he wants to focus on his career...not his
playboy status. So he cuts Marabelle a deal—in exchange
for Nick sponsoring a bachelor auction starring him and his
gorgeous celebrity pals, Marabelle will pose as his fiancée to
ward off unwanted advances.

"Will keep you hooked from beginning to end!"

—Harlequin Junkie for Not So New in Town

For more Michele Summers, visit:
www.sourcebooks.com